X

2

THE MYRTLE AND IVY

THE MYRTLE AND IVY

By

STUART MACGREGOR

M. MACDONALD · EDINBURGH
1967

Published by
M. Macdonald
1 & 2 Richmond Lane, Edinburgh 8

Printed by
Macdonald Printers (Edinburgh) Limited
1 & 2 Richmond Lane, Edinburgh 8

To the Brotherhood of Sandy Bell's
—especially as it was then.

Càit bheil gillean luaidh mo chrìdh
'S na nìonagan bha bòidheach?

EWEN ROBERTSON (1842-95).

AUTHOR'S NOTE

It is possible that in a book of this kind readers may find themselves tempted to identify settings and characters with real places and people.

With regard to place I do not really mind, being confident that the stone and mortar of the two great seats of Edinburgh learning—Sandy Bell's and the University—are capable of surviving with dignity the journalism of their most errant sons.

People, however, are more perishable commodities, and remembering with affection and gratitude how much happiness my youth owed to my friends and mentors in both institutions, I should like to stress that all characters in this book are imaginary, and that I have taken great care to avoid their confusion with the living.

There was a day in the glen when they were clearing the rubble from the road, for the blasting was heavy this summer. They were big men mostly, and cheerful, red and black of Mayo and Donegal, and in their midst a youngster was brushing away the lesser debris.

The old woman hobbled through them, and her scowl burned into their honest labour, for they had not always been here. She passed the boy, and his eyes twinkled as bright as the quick shaft of his brush.

She turned with a curse, rubbing her rump, and her other hand clawed for his face; some laughed, others shouted at the boy to behave himself. His hand was up to ward her off; she caught its wrist and ceased her attack. The parchment of her cheeks quivered as she saw the dirty hand and muttered, and the men were quiet and still, and so was the boy.

She moved away, and they turned to him, all laughing now, and asked what words of her latest wisdom he had heard. He laughed drily and answered that as usual he had understood not a word, and his face was pale.

There was another time and another place and other people. And the time was longer, and the place in a city, and few of the people were of Mayo or Donegal. When they tried to explain their need of the place, they rarely found a simple answer, but were content to conclude that they needed it in the same way that others needed God or Karl Marx. They knew that whatever they did not know, they were happy not knowing it here, that as long as this stream of consciousness had to be endured they could thole it where it crossed the place. The children of idiosyncrasy, they stood among its other children and were strangely comforted, likewise they claimed and blamed other parents, often calling them ridicule, frustration and failure. And they found a happiness of a kind, though the world outside the place scoffed and preached and wept and called their happiness a kind of shameful death. And because the time was a smaller thing within the Greatest it did not last, and the place changed with its passing; those who survived this looked back, and being human and perhaps dishonest, they called the time the best years of their lives, and the place by its older name, which meant the time and their strange happiness also.

I

THE CITY

Song of a Spring-time Dreamer

CHAPTER I

OLD WILLIE swayed over the gutter and shivered in the cold. "Hullo, Johnny. It's hellish, boy—they got Jesus. Cut him up in pieces over by the graveyard there. But God'll get them, Johnny. He's hanged yin o' them already ootside Connor's. The students'll no' be laughin' sae loud now, the sinners. Have ye got a shillin', Johnny?"

A silver disc slapped into the mad, grasping claw. "God bless ye, Johnny. Jesus'll come back for ye, Johnny."

March was dying in the City, in this year of our Lord 1958, but dying hard; winter was still very much alive, ably supported by a vicious east wind from the North Sea, which snarled around the grey streets, spitting sleet at nylon-clad legs that stung painfully as the icy moisture evaporated. Over in the Art College, however, a few bare legs shone white among the multi-coloured calves of fashion, and the bravest took their lunch break outside on the grass; spring tended to come quickly in this part of town. The rest of the University remained as yet in sullen winter garb and behaviour, but behind the polished bar in Connor's Stan was ordering extra draught beer and cutting his spirit stocks, and across the road Maria was storing away her Nescafé and installing a new refrigerator.

John Stewart Ferguson staggered out of the Medical Quad and away from the grateful insanity of the old tramp. He heeled his sparse flesh over into the teeth of the gale, his thin, sallow face contorted with the smirk of a poacher smelling new grass. He knew that spring was coming without consulting a calendar; he had been able to smell its approach ever since he was a freckled little shrimp fishing the young trout of West Perth with his father. A boyhood on the slopes of the Southern Highlands had filled him with a rooted hatred for the month of March, and with the approach of his favourite season he had shed his string vest this morning, an annual ceremony of his own fertility cult which celebrated the end of winter. He was just twenty-two years old.

A raking gust blew a gutterful of dust up his thin slacks; a pretty shopgirl fluttered her eyes and he felt the old spark ignite in his middle. His boyish, wicked-innocent grin widened. You're right, Johnny boy. The season of love is upon us.

He pushed his left shoulder against the glass swing-door, and let it bang. Connor's was already half-filled with students, clamouring at the long, narrow counter for their orders. He pushed his way to the far end of the bar and threw his books down sharply. A pint of amber beer slid skilfully to his elbow. Lizzie's fading prettiness followed it.

"Evening, Johnny. How's the pride of Perthshire?"

His grin returned in a slow ripple of muscle. "There's not so much pride about Perthshire these days." He looked at the last diluted beam of winter sunlight fading on the window. "Still, I think the old man's coming to life again, Lizzie. You'd better stay your side of the bar to-night."

"I was handlin' faster laddies than you afore I was sixteen. Dinnae be sae fresh, young Ferguson."

Her worldly-wise barmaid's eyes fixed on the rythmical movement of his lean thrapple; he was drinking quickly, grey eyes open, and fastened squinting on the bottom of the glass. She looked away quickly: this fierce young face with its untidy shock of black hair did not always make for quiet sensations.

Johnny set his glass down quarter-full. A large bubble of gas shot to the back of his throat, and he impeded its escape with a decorous right hand. He pulled a battered packet of Players from his pocket and lit a crumpled cigarette with a loose match which he struck on the rough tweed jacket of the tall young man standing with his back to him.

Murdo Macauley turned, exhibiting his wolfish leer. "Who else but the Ferguson? What are you bragging about to-night?"

"No bragging, Murdo. I've just got time for a Gaelic lesson and a quick review of our latest sexual successes."

"You could certainly do with a Gaelic lesson," said the Hebridean. "Your Gaelic's pretty putrid, despite those lines you shoot about your scholarly bard-grandfather. And I've beaten you to so many bits of stuff lately that you'll hang one on me if we talk about it."

"Rubbish—you damned Folklore lecturers are clueless with women. It needs the red blood of the Medical Faculty to show you the way."

Murdo grinned back, lean face creasing from ear to mouth. The small moustache was slightly lighter than his sleek brown hair. His long arm shot out in a swift, feline movement, and

Johnny's rebel forelock tumbled across his left eye. "It's a bitter experience being led astray by a child. I'm scared of going to cocktail parties these days, Johnny; I can see their scaly old heads shaking behind my back. The conventional conclusion is that I'm a promising boy with no sense of responsibility."

The hero-worship in Johnny's face summoned the shock unit of his seductive armour: the thin lips lost their cynical tightness, the slow ripple spread to the grey eyes until their intensity replaced pleasantness with well-defined attraction. He ordered two nips. Murdo watched, licking his upper lip in anticipation. True to his type, he despised the long sour drinks of the South.

"One of the girls is throwing a party to-night after the Folk-song Society."

Murdo cocked a long smooth eyebrow, sipping at the bulbous glass. "Can you get me in?"

"Of course, old boy, just mention the President's name."

"God knows why they elected you," said Murdo laughing. "Though I must admit I've heard worse style on the B.B.C.—you'll be a famous folksinger yet."

Johnny blushed: "I'm a medical student—singing's just a hobby."

"I'll be there," said Murdo. "We've a Japanese scholar from Tokyo staying for the week-end, so we'd better let him digest our contemporary culture."

Johnny ignored this jibe at the more trite Scottish folksongs presently in vogue. He finished his beer and reached for his books.

Murdo put a hand on his arm. "I've got a beauty for you." Before Johny could protest he was into the second line of his song. Murdo's thin, cracked singing voice was full of charm once you forgot its actual quality. It leapt across the subtle pentatonic intervals light-footed, yet it caressed vowel and consonant with perfect natural cadence, now clipping a note, now lingering a fraction longer on a stressed word, expert and guileless as a woman's hand in baby-hair. The song was the tragic tale of the maid of Cornaig; Johnny did not understand all the Gaelic words, but he felt a peculiar twist in his stomach as the song ended; Murdo's cool, emotionless voice consistently moved beyond sorrow.

He cleared his larynx noisily and stared into his glass. "Fine song, *a ghraidh*," he said. "To think that all this stuff's dying in Scotland." He shook his head, wise as the Sphinx, but as he gazed into the golden meniscus he reflected that the great tragedy of Scotland nowadays seemed to be that the only people sensitive enough to realise their country's spiritual plight were too neurotic to convert their theories of national redemption into useful practice.

This thought filled him with momentary sadness until he realised its hypocrisy. "Murdo," he said disarmingly, "I wish we had a dozen Highlanders like you—Scotland would be a different place."

Murdo frowned: a Gael first and a Scot second, his fear of Lowland Scotland, especially when stimulated by the sourer attitudes of the City, was often much more definite than any feeling he had about England. "Have another drink, you bum."

Johnny shook his head, fidgeting nervously. "Sorry. Got to meet Arnold. Don't get too pissed."

Murdo grinned condescendingly: his drinking capacity was legend in the City. "I promise. By the way, would you sing 'Arlin's fine Braes' to-night? It's one of your few reasonable songs, if you keep your instrument quiet."

Johnny nodded, and finished his beer with a loud gurgle.

"So long, Murdo. So long, Lizzie."

"Cheerio, Johnny."

He walked out through the clustering drinkers with a slight swagger, battered textbooks clapping against shabby flannels. Every yard to the door he was greeted by a grin, nod, wink, or "Hullo Johnny." His eyes took in each face in turn, some aggressive, some humorous, student, workman, sootstained, beery, downright pale and ill.

He read a roguish sincerity into each face, and felt an almost childlike sense of security, as if his mother had just laughed the ghosts out of the cellar. Connor's was one of the few places where he felt completely free of the evil spirits of adolescence.

It's a great thing to be a Connor's man. The hierarchy of the University may call us brawlers and wasters, but they don't understand. Connor's is different. If you're an interesting barmate, friend, come in and we'll listen to you even if *they* don't outside. If you're the biggest rogue on earth, come in as long as you're interesting. You're ashamed of yourself? Been in jail? Or a nut-house? Well, so have one or two of us—boredom makes people do queer things. Come on in—here is your refuge, as long as you don't bore us. This is the cult of Connor's, the local backwater of twentieth-century learning and drudgery, and yours truly is one of its most respected high priests.

Murdo watched him till the glass door closed behind his smallish figure. He lit a long filter-tipped cigarette and exhaled slowly. He held it between his long slim fingers, very near the tip, thumb ceaselessly tapping out a soundless rhythm on the brown butt. God bless Johnny, he thought, and God bless the Folksong Society. It's the one decent thing left in this terribly changed University. No decent rake could fail to be at home in young Ferguson's dictatorship. The meeting tonight should be good: the boys tended to be a bit young, but they were virile animals, often quite talented, and the girls who refused to go to bed didn't avoid you for weeks afterwards.

Pat Leitch, the big Glaswegian surgical registrar from the Royal City was enjoying his weekly escape from sterilised responsibility in his usual solitary position against the far angle of the half-horseshoe. Murdo wandered over to the sweating, red-haired giant and told Lizzie to fill up his gin and tonic.

"Hello, Murdo," said Pat, well-lubricated already. "Is this you on the piss again?"

"Just seeking a word within a word, Pat, and filling the vacuum of the week-end with the fragrance of this nectar," said Murdo grandly.

Pat giggled, man and voice seeming quite distinct. "Johnny's jumpy just now, isn't he?" he said with a suddenness that was almost profound.

"Yes," said Murdo, "he is. There's something wrong."

"Same old trouble? Trying to play the broken-down Sir Galahad, disillusioned by materialistic swine like ourselves?"

"It could be," said Murdo. "He's bored me to death twice or thrice recently, and it's been something like that every time."

"God help him," said Pat, and his gin fled at a swallow. "He'd better start doing a little work. He only just managed to sit his Professional last year on the strength of that concoction he told Price the Dean about having religious doubts and not being able to work. It won't work again—he could finish up a mess."

"There's certainly something wrong," said Murdo.

"Yes, with all of us,' said Leitch, granite chin bobbing in his cupped hands. "D'you know what Price did with Johnny, the old scamp?"

"No."

"He let him sit, but he put him under the personal care of some evangelistic bacteriologist. This bloke had Johnny at revivalist meetings till he was nearly crackers! We've never let him forget it."

They talked easily for a while, the undulation of Murdo's Lewis *blas* merging pleasantly with Pat's pleasant Glasgow drag. Their interests were too far apart for meticulous technical debate, but it was easy to chain-smoke and guzzle liquor in the wonderful warm ether of Connor's, to gaze quietly enthralled at the mint of character around you, careless of the fact that your sense of goodwill was bounded by the walls of your arteries and the efficiency of your liver. Their ordinary sentences became charged with emotion; the kaleidoscopic hallucination of early drunkenness filled their eyes with wonder.

Leitch was moaning about the career rat-race in Surgery, when Murdo glanced at his watch. "I'm off to the Folksong. Will you be at the party later?"

"I may be," said Pat. "I'll try to raise some of my friends with money." Again the red face split in a ridiculous smirk, and a treble laugh pierced the huge teeth, shattering the crystal ball of their quiet, poised composure.

Murdo felt the patrician nostrils of his intelligence twitch. "Cheerio, Pat." He stalked lithely to the door—medical people were always that bit barbarous.

Lizzie leaned casually against the packed shelves. Her feet hurt abominably and she had three more hours to drill up and down the counter. Then it would take at least twenty minutes to clear the abusive, the semi-conscious and the horizontal to the street outside.

But where would you find such men? Darling savages like Dr Leitch, or a charming young chap like Murdo, who always made you feel a lady—a real Highland gentleman. And young Johnny, who they'd been talking about, he always made her feel a bit soft, with that queer smile that nearly made him bonnie—at times she wished she was his mother so that she could tuck him into bed, kiss him on the forehead.

But the dream didn't fit. There was beer on the Bible. There was something else about Johnny Ferguson. . . .

CHAPTER II

One hour and twenty minutes nearer the world's creation the subject of Lizzie's reverie was stumping unglamorously down the Middle Meadow Walk, a smooth footway lined by elm and ash and bordered by scraggy banks of grass which panted asthmatically on a shallow bed of soil.

As he stepped off Woods Street on to the mottled grey surface he was flanked on his right by the massive ungainly frame of the Royal City Hospital whose lighted windows glared down in parallel rows, screaming hard work and tension; to his left George Square lifted its noble old Georgian mane to the falling dusk. Johnny marched on, head down, mouthing breathless curses; hurrying when full of heavy beer always gave him searing heartburn. The wind had now reached gale force; trapped between the two masses of stone it shrieked in captive fury and tore through his cotton shirt.

Once a sunburned little country boy came to this City urgent with what he called compassion, and burning with healthy ambition. But when he found that his dream was nothing more, he began to hate the reality he found in its stead, for when the new, cynical John Phoenix Ferguson poked his head out of the kid's funeral pyre he found himself surrounded by grisly monsters who called themselves Honest Truths. They laughed and told him that compassion can't exist unless self-interest is satisfied and that with the dream gone the scientific mechanics of his trade would become dreary to a mind whose passion was people. At first he laughed back, but he's cackling a wee bit shrilly now. To hell— I mustn't pity myself!

Johnny tossed back his forelock. Once again Murdo had succeeded in diverting him from his immediate purpose. He hated losing a battle of willpower, but the amulet of Murdo's voice seemed to gain in hypnotic effect every time they met. He smiled wryly as he considered the tall, lean islander and the times they had had together.

Had Arnold asked him to have another drink, would he have

delayed going to see Murdo? No. Arnold Ayton was now the complete reproach, food for a thriving guilt complex. This had followed hard on the heels of Arnold's Finals; he was now a first-rate house doctor, the guardian of thirty-eight surgical beds, conscientious, enduring and passionately interested. The old idol-figure, but now a source of fear that tore at Johnny's bowels with iron teeth, for when Arnold was around you could almost smell your own lost soul, and you desperately wanted to explain your lack of purpose.

Nevertheless, let's soldier on. With a bit of luck anyone can be like Arnold. Then along comes the most paralysing vision of a disgruntled, fleshy middle-aged man in a poky City suburb cursing the National Health Service and the rain that ruins the week-end golf. Death.

He reached the end of the Walk, still attempting to force an honest pattern into the tangled skein of his arguments. He strode briskly up the winding pavement of fashionable Chalmers Crescent where the solid grey villas sat in darkness behind their dapper green squares. In two hundred yards he had moved unseeing from the student quarter into a silent pool of ultra-respectability, but when he reached the crest of the hill and turned left into Grange Loan, vehicles and pedestrians suddenly assumed significance; Grange Loan stretched towards the far traffic lights, and the faint smudge of grey to the left of the lights was Newton Hospital.

Struggling to lift his depression, he reminded himself that this was the last Friday in March. He had not gone ten yards when he stopped and smiled. On the same Friday last year he had struck a winning streak at Musselburgh Races, and if his memory served him rightly he had scored three tries playing half-back with Arnold on the Dublin Easter Tour exactly two years ago. His need for a turn in the tide of fortune stimulated his Celtic paganism; superstition was easily translated into the realm of fact.

Good things come in threes; and it seemed that his excitement splayed and spun away from him the length of the Loan, and when it returned, saddling the wind, his pulse rose and his nostrils flared as though stung by the wild freshness of cordite.

CHAPTER III

FRIDAY NIGHT in the City was an hour of magic. It began when you skipped the 3 p.m. class, and wandered over to the Students' Union, secure in the knowledge that you could forget the stuffy lecture rooms until Monday. You sat yourself down at a marble-topped table with your classmates, and when you had hammered out the likely rugger matches to watch on Saturday afternoon and the likely women to dance with on Saturday night, you started to review nostalgically the pleasures of week-ends past, then abracadabra!—the hour hand was already slipping past the five. Up you jumped with a vision of Connor's, pregnant with warmth and wellbeing; you bade goodbye to your classmates, who, grinning, cursed you for an alcoholic, and in a minute you were out into the good clean smell of the City streets, rubbing shoulders with cheerful grubby-faced little Scotsmen clutching their week's redemption in a transparent packet, noticing with glee the moment's bloom on the faces of counterhands and cafe waitresses, and spitting with glee into the face of the cruel, cleansing draught that sought to ruffle your hair and good temper as it joined in the week-end assertion of character.

Then best of all the Folksong Society, with its weekly quota of sublimation, followed by some honest-to-God drunken student party. The Friday night routine was the climb of a multi-crested mountain, each peak presenting a wider panorama of pleasure and human fellowship, till eventually around the hour of Friday's midnight you turned your rump on the pretty girl beside you and proclaimed from the final summit that you were lord and master of the moment and thanked heaven that you were no other man.

But for the moment, a quiet jar with Arnold. Facing the back door of the Newton Hospital was the gleaming face of the Castle Arms, one of a chain of newer hostelries sprinkled liberally over this part of the City. It lacked the character of the older "howffs" in the part of town that Johnny loved, but it did boast a very comfortable cocktail bar with plush couch seats and a wide spectrum of malt whiskies.

The dazzling blue neon lights of the cocktail bar pained their eyes; there was hardly a scrap of space at the small box-bar. Johnny shouldered his way in brutally, slopping the pint glass of a large flabby customer. For a moment cold, menacing grey eyes and weak, bloodshot blue delivered a silent challenge, then the man muttered "bloody students" and moved ponderously away.

Arnold moved beside his friend with the speed and grace of a born fly-half. An uncreased split-new pound note flicked from his wallet to the counter.

The podgy owner's syrupy enquiry contained the affected vowels of the suburbs implanted amid the heavy glottals of the City.

"Large whisky and a Guinness please," Arnold answered. "Not that you deserve a dram, you young gladiator," turning to Johnny. "For God's sake, let's have no trouble to-night."

They leaned belly-pressed across the polished oak, sipping their drinks while the hum-drum chatter of the lounge orbited around their thoughts.

Johnny smiled around him. In every corner the balm of pay-night was dripping its way through the dreary hours of the week. Every table was loud with over-pitched mirth, the stuff of dreams; wonderful, stupid working people, thrilled at the prospect of getting drunk with their tails planted on a soft seat. Tomorrow the extra agony endured at the lathe or bottle-washer would be for the kids' sakes but tonight they knew the truth.

Arnold had noticed a woman with a goitre that bounced off her chin when she drank; it was a good job for her there was a National Health Service. No doubt she'd be across the road for a thyroidectomy soon, suing the hospital for giving her bedsores after she'd filled her bed with pie and chips. After a few months of a hospital residency you stopped believing that suffering ennobled.

The telepathic current flashed across two feet of clammy warmth and they faced each other guiltily.

Johnny broke the silence. "How's the job, Arnold?"

"It's great to be working for Rutherford, Johnny; that man must be one of the greatest surgeons in Britain."

"I've heard about him," said Johnny, "and I don't like him. He's knife-happy. He fillets patients at the drop of a hat."

"Maybe. But there's a big breakthrough coming soon. We'll

have conquered everything but old age in a few years. And we'll be in debt to people like Rutherford who take chances."

Johnny went through the motions of spitting. "At times I get sick of Medicine," he said. "Who wants to die of a hellish thing like senility? All these bright new boys are so full of scientific theories that they've no room for the old witchcraft—reassurance and personal kindness, the basic clinical principles."

"Rubbish," said Arnold angrily.

"And balls to you. Look at the way some Yanks fit their patients up with a ton of apparatus before a doctor has even seen them. Soon we'll be curing everybody inside five minutes and frightening them round the bend in the process. We're sick —we're science-worshippers like everyone else."

Arnold's good-humoured grin returned with effort. "Fifty years ago Medicine was an art; now it's a mixture, and in future it may be more of a science. It's still very worthwhile. But it won't adapt to suit you, you young megalomaniac!"

Johnny downed his whisky, needing it badly. The fire lay trapped for a moment in his throat before it flooded peripherally in a flow of comfort. "Lend me a pound, Arnold," he said.

Arnold produced a green note without question. "You're getting bitter, kiddo," he said. "Forget the moans and hit your books. You've got less qualifications than a Boy Scout if you mess up your Finals."

Something loathsome but intangible crept through the anaesthesia of Johnny's alcohol: defenceless against it, he attacked Arnold again: "Goddammit, who cares? What does success do? Look at some of our famous clinicians, who need to be reminded that absolute power corrupts absolutely. They care more about their petty little demigod status than their patients—or their staff."

"Rubbish," said Arnold.

"No!" shouted Johnny. "And all those slimy gents with influential names who get the good jobs—that shouldn't happen in Medicine!"

"You're talking like a silly young fresher who hasn't learned to wipe his arse with paper," said Arnold.

"Now, watch it!" He was twisting Arnold's lapel in temper.

"Go on, hit me," said Arnold evenly. "Use the Ferguson Law."

The pique left Johnny's face. "Don't be daft. I'm sorry, Arnold." He beckoned to a worried-looking barman. "Same again, please."

Arnold prodded the muscle above Johnny's belt. "Now, once and for all—listen. If you're going to preach Croninesque sermons to patients with boils and constipation you'll finish up sharing the bill with Bob Hope at the Empire. And some medical posts may be fixed, but no system 's perfect. And you leave our chiefs alone—look at Sir Norman and Professor Price. You can't beat them."

"Sure," said Johnny. "An actor and a—och, to hell, let's think about women for a change!"

"Thank God," said Arnold, stretching to six feet and smoothing his thinning fair hair. "We all fall out of love with the blood-and-guts trade at times. You'll get over it. Are you still sleeping with Nell, you cruel little scruff?"

"Cruel?"

"You don't realise it, do you? I'm a bit sick of getting my shoulder soaked by your cast-offs."

Johnny was beginning to feel the effects of beer and mixed whisky on an empty stomach. "You're too nice, Arnold," he said. "When you get to what the poets call the odour of stale ashes, the kindest thing is a quick surgical operation. A man needs variety."

"Yes," said Arnold, smiling. "And when I think of the slush I've heard in the dark corners of parties: 'I'm just a bar-tramp. You're a nice lassie who needs a good, stable husband—it's been wonderful': how they don't see through your corn I'll never know."

Uncomfortably Johnny repressed the moment of self-hatred. "I'll tell you a secret, Arnold. Every time I look in the mirror I wonder how any intelligent woman can bother with me at all." He was feeling very confidential now; this was one of the greatest sensations in the world. "You know, Arnold, I wouldn't spout this crap to anybody but you, but when I arrived here, I had only two shags under my belt, and they were poor stuff for the X certificate market. I assure you, old friend, that the uneven consistency of a Perthshire hillside and the harsh young hands of inexperience make a dreadful combination."

"Go on," said Arnold.

"When I first came down here, I tried to be smooth as Old Nick. An' you know something, boy? I got nowhere. You see, Arnold, all the country bumpkin has to do is to revert to type: the sophisticated young birds in this town like a boy from the backwoods; so you make them laugh, you tease them in your softer accent, and you're made. You know, I've had chaps come to me at parties—big muscle-men who fancy themselves, and they ask me how I do it. 'It's my looks and personality,' I say; and I don't understand or believe a word of it. Does that make sense to you, Arnold?"

Arnold shook his head and Johnny gazed in pity. How could this ruddy, handsome Northumbrian understand it, when his emotions were already immersed in their own Shakespearean tragedy? Arnold's unique vulnerability was his reticence to hurt a living soul, so he was now shackled to Betty Warren, a staff-nurse of the Royal City, simply because she had been head-over-heels in love with him since his first University Dance. And Betty Warren had the tongue of a viper.

They left through the noisy, throbbing throng of drinkers, and passed the table of the heavy gentleman who had been disturbed by their entrance. The man gazed them carefully up and down, then deliberately twisted his varicose cheeks into a sneer. Johnny discarded Arnold's hasty "Come on," stopped dead in front of the painted, middle-aged woman on his enemy's right, and with one slick movement raised her scarlet fingernails to his lips. As she started in yawning astonishment, he turned to her husband and flicked out his tongue. In a flash he had turned and was gone.

James Brown, fish merchant, turned an apoplectic shade of purple before the door closed. "The cheeky little swine," he hissed, lumbering to his feet. "I'll kill him."

"Sit on your backside," his wife said angrily, her long red talons clutching his wrist. "You've had too much, that's your trouble."

She looked through the smoke towards the door, then smiled at her angry husband. "He was only a laddie," she said.

In the raw damp of Grange Loan Johnny overtook Arnold. "I forgot to tell you," he said. "Something terrific is going to happen tonight."

CHAPTER IV

He sat next to the upper deck window, conscious of Arnold's warm, friendly figure beside him, and brooded contentedly over the long cartoon strip of scenes that flashed across his vision from the wet City pavements. The world required mere inspection without analysis: for once he could gaze at an unknown salad of humans without feeling compelled to furnish reasons for their existence, or anticipate their destinations. Life was incredibly simple at times.

The bus filled up as it swayed toward the City centre; after five minutes a small tipsy newspaper vendor in an old cloth cap sat down in front of them beside a large, elderly South Side matron wearing a fur coat. Steam rose steadily from his wet jacket.

"I'll sing yez all a wee song," the new arrival announced to the other passengers. "There's no' hauf enough singin' today—isn't that right, missus?"

There was no reply from the window seat, though the rouged cheek twitched fractionally; the bulky form pressed itself hard against the glass.

Unabashed, the pay-night Caruso broke into a lusty rendering of "Scotland the Brave." After two verses, in which every second line transposed key, he tired of the tune and informed his audience that he was about to sing an old City song which he had learned from his mother.

Arnold and Johnny grinned at each other. The fat lady turned towards them, throwing out a look that was part supercilious vinegar, part genuine agony. Arnold moved to tap the little man's shoulder but Johnny held his sleeve. "Let him sing," he growled. "We'll learn more from him than we'll ever learn from her. I'd rather have a week-end in a garret with a wee man that'll sing, than a week in the sort of bloody parlour she struts about in."

His words were audible: the lady's fur-lined neck coloured as she turned sharply away, but in an instant the promised song had begun, the artist apparently unconscious of what he was doing to his public.

His braggart brogue rollicked the length of the vehicle:

> "I'm no' gaun to Barrie's trip
> I'm no' gaun again—
> I'm no' gaun to Barrie's trip
> It ayeways comes on rain."

Johnny sat forward sharply. "I told you," he whispered. "That's a genuine street song: who said that people don't sing this stuff any more?"

He leaned forward and addressed the newsvendor, who was attempting to pull a large beer bottle from his coat pocket; the stout lady was receiving a small sharp elbow in her hip. "Where did ye get that song, Jock?" Johnny lapsed into an authentic City street-accent.

The small man grinned at them over his left shoulder. "As I said, young man, I learned this song from my deah old mother." Said resentfully, eyes on Johnny's University scarf, voice counterfeit of culture.

"D'ye know any more like that?"

Johnny's obvious sincerity penetrated the other's euphoria. "Of course I do," he slurred cheerfully. "I used tae be the life and soul of the First Royal Scots."

"We're getting off here," said Johnny. "Come on, my friend, you're coming with us to a party."

"Whit sort o' a pairty?" asked the drunk.

"A better one than you've had since the army," replied Johnny. "Come on, you'll be a star turn."

Arnold began a feeble protest as they rose but already the man was following. He lurched unsteadily to his feet, and regarded his female fellow-traveller. "I must go with my friends now," he stated categorically. "I'm sorry"—he belched—"that *you* cannae come as well, for I'm sure ye ken some smashin' dirty songs. I'll see ye again, Maggie."

"Really!" said the lady.

They placed the little man ("Bob to my freends") between them, and turned off the street into the Old Quadrangle of the University Arts Faculty.

As they walked through the pillared entrance, Bob looked about him in awe. "Mighty big hoose, this," he remarked. "Should be a guid pairty efter a'."

They crossed the gravelled Quad. diagonally and mounted a flight of stone steps to find themselves opposite an open door flanked by lighted windows. From within there came the sound of guitars and young voices singing.

"Aye, it's goin' well already," observed Bob, clutching his newspapers tightly. "There must be a fair stack o' booze in there," he added, eyes brightening.

Johnny paused for a minute before the clubroom door—here he was approaching his own version of Holy Communion.

Here lay the destiny of his infant musical promise, the accurate repetition of his mother's dandling-tunes which had sent his father into ecstasies of praise; of his childhood's indiscriminate hunger for his grandmother's Gaelic lullabies, the psalms of Sunday School, the popular songs of Vera Lynn. Here was the happy result of his teenage inclination towards the artistry of Leadbelly and the poignant, brutal balladry of his local Perthshire tinkers, whose art could work a unique miracle within him; of his early University days learning new Nationalist revival hymns and old American blues on the guitar with patient Art College friends. Here was the birth-product of his friendship with Hector Gunn, the brilliant English Language lecturer, folklorist and Connor's man, for he and Hector were joint founders of this, the University Folksong Society, the focus of civilised social fellowship for the elite of the campus.

A thrill of pride and anticipation shot down his spine. The room was shabby, but spacious, and several wooden benches had been drawn into ranks with a middle avenue facing a small oak table on a narrow rostrum. Various groups sat on these benches busily tuning guitars, writing words in notebooks, or singing together in their own brand of harmony. Johnny pulled little Bob to one side and sat him down at the back of the hall; Bob promptly went to sleep, newspapers folded across his knee. Several of the choristers detached themselves in Johnny's direction.

He received a friendly hug from his old Art College compatriot, Ricky Slater, the finest guitarist and banjoist in the City. Amid the group that gathered around him, two medical ties gleamed scarlet and gold beneath the only two faces that Johnny cared to call dear in Fifth Year Medicine.

Colin Morrison was a slight, dark City boy, incongruously

the University welter-weight, fleshly tough as his accent was smooth; a fearless rebel risen above the stereotyping of his fashionable education, and the ruthless answer to any vestige of academic pomposity that dared to invoke his satire. The hawkish, Norman features of the tall kilted man beside him were the most revered in the bars and brawls of Woods Street, for Jimmy Anderson of Hawick, after eleven years of undergraduate adventure and the fighting of a terrible secret sorrow, was the uncrowned King of Connor's, and a man whose fists and alcohol consumption were terrible to contemplate.

Johnny shook hands with them, then slipped through the circle searching the room with eyes that focused with effort. He found his quarry; a tall girl in a low-cut purple sweater and black skirt came towards him carrying a small Italian mandolin and a large Spanish guitar. Unquestionably, Nell Horton was a sight demanding attention. Her complexion was sallow, and the jet black sheath of her long narrow head ending in a large bun above the nape of her neck combined with her long straight eyebrows and violet eyes to give her a sultry Andalusian appearance. Her really fine features ended here, for her nose and lips were rather full and her chin too heavy. But if she missed beauty narrowly she was never less than striking, and the men who committed adultery in their hearts when Nell's figure was around were legion, for she was breasted and bottomed like a Greek statue.

She came gracefully towards him on shapely muscular legs. "Here's your guitar, honey," she said in husky, cultured tones. "Aren't you going to give your mistress a kiss?"

Johnny pecked her cheek; as usual she hinted French perfume. He pulled a small book from his jacket pocket and gave it to her. "Happy birthday, Nell," he said.

She pulled the mandolin to her breast with an impulsive childish gesture. "Oh, you remembered!" she cried excitedly. "I wouldn't have believed it." She looked at the title. "Rabelais! How did you get it, Johnny?"

"Never mind. I'm almost drunk enough to tell you where it came from and what it cost."

Her laugh was full and throaty. "It's the thought that counts, or so they say. I'll be telling myself for a few days that you *are* in love with me after all. God, Johnny, I'm twenty-eight today—isn't it fearsome? It's twelve years since I lost my honour, four years since I divorced my husband and one since I met you; regard with solemnity the milestones on Nell Horton's road to perdition!"

"If anybody goes to heaven it'll be you," he grinned. "I'll miss you, old pal."

Nell's look was haunted. "We're late already," she said.

"O.K.," said Johnny eagerly. "Where's our Secretary, Jehosaphat? I like to have him by my right hand."

"He's right over there," said Nell, indicating a long, scrawny, grubby individual: the face was pale and thin and its quaintness was accentuated by the absence of the spectacles that the short-sighted eyes required; David Algernon Smith's bewildered, vacant expression belied the true genius that flickered within his addled cranium.

"I don't know how you put up with the idiot," she said.

"You leave him alone," said Johnny. "He's the greatest literary intelligence I know."

"Of course, dear. And an authority on everything else, and a brilliant orator, who somehow fails all his medical exams. He's an idiot."

"No, Nell. Some subjects in Third Year, like Anatomy, are like eating mountains of pigswill. He's too bright to take it."

"It's nice of you to defend him," she said sardonically. "But then, you're his only true friend—he worships you, doesn't he, dear?"

"He knows I'm his friend, whether he's being clever or making a fool of himself. He likes being treated as a man instead of a super-intelligent circus animal."

"*And* you gave him his noble nickname," she said. "You hypocrite! I wonder if he's laughing at *me* now, for similar reasons. It's great to be weak; you're always useful."

Johnny beckoned and Jehosaphat sat down with him; the body of members began to settle in their places. Upwards of a hundred people were already gathered, and Arnold and Nell had seated themselves on either side of old Bob, who had re-awakened and was becoming restive.

Johnny hammered with the palm of his hand on the table. "Quiet, you Mongols," he roared. "Your leader has come, and for the next ninety minutes you will sit at the feet of the great and hear music such as the angels only dream about." Quickly he dispensed with a few announcements and introduced the first singer. A young science student made his way to the front carrying his guitar; he stood before the rostrum, tall, slim and bearded, a dreamy smile on his fine features.

And suddenly there was a kettle-drum in his bass strings, and the tinkle of treble bridles, for the Irish Dragoon was dying on the march, and the lass o' Fyvie far behind. The applause faded, and now the Appalachian love-strains were tender, for the colour of his true love's hair was black, black, and his voice the lonely lover to tell it. The Atlantic conquered again, a little island girl was percussing feet to life with the *puirt-a-beul* of the Hebrides, seagull-shrill for Lewis, lazier, vowel-drawling for South Uist; and again the tribute from a loving, writhing audience.

They writhed rather differently when Hector Gunn introduced the visiting Japanese lecturer whose eerie *belcanto* sorely tried the President's self-control. After keeping a straight face he felt bound to call on his own guest.

Little Bob Blane had been watching and listening with rapt concentration, only occasionally complaining that the "pairty needed mair booze," but the unusual sound-effects produced by the Japanese proved too severe a stress for his slender modicum of restraint. Despite vicious glares from Hector he informed Arnold and Nell in his piercing version of *sotto voce* that "this bloody Chink's nae guid—he ought to puke and get it ower with." The Japanese gentleman finished his song in peace only by the grace of Nell's strong left arm which clamped the little man's waist and Arnold's equally capable right hand which covered his mouth.

"Ladies and Gentlemen," said Johnny, gravely: "I now give you a special treat. After much wrangling with the War Office we have procured the services of the greatest folksinger that the British Army has ever known. I give you Robert Blane, late of the First of Foot!"

Bob shuffled forward to a great ovation. The sediments of his early drinking were scouring sour through his blood however, and he strongly resented his recent incarceration. "Whit'll I sing?" he enquired gruffly of Johnny, waving his newspapers in Jehosaphat's direction.

"Sing some of your army stuff," whispered Johnny.

Bob looked dubiously at his mixed audience, then burst into a bawdy memory of his Indian Army days.

"Sixteen annas one rupee
Seventeen annas one buckshee
Sergeant-Major, hollow-ground razor,
Queen Victoria very fine chap."

He cavorted around the floor like a performing bear, reeling off song after army song, and drew the young student audience into his pocket with consummate ease. He doffed his cap to the ensuing tumult of appreciation, sold several copies of the "Evening News" to the first three rows as a final encore, then returned to his seat to find a delighted Hector Gunn waiting for him with a half-bottle.

It was time to round off the first half of the meeting, and Johnny called on his own group, The Moonshiners. He jumped down from the platform, automatically tuning his guitar to the same pitch as Ricky Slater's banjo. Nell stood between them, hands folded in front of her, and on the far right Stella Davies, who arranged their songs, sidled fondly to Ricky's side, her dark Welsh features glowing with pride.

Ricky stroked a few opening bars, picking out an intricate rhythm on banjo with steel fingertips, and Johnny played a quick synchronised bass run that ushered in Nell's voice.

Nell's powerful contralto was a superb solo weapon, reinforced admirably by her provocative appearance. Born in Montreal, and the ex-wife of a British diplomat, she could imitate most accents with authority, and her stage personality tore into the audience in cogent lines of force. She sang sober, despising the aid of Dutch courage, her penetrating gaze sweeping the male element in the audience, steadily hypnotizing it into her power. They swayed into the refrain, Nell and Ricky taking the melody against Stella's lower fifth and Johnny's tenor third. The resulting blend was lordly, and the cracked chandelier rocked with approval. approval.

They had not recovered from Nell when Johnny was at them, thundering out of the bloody heights of Cromdale with Ricky's twelve-stringed guitar and Nell's mandolin on his flanks, his rough, turbulent voice taunting them to pride and anger. And finally they listened to "Can ye sew cushions" in a mood of twilight, and a few tears glistened furtively beyond the narrowing harmonies of pitch and volume before the light returned with a thunderous, thankful noise.

"Now," said Johnny, wiping sweat from his forehead, "we'll have our normal ten-minute interval. The second half will feature our esteemed Honorary Vice-President, Mr Hector Gunn; also the Josh White of the North of England, 'Jehosaphat Crazy-Fingers.' O.K.—scat!"

There was a rapid exodus in the direction of Paterson's, the small basement cocktail bar which was their traditional meeting-place during the interval. Equally traditional was the fact that the official ten-minute hiatus lasted at least half an hour; the second part of the programme was always calculated to be informal and mildly uproarious.

Hector Gunn strode majestically to the platform, an approving smile on his florid, handsome face. "The last ten minutes have castigated my laziness, Johnny," he said. "The Moonshiners deserve recognition. I'll have a talk with the 'Folkstyle' people; you're due for a record if they like you."

Johnny had a bizarre vision of packed concert-halls, and gleaming black discs spinning round their silver navels. Here was the first rung of the ladder.

He gripped Hector's hand. "I might as well be honest; this is what we've been waiting for. Bless you, Hector."

"In all modesty, I have the best contacts in the business," said Hector. "Let's drink on it in Paterson's—I have the thirst of the damned upon me."

"So have I," said Johnny, trying to remember how he had felt after scoring three tries in Dublin.

At half-past ten a motley column of students poured into their hostess's flat to finish off the evening in true Society style. They were in good spirits, for the final entertainment had been hell-raising; Jehosaphat, always emotionally unstable when drunk, had imbibed too freely during the interval, and had added two impromptu verses to "Beale Street Blues" which deepened their colouring considerably. Finally Jimmy Anderson had disgraced himself in unrehearsed but glorious fashion.

He had purchased a bottle of whisky and sponsored a private drinking competition with Murdo MacAuley and Hector in the back row. Called upon to sing the last two songs, he navigated the simple route to the front with great fortitude and on a slaughtered stomach; drawing his fine kilted figure to its full height, he rendered "The Thistle of Scotland" with heroic elan, but as the hall screamed "Encore," his flesh denied his spirit and sprayed a large quantity of it over Jehosaphat's feet. Johnny's closing remarks were lost in pandemonium.

At the entrance to the flat Johnny sat in a taxi with Nell, Arnold and Bob; Jimmy's prostrate figure was laid flat, his long legs twisted askew to fit his seventy-four inches into the small floor. His kilt had fallen back about his haunches, revealing among other things two large hairy thighs.

Johnny fumbled in his pocket while a small, angry City taxi driver demanded from the open door that they remove "this bloody comedian" from his vehicle.

Nell slipped her hand over his and he felt the hair rise at the back of his head. No matter how innocent her actions she was disturbing. "I've got plenty of money,' she said. "You and the boys take Jimmy up, and I'll pay the driver."

"God bless your sculpture, Nell," he said, resenting his own penury with a passing vehemence. "All right, lads, let's get the king upstairs."

Johnny and Arnold carried Jimmy into the bath-room toilet which was enjoying a rare moment of rest, and deposited him comfortably in the bath with a cushion under his head. They removed his shoes and backed away hurriedly.

By now the party was in full swing. A wide selection of spirits, ales and wines reposed in the kitchen sink—the result of a quick whip-round organised by the President. The guests who made their way through the large, old-fashioned lounge to this oasis were not all Society members; the grapevine had furnished many other public-house carousers and distant friends with a pleasant finish to the day; gatecrashing was a hallowed custom, and as long as numbers were mechanically manageable "open house" was the order of the evening. Colin Morrison and other unattached males were already scanning the wall in search of fresh talent.

Nell and Johnny danced cheek-to-cheek amid a mass of couples. She held his left hand tightly against her right clavicle, while her own strayed in minute caressing circles over the back of his neck below the hairline. In her two-inch heels she was only just short of his five feet eight inches, and she found it easy to tease his ear with the tip of her tongue. He was feeling quite drunk by now, and dancing with Nell brought home starkly the time-honoured statement of the Porter in "Macbeth." She thrust herself almost too hard against him; he felt the exquisite mould of her body contours, and a hunger rose in him that she obviously sensed. He moved back slightly as they turned, and she chuckled.

"You are a bitch," he said fiercely.

She threw back her head and let loose her throaty laugh, a blend of gooseflesh and warm honey. She looked superb, for in the semi-darkness her lower face assumed more shape, and the puffy dark pockets beneath her eyes had disappeared.

But the glance she delivered was not spurious. "Give me my moment of truth, Johnny," she pleaded. "Right here I can believe that I'm something worth loving."

He shook his head silently. There was no comfort in any answer he had to give; this was in fact a moment of lies.

The long-player finished, and Nell disengaged herself with some reluctance. She rubbed her abdomen. "I'm hungry, darling," she moaned. "I'll just nip through to the larder and pinch some bread and cheese." She moved away with a faint feminine rustle.

He picked up his glass and sat down on the floor against the wall. By any standards the party was a success already.

Ricky and Stella were necking on the sofa, interrupted on occasion by the people who fell over their feet. Beside them Jehosaphat was unleashing invective on the principles of Luther and a bewildered Pat Leitch, reeling off Aquinas with unerring fluency. Colin and a recovered Jimmy had discovered a couple of eager nurses; the dapper boxer had already reduced one of them to ground level in the corner. Murdo MacAuley, suave and collected, was impressing the prettiest of the hostesses by the door. "I feel that the Welsh are essentially different from the other Celtic peoples," he was saying, slipping a quiet experienced arm round her shoulders as he gazed down into her attentive innocence.

Johnny shut his eyes, cigarette between lips. Now the couples were plodding round the floor to the soothing strains of Harry Belafonte. He had forgotten that Nell existed.

Hector Gunn appeared beside him, produced the inevitable bottle and filled Johnny's tumbler to the top. "Come on next door," he said. "We'll get a good ceilidh going."

Johnny and he threaded their way to the small room next door, picking up Ricky and Stella on the way. Nell appeared clutching a hunk of Vienna roll and a bottle of Burgundy, and in a few minutes they had gathered the bulk of the party. The discipline of the Moonshiners relaxed and they allowed their voices to follow their fancy. Hector bellowed a selection of Irish rebel songs from his enormous repertoire—"The Croppy Boy," "Father Murphy," flowed from him wild, unvanquished, then they all sang "The Midnight Special" and "St James Infirmary Blues."

Nell took over with a mixture of French and Spanish songs. She played her mandolin softly and sang to the ceiling, her black hair loosened from its clasp and tumbling wild around and over her splendid neck. She performed with a minimum of motion, only the haunting throb of her voice and the slight rise and fall of her breast denoting her consciousness.

Johnny slipped away and wandered back to the lounge in search of another drink. For once Friday night was not sedating him completely; he still felt an innate restlessness born of his words with Arnold.

He found Arnold faithfully chaperoning Bob and discussing the colour problem with a West Indian without rancour or sentiment. Wee Bob took very little part, for he was again heading Lethewards. His head hung forward on his chest; very occasionally he joined in: "Never mind, Paul Robeson's a darkie, and he sings better than me, even." Johnny slapped Arnold's back fondly.

A few couples, Murdo and his willing booty among them, were still dancing. There was no whisky left in the bar, but behind Colin's prostrate body a wineglass lay untouched; this he quickly commandeered. Colin and the little nurse lay fast asleep in each other's arms. The girl's mouth was open and she was snoring loudly.

A small group of latecomers were grouped around the door, and he noticed with distaste that his old enemy, Allan Prentice, was one of them. Prentice hated medical students, and the editorial of "Halcyon," the student quarterly which he ran with vigour, was ever full of vituperative condemning their reprehensible behaviour. He was a powerful, ugly youth whose pale face glistened perpetually under a film of sweat; his cheeks were dotted with soft yellow pustules of acne. His deep-set brown eyes burned with an intense hatred of anything more balanced than himself and his opinionated pronouncements of his role in human progress often approached the Messianic delusions of paranoia. He looked round the room with quick, arrogant judgment. When he saw Johnny a characteristic smirk emerged, and he said something to his group which raised a slight titter.

Johnny shrugged his shoulders; he was too tired to fight tonight. He was about to turn away when a girl came from the back of the group to obtain a better view of the butt of Allan Prentice's scathing comments. He looked at her for what seemed an age before she slowly averted her eyes. She was a slim girl in a navy overcoat, with thick curling auburn hair which fell in long shining waves to her shoulders. There was challenging poise in the set of the shapely head; her small, oval face reminded him of Maureen O'Hara, the film star. A little colour glowed on the fine, high cheekbones under his rude appraisal. He was mildly surprised at the rapid revving in his throat. Downing the full wineglass he strode purposefully to the door.

The girl eyed him calmly as he approached. His gait was unsteady, and his flushed face and tousled hair did nothing to improve his appearance. He had discarded his sports jacket to sing, and his white shirt bore a few small beer stains. He tried to gauge her thoughts, but the firm green eyes remained neutral beneath the long lashes. At close quarters her complexion was not quite as flawless as he had at first imagined, but the small freckles which powdered her nose and cheeks in no way detracted from the aura of the goddess.

"Hello," he said awkwardly. "Can I take your coat? I'm afraid that you'll have to drink gin or Guinness." He tried a shy smile, cursing his flurried approach; before those cool, analysing eyes he honestly did not know what to say next.

Allan Prentice unwittingly solved his problem. "We're just going, Ferguson," he said. "I wanted to let Nora here see how the other half lives."

Johnny shot a diabolical grin at him, and Prentice advanced a pace, sensing trouble. His two friends closed order behind him. A small nebulous red spot was swelling larger before Johnny's eyes. Then the girl put a graceful hand on his arm. "Just you simmer down, little man—nobody's giving you an excuse to do a Marciano." For some reason he had expected her accent to be Irish, and it was; full of the lilting West, a song in itself.

"Well, now." Johnny looked at her appreciatively, slackening his tensed muscles. "I never met the Irishwoman yet who refused a drink from a gentleman: won't you please be our guest for a little while? The other half isn't so bad, you know!"

There was an almost imperceptible twinkle deep in the green fathoms. "Indeed, I believe it's not," she answered still without a smile, but her voice warm and friendly. "I'll have a small gin."

An exclamation of disgust issued from Allan Prentice. "Look Nora," he began angrily, "this is a bad way to introduce you to the University; you'll get the wrong idea completely."

"Now, now, Allan," she cut in sweetly. "I'd better get to know the bad characters along with the rest." She faced Johnny, and now her smile shredded his composure. "If you'll take my coat, Mr Ferguson," she said, "I'll join you for a while."

Allan Prentice hissed viciously through his nose, shot a venomous look at Johnny, and swept out of sight with his lugubrious bodyguard astern. Johnny slipped her coat from her shoulders with nervous fingers, ushered her into a vacant chair and poured two large gin and tonics.

"I'm Johnny Ferguson."

"I know. I'm Nora O'Brien."

"How d'you know?"

"Allan told me quite a lot about you. It seems that a respectable young woman has three worries in this town—American sailors, over-sexed Calvinist businessmen, and medical students like you."

His vanity purred. "Don't you believe that idiot Prentice," he told her in mock outrage. "What are you doing here?"

"The same as you. I'm studying, although rather more civilized material." She regarded him gravely, and he thought: she's got the face of a madonna, she's absolutely beautiful, beautiful—

"I'm doing Celtic at Trinity," she said. "I'm over here on exchange. I met Allan in the Common Room this morning, and he very kindly agreed to let me see the wicked University night life."

"The wicked night life." Johnny winked. "Of whom I am chief," he added, palm to breast.

"Don't be blasphemous, Mr Ferguson." It was impossible to tell how serious she was. "You have very little in common with St Paul."

"You know your New Testament very well for an Irish Catholic, young lady."

"But I'm not a Catholic," she said. There was real devilment dancing across her lovely face. "In the part of County Cork that I come from, they say that even the pigs are Protestant."

Not a Catholic! He decided to attack at once. "You know," he said, "me ould mother always said I would meet an Irish girl—"

A warning finger periscoped before his nose. "Your blarney's wasted, Johnny. I'm here mainly because those three pseudo-intellectuals were putting me to sleep."

"I see. You're not my type either, beautiful?"

"Of course not. I happen to fall for nothing less than tall, mature men full of Christian respect for women, the more ante-diluvian the better. Anybody can have loose morals, boyo—you're not original any more."

She looked at him quite impassively and her voice was barely guilty of irony. Then a flicker of regret crossed her brow, and he sensed that she had spoken on impulse.

Resiliently he kept his expression pleasant, and offered her a cigarette. She accepted it gratefully. "There was no need for that speech, old girl," he whispered. "My old mother also told me to treat everyone exactly as they deserved. A lady is a lady, and a whore is a whore; there aren't all that many in between, you know. But time is running short for all of us, and I'm damned if I'm going to waste any of it chasing a young lady who's just not playing. Now, if you'll drink your drink, you'll be back in your cosy digs in no time with nothing more sordid than your ideals of love and marriage to go to bed with."

She was genuinely taken aback. "I think I underestimated you, Johnny Ferguson," she said. "I live precisely four hundred yards up the road, so I'll be perfectly safe."

"I'll walk you there," offered Johnny. "No," he waved away her faint protest. "Whether you believe it or not I am at heart a gentleman and a romantic. I shall escort you to your door without laying rebel finger upon you."

She was toying with the gold band on her wrist. When she looked up she was admitting some reluctant respect. "That's nice of you, Johnny," she said. "I'll be glad to accept your offer." She smiled through her glass at the far wall; the sudden change in profile made her even more gorgeous.

"Like to dance?"

"No, thank you."

"O.K., I'll get your coat." He looked about him, suddenly conscious that he and Nora were under close scrutiny. Most of the males were still staring at this glamorous new arrival.

"I'll bet they think I've clicked," he said, lifting her coat. "There's no point in disillusioning them just yet. We'll be setting our foot to the street, and the winds of the night will pipe us on our way."

"You're no poet," she said, laughing. "But I don't suppose that's important in a medical student."

Nell and Arnold were standing in the doorway; he moved Nora quickly towards them, ignoring Nell's hostile stare. "Nora O'Brien —Arnold Ayton, Nell Horton." He introduced them quickly. "I'm taking this helpless young lady up to her digs," he said to Nell. "She's just come over from the emerald swards where men are still men and women are double-breasted. Wait for me about ten minutes."

"You bastard," Nell whispered after him, turning to Arnold's ready arm for solace. "If I start weeping, Arnold, lock me in the toilet. But, God—it hurts more every time. There's something different about her, not just her looks—I'm frightened!"

"You're far too soft, Nell," he answered. "You let him pickle his talents all over town, then you're ready with a warm flat and ready money whenever he comes running back."

Hysteria made her voice ugly. "One day, shortly after I took up sculpture in this town, I refused a Q.C.'s proposal. That same night, I literally picked Johnny off the floor in Connor's out of sheer pity because he was too rotten drunk to make it home. Since then he's cut me in pieces whenever he wanted to. How the hell can I explain it? I love the little rat—now go ahead and certify me!"

Her body surrendered miserably to the comfort of his cool hands. "What's going to happen, Arnold?" she sobbed.

Nora and Johnny walked up the road without haste, rejoicing in the purity of the chill night. He watched her effortless little strides and the easy carriage of her body: there was an air of accomplishment, of completeness—but, no, beggarly abstract nouns could not describe the assurance she carried with her. He had never felt so attracted to a woman in his life.

"Do you like poetry?" he asked. It was time for a new slant.

"But of course, young man. Don't you know that all Irish girls can recite Yeats backwards?"

"I think he's a bit mature for my taste," said Johnny. "You know—

'When you are old and grey and full of sleep'—

"We need to forget the future; it's far too frightening. Give me the poet who writes about contemporary experience and emotions that we can all understand, especially when we're young."

Nora gazed at the stars; it was certainly a night for poetry. She shot a puckish smile sideways. "What do you go in for?"

He frowned at her as they passed through a shaft of lamplight; for a moment she saw the perplexity of a little boy in pantaloons, and her warm heart wept for innocence wasted. He kicked a can into the street, and turned to her eagerly, hands in pockets. "Oh—Brooke, Sassoon, Thomas, Poe. No real criteria. And of course, there's old Byron. I love that man's stuff, even his doggerel."

"Well, now, I wonder why you admire Byron, Mr Ferguson?" she exclaimed in surprise so beautifully-feigned that he burst out laughing.

"He was certainly a waster, the old devil," he replied. "But his downright love of youth is so attractive. Listen!" He halted in front of her and threw a Roman salute to the moon:

'Talk not to me of names great in story
The days of our youth are the days of our glory.
And the myrtle and ivy of sweet two and twenty
Are worth all your laurels, though ever so plenty.'

They went on and she concluded that he looked nice in his serious moments, brow double-furrowed, eyes glaring angrily at the drying asphalt.

They turned a corner and she stopped at the first entrance. "Good night, Johnny Ferguson," she said. "And thank you, thank you very much."

The kindly cast of her smile aroused an overwhelming desire to crush her against him. Whisky fumes fled from his brain, vacating a need whose dimensions seemed unrecordable by finite measurements, more vast than all universes known. Sentences could not form, but in his desperate helplessness the wild melody of Murdo's song, the tragedy of Cornaig, found a communicative path, and filtered through his lips brokenly without words, yet conveying more than speech. I need you, Nora, need you as a cold dying planet needs the sun, as Christianity needs the Cross, as a young seed needs a womb of warmth—persistently the music pleaded the need of the woebegone features, and before the harsh, agonised crooning Nora O'Brien's face became tender, and her limbs were suddenly drained of their power.

When he finally spoke, he said clumsily, half in a dream, "Can I see you again, Nora?"

She stood unflinching before him: he took her lightly by the shoulders. Without taking her eyes away from his face she took a small white card from her handbag and slipped it into his pocket. "That's my telephone number," she said, and now her voice was gentle. "But Johnny, that girl back in the flat is fond of you, I know it."

"Nora." His voice was a hoarse breath of humility.

The green eyes were veiled with freshness as she stepped to him him and tilted her face close. "I've had too much gin. I don't think I care. You're a poor wild self-centred young devil, and you're dying for a bit of peace and security. It's an attractive mixture, Johnny, and it's too much for a sentimental Irish girl. I'll try, but I'm sure I've had too much gin."

"Never mind the gin, Nora, just try!" Relief and excitement surged fluid through him; something beyond his wildest dreams.

He felt her cheek, a pair of warm, soft lips brushed his own, then his arms were empty. A door banged. It seemed miles away. He staggered across the road in a daze. "Was it a dream?" he enquired of a privet hedge. He pulled the small square from his pocket: CENtral 2127 it said.

"No, by God, she's real!" he cried aloud. "Johnny boy, your redemption draweth nigh!"

"You know," said Nell, as she burrowed into his back two hours later. "I didn't think you'd come back to the flat to-night. I prayed that you would, and you did, and now I'm not sure that I'm glad. What's wrong, Johnny?" She clenched her teeth round the sheet, terrified of his answer.

"I'm tired, sweetheart," he said drowsily. "It's about time I gave you a rest."

She pulled his hand between her thighs. It lay there motionless; she shuddered as if she had touched death. Johnny baby, she thought, I can feel something awful approaching. Don't let her take him—she's far too perfect. She threw herself across him, as if to save him from the anger of the world.

"Come on now, love," he soothed her. "Let's dream the dreams of youth while the cold old earth sleeps dreamless. Tomorrow we'll crack the sun wide open."

But the world was still awake.

Professor Price, Dean of the Faculty of Medicine, stirred the embers of a magnificent log fire with a heavy iron poker. "I wouldn't have believed it," he said. "All those years I've known Malcolm Nesbit."

"It's the truth, I'm afraid." Sir Norman Parker sipped his brandy and regarded his old friend across the spacious fireplace. "That's why young Elliot got the sack from the Royal City—Malcolm threw him to the wolves. And as you know any young surgeon can run into an abnormal hepatic artery; it's just bad luck. I was having coffee with Malcolm when the Superintendent rang him. 'I'm not surprised,' he said, 'I have no confidence in Elliot,' and yet he had always demanded that the boy do his private cases with him—Elliot was such a wonderful assistant. But there and then Nesbit was only bothered about preserving the integrity of his own judgment in the eyes of the Board, the old pig, and we lost one of our best surgical prospects ever. You know, Gareth, we've had some great times together—when you're around I'm still proud to wear a white coat. How's that for the sugary snivellings of an old man?"

Gareth Price shook his head. "I'm flattered. I know how you feel. There are times when I look at those young first-year faces, all adventure and inexperience, and I feel like telling them to beware the human race. Still, you can't beat Medicine, Norrie; it's always chock full of interest, and only God knows what's coming next."

Sir Norman smiled and rose, holding his lower back. "Of course you're right, but I often wonder—if those young kids knew the inside story about people like Nesbit, what would they think of their chosen profession?"

CHAPTER V

Mr Rutherford laid the wet film back in its rack. "Right, Ferguson, we'll do him tomorrow. That's a nasty stone he's got in his ureter. Don't forget to X-ray him again tomorrow morning; these things have a habit of moving overnight."

He nodded an answer, writing busily in his notebook.

Outside the City lay in blistered subjection under the fierce loving of a sun whose unexpected faithfulness had lasted six weeks, and had exhausted it completely. It was early July, and the fruit shops were scarlet with ripe cherries. And everywhere the dry, exciting smell of summer arose from melting tarmac, as the women of the City rejoiced in their tanned skins and print frocks and their menfolk rejoiced at the sight of suntanned women in print frocks. Church attendances were low, except for the City Baptist Chapel, where body-odour was stronger than usual; on the whin slopes of the Corporation golf course Peeping Toms were enjoying an unparallelled season. But the succulent odour of new-cut grass which filtered through the windows of Newton Hospital carried a dry tang of warning—the lean, burned men who drove in from the Border country were smoking heavily.

Johnny shoved his hand across his face to remove yet another rivulet of sweat, and hoped Nurse Perkins wouldn't pass out in theatre tomorrow.

He accompanied Austin Rutherford to the door of the hospital. The nurses who passed smiled pleasantly but without devilry. Johnny Ferguson's reputation was a myth.

He had been asked by Arnold to act as locum house-surgeon, while Arnold sunned himself during his fortnightly vacation. Arnold was happy to leave his beloved wards in Johnny's charge; the irresponsible skirt-chaser who had been cheerfully bar-crawling his way to disaster during the winter was gone; in the summer term lectures and cliniques had been attended with astounding regularity, and his passing of the Forensic Medicine and Public Health Professionals, together with excellent class marks in Surgery, bore testimony to solid evening bookwork. Johnny still found time for the occasional drink and guitar session, but now his day started and ended with purpose. And, of course, there was herself; the source of all purpose. No wonder those titless little hags were disappointed in him!

The night before Arnold left for the south was cool and quiet. The cocktail bar of the Castle Arms was deserted, and they drank their chilled lagers in tired contentment.

"You know your stuff, kiddo," Arnold admitted after an argument over the merits of the upper abdominal incisions. "Sorry as I am for Nell, that colleen has made a real man of you."

"Poor Nell," said Johnny with a sigh. His only regret was that in avoiding her he had been forced to shun the Society; Jehosaphat had been holding the chair. But at long last he knew the face dreamed by the salmon pool, and a sweeter scent than late blackthorn. It was worth a lifetime's guilt.

Mr Rutherford left, and Johnny stood contemplating the huge shoulders that thrust through the revolving door. He makes you wonder, old Rutherford—there's a man climbing the ladder with bitten fingernails; he'll be a nation-wide name one day, but his staff are too frightened of him to like him. Who said ambition was a healthy thing? It's difficult to be human when there's a holy flame licking your arse.

He entered the surgical corridor. Sister Glen, the handsome shrew of the theatre, was coming towards him, hen-toed and heavy on her wedge heels, white uniform gleaming against the pale walls.

"Afternoon, Sister."

"Afternoon, Mr Ferguson. What mischief are you up to now?"

"I've just tried to persuade Mr Rutherford into the 'Castle' for a pint, Sister. It's no use, though; I think he loves his wife."

She smiled at him levelly, displaying perfect teeth. "Your powers of persuasion must be on the wane, Mr Ferguson. What a pity, after your fame had reached as far as my decrepit ears."

You bitch, he thought, regarding her lined, pleasant face. You've been at this game so long, sublimating your heat into remarks like that, that you know just where to place the barb. By God, a year ago I'd have had you laid on your back by now, even if you are nearly forty, and built for comfort.

"You're right, Sister," he said in a sudden fit of sly inspiration. "I'm afraid we aren't all endowed with the persuasive powers of Dr Ayton."

Sister Glen blushed to the roots of her dark hair, and Johnny felt a heel. Her fondness for Arnold was known throughout the hospital and the more malicious elements of the staff made oblique insinuations regarding the time Arnold spent in her duty-room.

"I must go for tea, Mr Ferguson," she said, deliberately avoiding his eyes. Her cape brushed past his hand, primevally female. He wondered if what they said about her was true, that she had carried a torch for some registrar for years, only to discover in the end that he was homosexual. One never knew.

Tonight was his night off, and he was meeting Nora for supper. After that they had promised to pay a visit to a Scottish Nationalist meeting at the house of Torquil McLelland, the fiery political genius of Connor's.

Nora had developed a great admiration for the lean and long-haired Torquil, but Johnny was unimpressed by the promise of "A New Line," remembering fruitless years full of harangue and inferior brands of hot air.

"A fine Scot you are!" she had chided him. "Do you think that Ireland developed a powerful movement in a night? Torquil has real talent. We'll go."

He finished in the wards, and phoned the medical resident. "I'm going out in half-an-hour, Gerry. I'd be grateful if you'd have a keek at Wilkie's drip when they change the bottles."

"Will do, Johnny, and have a good time. Don't put your right hand anywhere I wouldn't."

"Certainly not, boy—I'm left-handed."

Outside in the warmth of the evening he told himself that he'd never been so happy. The inimitable hot, dry flavour of July lingered in his nostrils: the spice in the air intoxicated the blood with all the alchemy of Araby; the only jarring sensation lurked in the ugly tint of yellow pythoning its way into the green slopes of the hospital lawn.

He had time for a pint of amber in Connor's before meeting Nora. For a moment the urge to save one and fourpence was strong, but the moment was short. He lengthened his stride, short, stocky legs pistoning their way ruthlessly over the hot pavement.

An old man staggered past him, mumbling drunk; the magic of summer vanished.

Back into your dreamworld, boy; there's a nasty, old, familiar feeling inside you again. You're the youngest surgical registrar in the Royal, you're at the Royal ball, and Nora looks like a spring morning in Heaven with all her lustrous hair swept back from that gorgeous cameo of line and colour, and you're enjoying the lust that ogles her evening gown, for these bastards all envy you, and afterwards you're taking her home to your pretty bungalow in Colinton, to a warm bed where she won't be wearing that black dress, and tomorrow it'll be Saturday so you'll have an easy wander round the wards in the morning, and you'll say 'Yes, Sister, no, Sister, how fucking nice of you, Sister,' and you'll give your patients the old Ferguson charm, then you'll come outside into the freshness of a lovely East Coast wind, but it'll smell different for as far as you're concerned the smell of Connor's ale is a thing of the past and so is the guff of new sweat that comes up between your skin and your old shirt when you're half-way through the last verse of a chain-gang holler, and young surgical registrars don't go into Connor's because it's a bloody dive and they don't play guitars in smoky clubs because it's just not done.

No, boy, home you'll go, home you'll drive in your Ford Consul to a lunchtime drinks party that you're giving for your neighbours, and you'll talk Forensic Medicine with the impoverished young barrister across the road, and gardening, and cars and nannies, and you'll be happy in the knowledge that but for one flickering smile from Dame Fortune that sunburst into a big, lasting beam you might be boozing your Saturday away amid the clamour of C's and G 7ths, Jehosaphat's ramblings, and the profanities that have their dwelling-place on either side of Connor's counter.

In mid-stride he felt sick.

He looked up as a young woman approached him, and admired the heavy black tresses that half-veiled her face, and the voluptuous sway of her tanned body whose limbs sprang in dusky promise from her green floral frock. He looked again in horror.

She stopped, awaiting him in her old, easy stance, one leg thrown forward with instep turned to show the full curve of her calf. He looked at her with stubborn distaste, and nodded a gruff welcome.

"Well, now, aren't you the smart little boy these days?" she drawled. Her eyes flicked over his new 'Varsity blazer, his pressed white shirt with the red and gold tie drawn tidily at the neck, his immaculate grey slacks and polished brogues. "I scarcely recognise the notorious rake." Her breath was fiercely scented with gin; the eyes were torpid and the flesh under them pocked with shadows.

"What are you doing here, Nell?" he muttered uncomfortably, not slackening his pace.

Her voice became shrill: "Damnation, Johnny, you know what I'm doing here. I've been hanging around for the past hour. What's so special about her, Johnny?"

"We've been through this already," he rapped out. "We lived our sex and songs together, but I've found somebody who's got much more to give. You just can't compete, Nell—surely you understand?" He patted her bare arm with synthetic kindness.

She shivered at his touch. "I wish I didn't know you so well. You've been dreaming up your ideal woman ever since you were a kid—a good Celtic pedigree, pure, sweet and beautiful, and you're not prepared to look any further. For God's sake, throw away your rose-tinted glasses—it's your own stupid imagination you're in love with!"

Seizing her by the shoulder of her dress he shook her savagely. "You keep your jealous filth to yourself, you bloody shrew-cat. If only you realized how differently Nora talks about you! She never had an evil thought in her life!" He was shouting: a hundred yards away an elderly gentleman walking a fat spaniel turned around and stared.

Nell adjusted her shoulder bag slowly and he loathed the dignity in her voice. "That's the trouble, she's just too perfect. She's a little porcelain vase, made in Ireland, and she's the loveliest trophy you've ever set on your vanity. But it's no good, Johnny darling. One day you'll hit one of your rough top notes, and she'll crack right down the middle." She turned on her heel and left him.

"Nell!" he called, bathed in a broth of emotions quite beyond analysis. But her hips swung away from him round a corner. He walked the remaining distance to Connor's in record time.

The swing door was hardly still behind him when Johnny noticed Ricky Slater and Stella sitting in a window alcove. They looked uncertain as he approached them; the reason was so obvious that he took it for granted.

"How are you, my young lovers?" he greeted them with affection.

"Fine, Johnny," Ricky answered. "Where have you been?" Stella, he observed, was glaring stonily at her folded hands—she had always been very thick with Nell.

"I've been very busy, Ricky. Work and Nora take up a lot of time these days." He was going to stick to his guns, by God!

The question had to come. "What about the Moonshiners? Are we still going on?" Stella asked it, and there was no resentment in her voice. With a sudden jerk of pain he realised that their singing had been the breath of life to others beside himself.

Ricky had more fuel to add. "I've just seen Hector: there's a Yank in town who wants to audition us—we can probably make a record by the end of the year if he likes our stuff."

Johnny sat up startled. "That's wonderful, Ricky. Of course we'll carry on. I'm sorry that I haven't seen you lately, but what with—" his voice trailed off. Stella was looking at her hands again; he felt himself losing control of the situation. "When is this audition to be, Ricky?"

"A week on Saturday morning, down at Hector's place."

"Right," he said authoritatively. "If Stella can get in touch with Nell, I'll be free. O.K.?"

"O.K." Stella smiled at Ricky, and Johnny felt a desperate urge to be close to both of them. He noticed the guitar on the window ledge. "Come on, Ricky, move along a bit. Let's liven this place up a bit." The old, restless spirit.

Ricky's arpeggios rippled over their drinks. The wheel of time had slipped back a few revolutions and truth was again an Aberdeenshire bothy song: loud, utterly unapologetic, but meaningful beside the clink of glasses and the smoke and talk of leisure.

Yes, boys, the fleeting night of revelry is often birth and always life to such a song, and until the barman objects, is never less than joy to those who sing it.

But wait a minute—there's drama in Connor's again. At the far end of the bar there's a dark-suited form writhing and screaming on the floor. Stop the music, Ricky, for if I recognise the signs correctly, poor old Jehosaphat has been crossed in love for the seventh time this month.

Nora O'Brien was brought up in a part of the world where young women learn patience quickly: where if a young man agrees to meet you at six, it is not unusual for him to make his grand entry at nine in a somewhat alcoholic condition.

It would seem that when she agreed to meet a Scottish medical student in a small City cafe, she should accept the fact that he was forty minutes late and smile phlegmatically. But to-night Nora was fuming. She drank the Scala's coffee slowly, one hand thrust in the pocket of her full blue skirt: flattering glances flashed her way, for students passed her as they went to pay Maria at the counter; she accepted and ignored them as automatically as she did the sunshine. Maria, ever the intuitive psychologist, noticed the throb in the small throat and wandered up to her.

"Don't-a you worry about-a Johnny—he'll come O.K. He's a bad-a bugger." She lowered her voice in confidence.

Nora grinned in spite of herself at the young Italian woman. She felt comforted in the fact that Maria had noticed her anger and was sympathetic, for Nell was very popular in this part of town.

"He's far too selfish, Maria," she answered. "I'm not letting him away with this."

Maria smiled and picked her yellow teeth. "I dunno, he's a good man. All-a them people who keep sayin' he's lucky gettin' you, never say you're lucky too. I used to hate 'im when 'e come in 'ere drunk and fightin' and doin' bad things with the nurses up in the corner there, and then one night a man call me a dirty, Woppish-a Pape and Johnny belt him right in the guts." She chuckled in evil reflection, happily unaware that she had intensified Nora's gloomy mood.

"I do believe you're very fond of him yourself, Maria," said Nora with a small devil in her voice.

"Oh, yes, I like-a Johnny, but don't-a you worry, I got no crush on him," Maria replied modestly. "Johnny's a good man, but some of his friends are verra bad buggers. You look at that-a Jimmy Anderson: 'e come in here drunk last week, and we give 'im a meal on the slate, and 'e starts-a liftin' up the waitresses' skirts. Then 'e try it on me so 'e got a cup of hot coffee up his kilt. Mr Smith tell me that 'e needed plastic surgery on his-a backside, but I think 'e was-a kiddin!"

Nora could not contain herself. Johnny appeared at that exact instant; her advantage was lost.

"You seem to be enjoying yourself, sweetheart." She recognised the tell-tale flush on his cheeks. He turned to Maria. "How are the bowels, old girl?"

"Now Johnny, don't-a you start bein' clever. You're just a young-a-ster." She made a diplomatic withdrawal.

Nora glared at him across the table. "I suppose you think I enjoy sitting on my own while you're boozing it up."

"Had a bit of trouble across the road, honey. Jehosaphat got terribly drunk, and I had to sober him up."

"How? I suppose you've stood in personally for the stomach pump!" Her Irish temper was rising. "This is your old game, Johnny, and I thought I'd pulled you away from it."

Into battle—his grasp was rough on her hand. "He'd just been let down—by a woman. I couldn't leave him howling on the floor, so that I could be the attentive lover. Surely you respect loyalty, Nora."

She stood up. "Of course I respect loyalty. But your loyalties come in a queer order, Johnny. The last few months have been something out of a fairy story, and I don't want them spoiled by your drunken friends."

She's called my bluff, he thought. The pit of his stomach sank craven, enjoying a tiny thrill of fear.

His lips were pursing against an abject apology, when she said, moving away: "I suppose you've left him to drink himself senseless again?"

Slumped in his seat, he told the truth. "Lizzie made him a pint of coffee, and he seemed to sober up. But now he won't speak anything but Latin—I've always distrusted Connor's coffee."

Nora sat down with a thump. "Lord above," she said, laughing, "No woman with a sense of humour could ever leave you. I lose!"

He smiled with relief. "Women!"

She ran her finger coquettishly down his nose. "My silly pride was hurt, Johnny. Don't put me on a pedestal too much: I have my faults, and I'm vain as the devil where you're concerned."

His monosyllabic retort was vulgar, but he clinched the battle with a kiss.

Derek Paton was in top gear. The newly-elected President of the Scottish Free Party held the floor.

"The trouble with the English is that they exist," he shrieked, drooling over his hairy chin with the thick meat of his lips. "They must be driven from this fair land of ours until not one vestige of their venereal filth remains; then indeed we can set about rebuilding the glories we have been denied, and regain the birthright which was sold by the shameful few for a mess of Saxon pottage. The time is ripe! All over Scotland young men are prepared to rise, to spill their blood. They are waiting for us, the mentors, to light the fiery torch. Once it has been ignited, dear friends, it will burn with valour until the last drop of alien blood has dried on our pavements and the night has taken the last swaying shadow from beneath our lamp standards. They are lice—lice! Forgive me if I employ the assistance of our great Lowland bard and indict England with all my rough Scottish honesty." His bald mushroom head went back on its stalk.

"Ye ugly, creepin', blasted wonner,
Detested, shunn'd by saunt an' sinner,
How daur ye set your fit upon her—
Sae fine a lady?"

"That is the answer to the English Louse that drags its broken, failing members across our soil. Take it, fellow-Scotsmen, take it between your sturdy fingers, and squash it forever!" He sat down and mopped his dripping forehead, smiling a cat-and-cream smile as an enthusiastic burst of appreciation clapped round the room.

Johnny yawned and gazed through Torquil McLelland's front windows at the flawless pastel of the evening sky. He had set his mind against listening to the bulk of Paton's tirade; he disliked the bearded little man intensely.

Earlier in his speech, Paton had quoted Hugh McDiarmid's lines on "the little white rose of Scotland. . . ."

You little seagull-whited sepulchre, thought Johnny, who loved the words viciously. You're standing up and inciting all those fine young lads to acts of violence, and you've never done an honest day's law-breaking in your carefully-planned life.

The meeting developed into a discussion over tea and sandwiches, and he took stock of the new conscripts. The inevitable schoolboy, bespectacled and beautiful in his innocent sincerity, was trotting out the Declaration of Arbroath to a grimy little sweep who did not know where the place was; Murdo, between two pretty girls, was indulging in a learned exposition of the need to re-Gaelicise the Highlands; a tuberculous laboratory assistant was discussing the Treaty of Union with a University soccer blue. The most heated discussion was sited by the Rösener piano where Paton and the nucleus of his new committee were defending the tactics of the I.R.A. against an irate twelve-stone female pacifist who appeared perfectly capable of clearing the room.

Johnny groaned inwardly. My brethren, my Scottish rock-salt-of-the-earth darlings, don't let yourselves be led until your heads are clear. Your country's issue doesn't warrant the bloody rebellion that these people are advocating from their comfortable armchairs; evolution, not revolution, means progress, and in any case apart from dear old Torquil not one of them has heard a shot fired in anger. Nothing but good hard graft will give us a better Scotland—only unrelenting socialist endeavour can break London's economic stranglehold, and give us a breathing-space to review our ideals. At the moment how can you tell a penniless Glasgow boy that it means something to live in Scotland, or remind parents in the Hebrides of the glorious poetry of Gaelic when their children can only make a decent living in an English-speaking society? It's downright bloody immoral. But we've tried all the political avenues, and the country wouldn't accept Marxism in the days of the Depression. There was bound to be a simpler line after all our milk-and-water liberalism had failed: now the propaganda is focussed on individual temperament, an exploitation of scorned dignity—it's relevant enough to the hearts of men, but it's got the wrong perpetrator, a minor repeat of Germany's unhappy accident, ready now to have a go with his jackboots.

He had lost Nora, and saw that she was listening to Murdo. He went across the crowded room and slipped an ostentatious arm around her.

"I admit I'm a bit of a hypocrite," Murdo was saying to two young City typists, "but in the end I always admit that in this country one cannot be a good Gael without being a good Scotsman. On the very few occasions when we've had a Scottish leader capable of uniting the country we have seen moments of unsurpassed splendour—Robert the Bruce is perhaps the best example."

Torquil McLelland made for them. "Have you decided to join us yet, Johnny?"

"I don't know," he said. "I'm a bit sick of this hate-the-English policy."

"Sacrilege!" said Torquil.

"The Derbyshire miner or Devonshire farmer is a good bloke, Torquil. He couldn't give a damn whether we have Home Rule or not. Most of your ammunition is being fired at empty trenches—point your cannon at the stinking Government."

Murdo agreed from behind him. "Let's sort ourselves out first, Torquil. I wish I could make my people in the Hebrides realise how cleverly their language is being civilised away from them, but the only people they'll listen to are their bigoted bloody ministers."

"Och, but we're being anglicised in such subtle fashion," said Torquil. "Think of newspapers and the radio. We've got to teach hatred of the English."

"I met some grand Englishmen in the army," said Murdo. "But there was one four-eyed reptile of a major who asked me to leave my accent at the mess door—he turned out to be an anglicised Scotsman. There's your real enemy."

"Yes," said Johnny. "Let's stop tirading against individual Englishmen—if a man's a reasonable human being, to hell with it!"

"You're getting wound up, De Valera," said Nora. "We'd better go before you hit somebody. I enjoyed the meeting very much, Torquil—Paton's a bit fierce, but I was bred a rebel."

Torquil McLelland saw them to the door. He was followed by the red, throbbing forehead of Derek Paton.

"You'll come in with us in the new Party, won't you, Johnny?" said Torquil in his soft Inverness-shire. Conviction lay rocklike along his lean jaw—his love for Scotland seemed almost pathological.

Johnny shook his head, but he grinned affectionately at the cadaverous economist. "I don't know, Torquil, so many of my thoughts haven't crystallised yet. There are too many cranks around these days." He gazed pointedly at the smirking Paton.

The latter guffawed and slapped him on the back in what was obviously considered to be bluff bonhomie. Johnny wheeled to face him, clenching his right fist into a stony ball, regarding with love the small hairy chin. Paton stepped away.

"I'll think about it, Torquil," said Johnny. "I'll see you in Connors' some time."

"If you're lucky," said Nora. "I'm keeping you out of that den of iniquity."

The door closed; McLelland frowned. "I think we're losing him," he said.

Derek Paton did not hear this. He scrutinized the door; in his pale, cold eyes disease flared madly. His dropsical eyelids flickered in fury. "You wait till I have charge of the concentration camps," he jerked out. "I'll sort you, you tough little bastard!"

CHAPTER VI

THERE WERE so many larks about that you used their song for silence.

All around you the whin bushes sprawled, an endless untidy protection; within and about them the grass was long and cool, freckled blue and yellow, fragrant with pine-scent. Further up the hill the ground was rocky; the summit was smooth and bald against the unflattering heavens. At this time in the afternoon the sun was rampant, but the hill was uncomplaining, for two days' rain had sweetened the earth and it welcomed your tired body with a mother's love while you lay in the shade of the old stone dyke that snoozed along the gurgling ribbonlength of burn. Through the gaps between the mossy stones the golfers marched up and down the precipitous fairways of Lothianburn Golf Course in an interminable procession of futility, and you grinned as obscenities mingled with the click of club on ball. On the far side of the narrow ninth fairway the woods spread a southwesterly finger, shimmering dark green, a haze of brassy anger that dared a steady appraisal. But on this side of the dyke the world was mild and gentle; if Eden was a human concept this was the sort of wild garden that inspired it.

Nora's mouth clung to his; his tongue flicked with skill across her palate. One hand maintained a steely hold on the small of her back, the other roamed splay-fingered through her hair. She broke away with an expression of pain on her face, then hurled her body back at him. His lips pinched the scented flesh of her neck; again she squirmed away only to return; slim brown hands moved hungry underneath the back of her dress. She felt the catch part, but as her breasts panted in freedom against their slender leash of cotton, she shuddered, threw herself into a sitting position and buried her face in her hands. Johnny leaned forward on his arms, burrowing his chin into the dampness till he felt the gritty scrape of moist soil.

"Crikey, how long did that last?" she gasped. "I've just lost a bit of my life. Oh, I'm disgusting."

He regarded her over his folded forearms. "Come off it, sweetheart. There's nothing to be ashamed of just because you feel like a woman. God Almighty, don't you trust me yet?" The face was a pouting little boy's—mother still kept the larder key.

"I don't trust myself, darling. I've always enjoyed kissing boys, and occasionally I felt a little bit bad, but when you've got me in those clinches I feel as if there's a fiery sword right through me. And I keep telling myself that it'll spoil things if we—oh, you blighter, I feel so dreadful!" But she cupped his face between her small hands and pulled it against her. She gazed far beyond the southern horizon where the main road vanished. "I'd just love a little boy like you," she said.

His cheeky grin appeared from below. "What a wonderful idea!"

"Easy, Casanova." She pulled his tweaking fingers from her nipple. "There's a place appointed for the consummation of desire, and it lies at the end of a rugged ould road that you're never likely to travel." What was going on in that head of hers now? That grave nobility could mask a Roman triumph or a Greek tragedy.

It was then that the thought struck him—brutally. He erased it from his mind, but it came back within the space of a split second, and a split second after that he honoured its sense.

"Nora darling," he said. "I want to marry you."

From the direction of the wood she heard a small, vague scream of pain. It was animal but very vague—she wondered if it belonged to weasel or woman. It awakened a kindred cry inside her and she held him closer.

She said: "Don't say that, Johnny. You're playing with a feeling."

In the context of the moment he felt bound to repeat it.

"If only you meant it," she said. "But for all I know this is just the hunter producing his most powerful weapon: you're such a romantic, Johnny, you could deceive yourself very easily. Let's wait a while; your career's not started yet."

"So what, Nora? I love you, dammit."

"Because a tiny flat and a howling baby are a far cry from a choir of birds in the grass." She poked him half-playfully with the heel of her white sandal.

"Nora, you sound like a women's magazine. Look! I've

never felt like this. You're the one thing in the world that can make me feel a wee bit idealistic again. I could take you right now if I wanted, but you've still got a lot of daft Victorian brainwash in you, and I don't want you hating yourself. Surely a ring is the only sensible answer?" He felt like a Catholic after a self-satisfying confessional.

Nora smiled, the way nobody else could. "It's a lovely thought, Johnny. But don't rush me, love—for the first time I'm in the middle of an affair that I'm not controlling, and I'm a little frightened of you. I wish I didn't see the moon and stars in you so much—it's the ould pride again!" There was a new, smoky fire in the green eyes: he had a feeling she would lie here for ever if he asked her. The ball was in his hands, and the line lying open—and yet he was not desperate to score.

They raced each other down the hill. On the lower slopes they twisted in and out of the picnicking families clumped around the burn. Nora's legs moved with deceptive power, and as she took his arm breathlessly at the iron gates of the Corporation park, he thought: Nell could never do this.

On to the smooth, dry road, my dear, with its white, perforated line in the middle. When you're drunk that line gives you the impression that you can tear the road in half, and by God, with a girl like this one in your pocket, why not?

"Wake up," said an Irish voice beside him. "For the third time, who are we meeting at the Union to-night?"

"Oh, Colin and his nurse, and a chap called Jimmy Anderson—you'll like him. He's only managed to stay in Medicine by the skin of his teeth. He's always had a weakness for the bottle, but it's got much worse since his twin brother died of cancer four years ago."

"There's not a Connor's regular who doesn't have some excuse. No doubt he'll have some poor woman with him?"

"Of course. All the lads will have their girls with them. But I know whose girl will be the prettiest." He beat his breast like an Old Testament prophet.

"Thank you, Mr Ferguson." Nora curtsied, displaying a graceful sapling of golden thigh. She looked almost afraid at the heat in his face. How much longer?

They approached the hilly South Side suburbs. Shrubberies were trim and green, rejoicing in a near-audible juiciness, but

Johnny regretted that the wallflower and lilac were past, for in May this part of town smelled sweeter than a Paris boudoir. Courting couples were in bloom everywhere, wrapped around each other with the tireless power of young muscle. The boys all glanced at Nora, and turned away shamefaced to their own girls as if to apologise for their weakness; she let a dimple tug at the corner of her mouth as the preening conceit shone from Johnny's face.

The heart of Scottish bourgeoisie lay here, in the semi-detached villas, the crescents of grey bungalows, the lush green parks and weedy streams overhung with weeping willows, the tidy youths and girls in their blue and maroon blazers, the bank manager flaunting a shabby old school scarf, the schoolmaster walking his pigskinful of soul-mutilating correction home, the narrow vowels, the heavy overdrafts, and the stiff upper lip that complained less than most. Here "sex" were carried by coalmen, here, as the tenements of the City centre declared, "the weemin a' wear fur coats and nae drawers"—here was a land that gave more than its share to the green sward of Murrayfield, and had given the same to the mud of Paschendaele and the sands of Alamein. Here a wealth of endurance awaited discovery beneath cold East Coast reserve.

"The pubs won't be open for twenty minutes yet, love," said Johnny. "Let's go up to Torquil McLelland's; he's sure to have a beer somewhere."

"Fair enough," said Nora. A cluster of tiny sweat beads encircled her nostrils.

Amid the pleasant chatter of business the bell of the merchant's till sallied out through the open doorways, wreaking death and destruction on the housekeeping money. An ice-cream vendor, lathered in sweat, was dishing out sliders and cones to a restless queue of children; in passing, Johnny noticed with a professional eye that the man had a large boil weeping on his hairy wrist.

"I wonder how many of that lot catch the dreaded diarrhoea and vomiting?" he remarked to Nora. "Just think of all the assorted bacteria crawling down his arm, ready to leap into the bowels of small, unsuspecting innocents."

"Johnny, you think up the most ghastly things at times," she complained. "Let's talk about something a bit cleaner."

"Agreed, m'lady—how's your sex life?"

"Oh, Johnny!" She smacked his bottom, naughty-little-brat

fashion. "Darling, do you think we could?" she asked. "You know, my brainwash and all that."

"Of course. Surely we should give each other all we can. We're both intelligent adults, and most problems can be handled by intelligent behaviour."

"Do you think you won't secretly despise me?" she queried doggedly. "Look how you run down Nell and all those others."

"My dear girl." Johnny was growing irritable. "I needed them in the same way as I needed a pint of beer. But with us there's a sort of spiritual bond that's bound to pull us close at all levels, and what goes on between clean sheets is one of them. You want me too, and damn well you know it!"

They reached the entry to McLelland's flat, and she stopped in the huff. "Every woman doesn't fall for the same fast patter, Mr Ferguson. I'm getting tired of hearing about your past amours."

"Then stop trying to extract the gory details. Do I keep casting all your past misdeeds up?"

"There's nothing to cast up," she retorted. "Compared to your record mine has scarcely a black mark on it."

Thunder rolled across his face. "What d'you mean 'scarcely'?" He had lost colour below his tan.

"You know what I mean, Johnny," she answered in hurried confusion. "That one night with Kevin on the beach, when he nearly went too far—but that's absolutely all. I'll bet I'm the first virgin you've had for a long time." She stopped, for he had winced in pride.

He opened the entry door and ushered her in. "Let's have a beer with Torquil and forget it."

Inside she threw her arms around his neck. "I'm not a bad girl, darling. There's never been anyone like you, honestly."

A cool breeze swirled around the well of the stair; it fell fresh as ice on his hot cheeks. His smile was soft. "Forget it, Nora. It's just that the thought of anyone else touching you makes me feel sick. We don't need to delve into any old cupboards—I know an old song that's written just for us."

"Trust you to find the right song," she said. "How does it go?"

"Aha," he murmured, eyes bright and menacing. "I shall sing it to you between clean sheets!"

The bus took him up Lauriston Place; he disembarked opposite the Royal City, and moved quickly in the direction of Teviot Place, where the University Union lay in wait of a Saturday night for young people with adventure in their eyes and pleasure in their pockets. As he turned into the wind, a tall young woman passed him. She was a working-class lassie; ugly, black seams on her stockings, and a garish red coat. She was also attractive in a pale blonde sort of way, and he stared at her harder than he should have. She quickened her pace; the black patent leathers clipped away angrily from his candour.

Why did I look at her like that? I've got a girl who's streets ahead of her. Surely the old eye's not roving again? I love Nora, I love Nora, I love her. . . .

Colin and Jimmy were late. In the Union beer-bar he ordered a pie and a lager, scrutinising the confident young blood in the mirror opposite. White shirt, red tie, clerical grey suit, £12-ready made, white arrowhead of linen in breast pocket. Thick hair parted neatly, and poised in a rakish sweep over right eye. Not bad on the whole but no match for Nora. Women were weird creatures, thank God!

He looked at the frosty lager glass until the sand in his throat became unbearable, then lowered it three pegs at a gulp. The pie-crust was hot and crisp, and the peppery meat melted in his mouth. The big, lazy room was peopled mainly by tables of bridge fiends: they played silently, their pale faces bereft of meaning.

He looked along the bar. He did not know the small shrill Indian who was boring the barman with a garbled shaggy-dog story at the other end, but he could not help admiring the golden tiepin which flashed between the narrow lapels of his blazer. It vanished suddenly; a shabby brown suit had blotted out its brilliance.

"McEwan's Export," said the newcomer. A big chap, about six feet. The massive spotty face sucked beer noisily while the heavy dewlap quivered. Allan Prentice of the "Halcyon."

He saw Johnny half-way through a mouthful of meat pie; there was cold menace in his recognition. He did not move, but stared rudely, hands pushed deep behind his waistband. "Look at that ugly bugger." His voice was thick with earlier ale.

Johnny gazed steadily over the bar. He counted the number of full Guinness bottles on the bottom shelf; there were eleven.

"There are some things I can't stand," said the voice. "One of these is a medical student, another is a Scottish Nationalist. But when you get the two together, boy, you've found something really sordid."

As always Johnny felt dreadful at first; trouble was in the offing, and he was sober. His heart beat too fast, his breathing went coarse, and the floor seemed to borrow his legs. And then his whole body was instantly charged with a venom of power, generated in the part of him reserved for one thought only: your name is John Ferguson, and you'll crawl to nobody! It was all done so easily—you turned on the switch, and in a minute you were a different person, panting with the knowledge of what must be done, hypnotised by the cruel pain that was cleaning you inside out.

He walked across to his aggressor. "Are you talkin' to me?" His head was on one side, and he was grinning without knowing it.

Prentice sneered. "If it's possible to talk to a bloody —"

Johnny dared not wait longer lest the fury should leave him. He smashed his right foot across Prentice's shins at an angle, and as the other's arm groped downwards in pain, his jacket was seized by Johnny's two swift hands and a flail of solid bone hammered two front teeth into the back of his mouth. He gagged and retched as his throat filled with blood, but he was helpless, for a right leg had advanced in mid-air and the momentum of this ferocious little warrior was throwing him across it. His head struck the wooden floor with a sickening crack; all his strength had been replaced by pain, but his chief sensation was one of sheer disbelief. Far away the barman cried in protest.

Johnny sat astride him. His left hand was savaging his enemy's throat; with his right fist he smashed forehand and backhand punches into the bloody mouth that he could scarcely see. "You dirty big bastard," he hissed through his teeth. Then Colin and Jimmy had his hands behind his back; he leaned against their legs exhausted.

The bridge tables were empty. A crowd of students were regarding his handiwork with a mixture of admiration and horror. The big man sat up slowly and a shudder went through him. Johnny was now temperless and attempted to help him up, but

Prentice pushed him off. Tears streamed from his eyes, and he thrust a dirty handkerchief against his lacerated lips and gums. Blood was welling through the gap in his teeth, staining the stubby fingers.

"All right, Ferguson," he muttered thickly. "You won't always win." He staggered to the door; before he opened it he stopped to examine his legs and spit.

The crowd was dispersing. Nobody had made a move to apprehend him. He heard the comments that filled the room, however: "Did you see that? Just like a Ted, in with the head . . . hard case, Ferguson, shouldn't have tangled with him . . . no committee around, lucky for him . . . Prentice asked for it . . . this used to be a gentlemen's club. . . ."

The barman wiped the vampire's kiss on Johnny's forehead with a wet towel. "Have a drink and forget it, son," he said. "It wisnae your fault."

No, he thought, if you don't do one of these big bums once in a while, they'll never leave you alone—we need another war to get rid of them.

To Colin he said: "Don't tell Nora about this. She wouldn't understand."

"Of course not," his elegant friend replied. "I wish you'd killed the bugger. Wait till I get Jean going on the drink tonight, Johnny. It'll be the easiest seduction in history."

Johnny's laugh stifled in his throat: the room was filling up with suits and blazers; between one of each he had glimpsed the second barman mopping up two dull white objects that sat in a pool of red by the door. The cosy room was suddenly a dungeon of imprisoning, accusing vileness—the site of the murderer's lust, the Gauleiter's *Ofen*, the ring of the rabbit-punch.

"Let's get a good lining of Guinness in the "Woolpack," he said. "Come on, drink up."

The Union Palais was held upstairs in the Debating Hall, a brown study haunted by the ghosts of laborious wit and restive benchloads of malice, but the dance did have therapeutic value; you could stagger round the sardine-tin of floor clasped to a taffeta belly, and sweat out your beer without the slightest danger of falling down.

They had drunk seven pints of draught Guinness with Hector Gunn in the Woolpack, and Hector had sung "Reilly's Daughter" with elbow-swinging panache, and he had knocked a drip from the beaky nose of a little man into the little man's pint, and the beaky little man had objected. They had left hurriedly when Hector began to inform the bar that the City was an uncivilised cesspool, and no fit place for a nobleman to live in; one fight was enough for one night, and the University and the City were always potential foemen in the public-house arena.

They sat with their girls on the balcony that encircled the dance. Tonight had drawn the usual gumbo of adolescence and early adulthood: freshers screaming drunk on a smell of cider, steady Union twosomes in their third year of a better-than-nothing-to-do routine, Rugby stalwarts, devout in their faith that last year's muddy glory and tonight's kudos-crested navy serge would render conquest a formality—and the sly stranger, who stuck out like a sore thumb, with his oily black waves, Windsor-knotted tie, and the big gold ring on his left hand.

Johnny made a quick survey of the girls, and was satisfied that Nora was queen. She had caught her curls at the back in a narrow fillet; they emerged in a long burning bunch that kissed her right shoulder. Beneath the sheath of her green dress a frothy flare of underskirt guarded her crossed legs. Colin's Jean was a pleasant little nurse of five feet; Jimmy's current mistress was a tarty blonde of five feet ten.

Their present position afforded a fine view of the carnage below.

The five-piece band was blaring forth a hideous samba, simultaneously drowning the voice of their middle-aged female vocalist, whose massive bosom gleamed glistening wet out of a sagging white blouse. The bulk of the hall was occupied by dervish hordes of couples gyrating around each other like unstable electrons, but in the middle of it all a few were scarcely moving, clasped together in an oblivion of mixed ancestry. The purple beam of the spotlight was focussed on the plump pimpled back of a girl whose head lay on the shoulder of a tall, bearded African.

Nearer the door the cattle-market was still in session, but the good stock was all on the floor. The remaining women huddled together in shame and desperation under the scrutiny of the equally desperate faces which moved about them, searching their ravaged ranks for a reasonable feature or form that would not qualify their classmates' Monday morning greeting with a smirk.

"It must be hellish for these poor birds," Johnny said to Nora, pointing to a small group who were devouring the whirling figures with starving eyes. "It's enough to make you cry. They stand there all night, poor plain horrors that they are, until it's obvious that nobody's drunk enough to stand the sight of them, then they slink home down the back streets."

"Have you ever danced with them?" asked Nora.

"Good God, *no*!" Johnny's face was outraged. "A man's got his self-respect."

This was the stage of the evening when wit and laughter were easily mass-produced. Jimmy and Colin indulged in their customary cut and thrust to the great amusement of their women, whilst Johnny fanned the flames with the odd quip, or insulted Nora gently, drawing a crack bead on the line between vulgarity and forgivable earthiness.

"Happy, darling?" he queried.

"Of course I am." She moved closer to him, and slipped a slender leg across his knees; the warmth of it flooded him.

"I always knew I could enjoy a Saturday night in civilised fashion," he bragged. "It took you to force the issue, though. You're the beacon that this old ship's been tryin' to sight for years."

"Nonsense." She dismissed the image graciously. "It's obvious to any sensible girl that you're worthy of a better life than the one you used to lead."

"Its getting better all the time," he said. "You've saved me, Nora. We still have the odd scrap, but we're climbing in the right direction. Just a little effort, and we'll be on the plateau of perfection—and then it'll be a case of living happily ever after."

"I hope so," she said, without allowing doubt into the conviction of her rich voice. She bit his lobe gently; this was something novel. An action worthy of Nell.

The Hell's Bedlam of the band died on a sharp seventh, then a great voice issued from the sweating floor. Jehosaphat had appeared on the balcony-head above the clock, and student heads turned with enquiring female faces. A hush fell.

"Where will you spend Eternity?" he roared at the throng.

"Connor's must be closed," said Jimmy. "And Jehosaphat's drunk again."

Colin stroked Jean's shaven armpit. "Impossible as it may seem, old boy," he drawled, "in two successive sentences you have delivered the understatement of the year, and capped it."

"—In the arms of whores and immoral women!" bawled Jehosaphat. He swayed over the rail, an oafish leer on his face. "You will perish in hell, where the worm dieth not. Be not deceived, God is not mocked; for whatsoever a man soweth that shall he also reap!" His audience howled another ovation.

His friends were all laughing, but for once Johnny was not amused. Jehosaphat's drunken tirade had awakened uncomfortable memories of childhood. He felt relieved when the band struck up again, drowning the tipsy preaching.

"Come on, love, let's go down to the flat," he suggested to Nora.

Jimmy was eavesdropping. "We're all coming!" he pronounced. "Fellow-Bacchanalians—the lady Nora is about to throw a party. I'll just go and get a bottle from Lizzie before she leaves."

"Look what you've let me in for," complained Nora. "My neighbours will have a petition ready in the morning."

"To hell with it," said Johnny. "What about tonight, when they've all gone?" he whispered aside.

"I wondered when this would come," she said through dry lips. "But I'm not long into the flat, and if the neighbours see you slinking out in the morning, that will be the end. But we'll see—you've got me in a naughty, curious mood tonight."

He felt a minute suspicion of ice very deep inside him. Dear Lord, let me be kind to her.

"What's happened to your head, honey?" She had noticed the tooth mark on his forehead.

"I bumped it on the blasted wardrobe," he lied easily.

"Oh, you poor thing," she crowed. "Here, let me kiss it better. It's terrible—the things that happen to you when I'm not around to watch over you."

It was now quarter to eleven; most of the floor shuffled slowly in languid love, but in the Art College corner buttocks still oscillated obscenely and arms and legs flew through the air in all directions.

They collected Jehosaphat and moved through the spacious ante-room, where the portraits of nineteenth-century Union Presidents observed the rabble with taciturn contempt. As they moved downstairs, Johnny, who was in the lead, shouted: "Gardey-Loo the feet, citizens!" Several steps were sprayed with a mess of pale, congealed vomit. The sour odour lingered with them for two flights, at the foot of which they found its author lying prone on a broad window sill. He was small, about 18, and his green cavalry cords were stained stiff.

A precious small pleasure of life is to step a doorsbreadth from a hot stuffy building into the balmy surprise of a mild night. Most of the company bounced toward's Colin's car, but Johnny remained on the top step savouring the swiftness with which the perspiration of his brow was chilled, hardly able to conceal the mounting excitement that needed more than this face for expression.

In the flat they dropped exhausted on the ugly antique furniture; after half-an-hour Jimmy returned with Murdo Macauley, a bottle of Gold Label and a terrifying anger.

"Sorry we're late, gentlefolk," said Jimmy. "I was jumped outside Connor's by a couple of Teds."

"Surely you didn't let them away with it?" said Johnny. There was an ugly blue weal between Jimmy's right eye and his fine aquiline nose.

Jimmy shrugged. "They hit me with a chain from the side, then beat it before I got going. Some High Street gang are talking of clearing the students from all the pubs this side of the Square. This is what happens when our hard men desert us." He winked at Nora.

She smiled woodenly: Jimmy Anderson, like Murdo, should not come near Johnny too often; here again was the pined-for charming elder brother he was lucky not to have; no Highland hero this time, but ten talents unsullied in adversity, a seeker of aesthetic nothingness with glass in hand and friends ever-present, and a personality as irresistible as the sea—the uncrowned King of Connor's.

Nora produced deep crystal goblets from the large mahogany sideboard together with a jug of water. She turned on the wireless. "If you want to dance, take your shoes off," she warned. "There's an old spinster living below."

The room filled with smoke, for all its windows were closed, and the fat bottle lay empty in the fireplace. Nora brought another half-bottle from the kitchen. No complaints yet from the neighbours.

Johnny finished the whisky with Murdo by the unlit fireplace. "This is a lot quieter than the sort of hoolie we used to have," said Murdo.

"It's a lot better too," said Johnny. Fearfully he imagined Nora at some of their former orgies.

"That's a lovely girl you've got." Murdo's dark eyes were ravaged with drink; ugly red streaks flared in their whites. "Yes, you keep on the way you're going."

"She's too good for me," said Johnny, hiccupping. "How much should I tell her about the old days? Remember those two old whores Jimmy and I picked up down in the Fishmarket? I want to be honest with her, but I'm scared."

"If the truth's going to hurt her, forget it," said Murdo carelessly. "Remember what Caesar said, and let people believe what they want to."

She came out of the kitchen. "Where are Colin and Jean?" she asked.

Johnny's eyes travelled the room, his memory the evening. He saw Jimmy's head incline ever so slightly towards Nora's bedroom, and he remembered something said.

Quickly he turned her round and kissed her. "They've gone down to the car to get fags. How about some coffee?—we could all do with a bit of sobering up."

He waited till he heard the spurting of hot water and the dull click of china on oilcloth. He crossed the room in three strides; one more for the hall, and he was into the bedroom. "Colin," he called softly. A hazy shape detached itself from the bed and performed a lopsided mitosis.

Colin padded across to him in stockinged feet. "What's up, old boy?"

"Come on out of there—Nora'll be annoyed." He felt sheepish and out of character.

Colin wagged an upturned thumb beneath his nose. "It's O.K., Johnny. The *alea*'s *iacta* already."

"I see," was all that he could say. The little shape by the bed appeared to shiver in the half-light.

Colin's a bit of a lad, but it's a pity—she's a nice kid. He opened the main door, said loudly: "Oh, there you are," and slammed it again. They followed him into the living-room. There were fierce creases in Jean's dark skirt and patches of wet skin beneath her eyes. Jimmy and the blonde did not bother to look up; Murdo was asleep; Jehosaphat was discussing solipsism with himself on the floor. Colin slunk into an armchair and drew Jean on to his knee. She sank like a stone, and sat uncomplaining as he held her against him, but her hands hung clenched by her sides, and her small stupefied face brooded sorrowfully over his back.

They left just after three o'clock into the friendly warmth of the deserted street, that lay proud in its possession of the early east. Johnny shook hands with each of them in turn—Jean's hand was as cold as February. Nora's eyes had been riveted on the little nurse for the past hour, and she bent and kissed the tired face. Jean appeared not to notice. Nora's hand went to her throat; the moment had an eloquence which Johnny did not like.

The door closed, and for an awkward moment they faced each other. The look was there, unreasoning horror, draining her prettiness. She knew.

He took the bull by both horns. "I'm going for a walk."

"Are you coming back or going straight home?"

"What do *you* want? Maybe I'd better go back to the digs."

"Maybe you'd better."

Silence.

He opened the door again. Colin's impetuosity had outflanked him; strategic withdrawal was a necessity. "I'm really sorry, darling," he began. "I honestly didn't know."

Silence—then she smiled, and the smiling aged her ten years, not in a haggard direction, but bestowing a new maturity that cast her the happy mother of eight. "Come inside, you little clown," she said. She led him into the lounge by the hand, hauled him down beside her on the settee, and wrapped herself around him as completely as her supple limbs allowed.

Afterwards, when he remembered nylon and rustling silk, and the silkier press of something warmer, the muttered curses that came as he sweated in haste and gave pain, and his final rueful apology for what should have been much better, he wondered if the smile at the door had been a greater gift than flesh.

"I thought you'd never let me touch you after that bloody business in your bedroom tonight," he whispered.

"I nearly didn't," she said, her hands still working masterfully.

She was flushed, and the corners of her mouth were smiling. His mouth had left a red mark on her neck.

"You hated us all for a minute, didn't you?"

"Who?" she asked.

"Oh—men." His hand drew a film from his forehead.

"Yes," she said. "You all consider it your divine right to take. Poor little Jean—I was a raving suffragette till you made for that door, then I remembered that you and I are alone and in love, and who knows what's coming tomorrow?"

"Nora." He sprang her firm breast from its shell and nuzzled it gently.

"You're a saint, love," she said. "You were dying to get your hands on me, but you'd have tramped the streets because I was terrified; that's love, in my book."

He looked at his bare feet, not feeling saintly at all. "I'm sorry it wosn't too good, Nora. I'm losing my touch."

She gave a delicious little chuckle. "It'll be better next time, Johnny."

But a black wave of depression had swept over him. Their first time shouldn't have been like this. Somehow the initiative had been taken from him, and he resented it.

He rose slowly to his feet. "You've been an angel, Nora—not me. Do you mind if I go out for a wee walk now? I'd like to clear my head a bit." She was rearranging her clothing; he turned his back in sudden embarrassment.

"On you go, love," she said. "But come back. I want to see those eyelashes of yours tight on your cheeks first thing in the morning."

"Bye, darling. I love you."

"I love you too."

He left the flat and wandered across the green expanse of the Meadows. The dew was gone already, but a few grassy dells were still flattened from last night's moongazing. He was filled now with a hunger to feel real grass under him; good Perthshire hill grass, and scrubby heather and dry pine needles. He was sick of the City, and all cities.

His mood mollified as the sun caressed his tired limbs. Leaving the Meadows, he headed back towards the Old Town and his favourite streets. At this hour the City was as quiet as a Scottish country Sabbath, and he dreamed himself ninety miles northward without any difficulty. By the Cathedral he heard his father's sermons, and by the Mercat drinking font a fountain much purer; the odd shamefaced pedestrian was a renegade from the dance at Killin and the grubby North Bridge shrank to occupy a wooden station over a narrow mountain river. Reaching the magnificent main street of the New Town he awoke from his whimsy, leaned against a jeweller's window and feasted on the skyline. The Old Town gazed autocratically down from its rocky height, splendoured and craggy along its horizon of sun-bright slate and dark gable, shaming the elaborate gardens that clawed at its prehistoric shins. Turret and spire competed with the embroidery of the flowery carpet for the eye's attention, and won the unequal contest hands down.

"You old bugger," said Johnny to the City. "Given half a chance you'll have me in love with you again." He retraced his steps homeward.

It had been quite a night, but at the end of it all he was strangely disappointed. Life brewed more paradoxes every day: the moment of fulfilment which should have levered them up to the plateau of perfection had moved him less than the misfortune of a diffident little nurse. He had said that they were climbing well, and they were, but he should have known that for him perfection could be easily attained in one place only. Glenellin.

That's the answer—the final consolidation, in the finest place on earth, where Johnny Ferguson really belongs.

When he asked her in bed she concurred drowsily, burying her face into his shoulder. He slid into a coma full of soft arms and sweet hair; the dream deepened, and the images became confused. His father, clad in black and imprisoned in his dog-collar, was standing in the distance and admonishing him with his forefinger. The vision came nearer. But, my God, it wasn't his father, it was Jehosaphat dressed in his father's togs, leaning across the balcony, and leering at Nora and him. He turned to Nora in panic and saw that she was naked and that she had that awful look of terror on her face.

"Be not deceived," shrieked the black Jehosaphat. "God is not mocked!"

Nora started up as Johnny screamed in his sleep.

II

GLENELLIN

The North Road to Decision

CHAPTER VII

ARNOLD RETURNED from Brighton on the following Tuesday, happily bleached and browned by the healing sun of the Sussex coast, and worried by the seeming inevitability of marriage to Betty Warren.

He was sure that his love was genuine—how else could he have refused affairs with much prettier women over the past few years? Matrimony demanded a strong, durable relationship, a marriage of like minds, and there was no doubt that Betty and he had much in common. They had whiled away the cool evenings with excellent medical discussions; he could imagine a very satisfactory mental climate around their future fireside.

Against this was her malicious slanderous gossip regarding the sexual behaviour of her colleagues, and her fiendish delight in recalling their disasters; Arnold blamed her strict up-bringing, but a more objective observer might well have indicted the scanty physical experience occasioned by her own mortal terror of "going wrong" and Arnold's deep-rooted shyness as a lover. She was becoming a more vicious possessor daily: their holiday had been particularly marred by a tantrum which she had thrown after finding him joking innocently with the pretty waitress at their hotel. On the return journey she had made several spirited attempts to fix a marriage date, but he had successfully evaded this on the grounds of his impending National Service, stating that her widowed mother should be consulted before she suddenly found her only daughter somewhere east of Suez.

He was glad to be back. Johnny had left his wards in good condition and Sister Glen had welcomed him with tremendous enthusiasm; for some reason she could raise his morale in a way that younger women never did.

He sat in her duty-room after a short morning operating list, teasing her gently about the usual theatre topics. She knew more about his innermost thoughts than any other person save Betty; he had never met such a loyal soul whose integrity was so complete.

"No, I don't think we'll marry till after my National Service, Sister," he said. "I think that a little separation will do us no harm."

She averted her eyes, stroking the brooch he had bought her in Brighton. She knew now that Betty was not for him, as she had suspected all along. She herself had no real physical passion for Arnold, despite what her nurses said—she was past the stage of longing for a man's mere flesh. But he had filled part of the chasm inside her which had been vacant for years, and whose pain had become part of her crusty antiseptic starchiness. This was one of the few real things in her life, and in her devotion she longed to see him happy.

"Think about it carefully, Doctor Ayton," she advised steadily. "In my own experience I've found love a bit like Guinness—it doesn't travel very well over water. But whatever you do never act against what you really want. If you do that, you'll warp yourself terribly."

Hurriedly he turned the spotlight on her: "It's time you got yourself married, Sister. It's awful to see a fine woman like you going to waste." And indeed she did look fine today, with that slick, new hair-style and her buxom freshness.

"My day is past, Doctor," she replied. "If I had done what I wanted to do at the right time—but, hell, what's the use in talking? All I'm good for now is keeping penniless young housemen in cigarettes."

The telephone rang.

"It's for you," she said. "A woman."

Nell's voice slushed into the earpiece—drunk again. "Hello, Arnold," it said, "I'm glad to hear you're back, dear."

"Oh, its you, Nell." Sister Glen tiptoed off to lunch. "Is something wrong?"

"I went up to Connor's on Saturday night."

He snorted in amusement. "What's so unusual about that?"

"Let me go on, dear." The voice broke, then continued: "Allan Prentice came in about nine o'clock. He was in a hell of a state . . . blood all over his face . . . you know why? . . . Johnny . . . big fight at the Union . . . looks like that Irish bitch isn't controlling him so well. . . ."

"Nell, you'd better go and sleep it off," he said sharply. The young idiot—just when he's doing so well!

"I'm not finished, dear," she insisted. "You should have seen his face, Arnold; it was terrible. You know what I did, Arnold? I took him home, and patched his face up—then I—I asked him to sleep with me, Arnold. Oh it was dreadful!" Her voice shattered.

"You what?" The strength of his anger shook the telephone.

"I don't know why I did it," she sobbed. "Except that when he stood at the bar there all alone and ugly, with Johnny's cronies laughing behind his back, I felt a kind of kinship. Here we were, two poor devils who had been hurt by that bastard Ferguson, and I thought we could lick our wounds together."

"Lord on high!" said Arnold.

"But it was so utterly bloody, and he left with a funny smirk on his face. I've never felt remorse like it. If Johnny finds this out, I don't think he'll ever take me back—you know how damnably proud he is." A queer variety of sound effects succeeded the moaning despair of her confession.

"Nell, listen to me," he said soothingly. "Come up to the hospital right away—you know the back entrance through the scrapyard. I'll get some coffee for you in my room, and you can rest here until you feel a bit better."

"Thank you, darling," she slurred. "Why can't I fall in love with a big hunk of goodness like you? You've got everything I should want."

"Come up as soon as you can," he repeated gently. "You can get it all off your chest to Uncle Arnold." He put the telephone down and said to himself aloud: "I should have been a priest."

When Sister Glen returned he was still standing before her mirror, smoking furiously and staring at the smooth baldness of his left temple.

"Off you go and get your lunch," she said. "The cook's produced a nice bit of roast beef and Yorkshire for once."

He shook his blonde head, grating his upper teeth on the skin of his lower lip. "Women never cease to tear the stomach out of my worldly knowledge," he said. "They live by their hormones, not by their thinking processes."

"What's wrong?" she asked.

"Mr Ferguson's been at work again." He cut the truth in half.

She looked annoyed. "I've got nothing against that boy," she said, "but you can smell trouble when he's a mile away. People like him have a habit of involving their friends too damn much. And I don't want to see you with any more burdens on your shoulders at the moment." She banged her heavy ruler on the walnut desk in temper.

"Well, Sister," he said, smiling, "I didn't realise you felt so strongly about my peace of mind."

"You didn't?"

A post-prandial beauty session in the Sisters' Residency had added rouge to her cheeks, and her lips were a bold curve of scarlet. From beneath her frilled cap black curls peeped over her forehead; her dark blue eyes were blazing with fury, and the same emotion gave her big breast a thrust that belied her years and compelled his eyes. He slipped his gaze to the long white fingers that pointed at each other across her apron, and as he stepped towards her sudden perception of her desirability burst through his reserve like floodwater, and a new foreign excitement was challenging his precious principles of self-discipline.

Her eyes narrowed, and she stepped back a pace. He halted uncertainly, confused by the uselessness of his body. The theatre was as silent as a graveyard, but for the harsh whisper of their breathing.

He moved again, and she placed the flat of her hand lightly against his shoulder; the perfect block to the killer-punch.

"Go and have your lunch, Doctor," she said.

He went quickly, slamming the door behind him, and the swing doors when he stepped out into the corridor. He raged unseeing towards the Residency, all but bowling over the theatre staff-nurse as she strolled back from the dining-hall. "Oh, Lord," he groaned. "What did I nearly do?"

Sister Glen settled herself in her chair and lit a cigarette. She would be a little more careful of him in future, bless his heart. It would have been so easy, and it would have spoiled everything.

The clatter of tomorrow's tools, steel on steel, jarred through the closed door. Waves of cruel, necessary heat blasted from the pipes, and the acrid smell of anaesthetic blended warmly with the midday vapour of the open window.

Tomorrow Mr Rutherford's skilful hands would be fighting to prolong the existence of the little barber in Ward B 1, who had cancer of the stomach, and would remove the leg of old Mr

Coates, who had arteriosclerotic gangrene. There were ten cases in all; they would probably be at it all day.

In the top storey of the tenement opposite a woman was hanging out her washing. She moved about with ponderous calm, and as she worked she sang. Her harsh, powerful voice slipped through the window with the sun, adding another dimension to the early afternoon.

CHAPTER VIII

A KEEN SHAVE, and the comfort of light summer clothes. The harsh heat of a gulped nip, and the soothing cold of amber beer on top of it. A flat, clipped, working-City voice telling a good story, and regular bursts of male-voiced laughter. The mild astonishment that an hour ago life held the odd problem. A jazz band on the wireless and the door open to the street. Connor's and a Saturday morning.

As far as the inner circle was concerned, this was a good turn-out: they stood seven, the perfect number, in their favourite spot by the old wooden arch. Joe The Rat, the tiny local postman, had done well on the horses, Johnny had his locum's pay untouched, and Jimmy Anderson always had money: thus they were drinking whisky with their beers—nips and pints in City fashion; talk was always good in such a well-heeled company of sinners, and today was no exception. At the moment The Rat was narrator, resplendent in the strong-smelling tweed suit in which he had slept the previous night. A shambling pygmy, he was one of the best raconteurs in the drinking business.

"Talking of nuts," he said, "do you remember that big negro burglar from the States called Ollie the Bull who used to be around here? He was a skisofannic or somethin', an' the poor bugger had spent most of his life between nut-houses and jails. Well, remember—he got this queer taste for culture, an' he used tae paint and write poetry half the time. Hector took him under his wing fur a bit, an' he used tae come to a' the ceilidhs and concerts."

Torquil imitated Hector. "Indeed, he was a black prince—a true nobleman. We all liked him, indeed we did."

The Rat continued. "Then he got some mates thegither an' they broke intae an Insurance Office on the corner o' Victoria Street, an' it was one floor up. When they got tae the safe, it was far too heavy tae cairry doonstairs, so they rolled it tae the window, and tipped it over the sill, and it nearly killed a polisman comin' roond the corner! Poor auld Ollie the Bull, he was the most reliable burglar in the world; he never did a job withoot gettin' caught!"

"We've certainly seen some cheracters around," said Starkey Shearer through his nose. He brushed a few specks of ash from his immaculate suit. The others followed the action, united in thought: the suit represented about a month's wages that his wife Ellen had sweated for in front of a towsy class of Corporation schoolchildren. Starkey was an idle, well-bred, lovable swine: since his wealthy father had cut him off without a penny, Ellen had earned his bread and beer without complaint.

He thrust his small head forward. "Thet was a great night lest year when Jehosaphat won fifty pounds on the football pools. He tortured us all night with his theology, but he bought us about ten drems each. We took him out to the cottage for a party, and he pessed out singing 'Abide with Me' so we put him in the beth under the cold tep, and somehow he bunged up the bloody plug-hole. When Ellen found him under three feet of water, she got scared, the silly bitch, and started yelling. Jimmy and I were a bit pissed, but we hed great fun giving him artificial respiration, and after a while he started breathing again. My God, thet was a great night." He crooked his finger around his Semitic nose, giggling.

Johnny left the laughter to the others. He was remembering other nights and scenes from Connor's: the cottage parties when they burned Starkey's furniture to keep warm; that was funny enough, but you didn't laugh when you remembered gallant Malcolm Anderson forcing his whisky past the cancer in his gullet, or Joe The Rat lying bleeding in the close where the Celtic supporters had bottled him.

He could cheerfully spend hours at the bar among those loved faces and voices, but he had a train to catch in twenty-five minutes. There was a louder call ringing in his ears than the barman's, for today he was taking the woman of his choice home to the hills of his fathers, and his heart swelled within him with pride.

He shook hands with them all in turn. "I'll see you all in September," he said.

"Don't be such a stranger next term," called Starkey. "Even if you *are* one of the gods of Final Year, we don't mind your money." Johnny grinned: just one more session like this, dear Lord, and I'll qualify happy!

On the way to the station he savoured the dream of the holiday that lay ahead of them; his only worry was his fundamentalist mother. He descended the sixty steps to the Station Row, and found Nora waiting for him. They bought a few newspapers and magazines—there had been three more killings in Cyprus. Nora was wearing a hat today, a little feathery cup inverted on the mass of hair she had piled up behind, and her apple-green costume was tight to her body, with a narrow skirt that tautened in full stride to show the mould of her legs.

They found an empty compartment and settled down cosily in the stale upholstery. Johnny felt a surge of exhilaration as the heralds of departure were loud in their banging of doors and clattering of tardy feet. Finally, that Godsent old whistle opened its banshee throat, and he leaned back in luxury when the first jolt of movement shook the carriage. Nora was pulling her magazine from the rack, and was thrown against him. He pulled her shoulders to him, and kissed her. There were times when you wondered just how much you could love one woman.

"You've been drinking," she said. She went back to her corner seat and began to turn over pages.

They sailed through a tunnel for two full minutes; daylight appeared again and the City gave way to rows of playing fields, a green wood-tipped hill to starboard and finally open country. He stood at the corridor window to see the metropolis in final perspective beneath its light blanket of smoke. When it was out of sight, he slumped down with a contented sigh, then a cruel flash of recollection jabbed his complacency; he had completely forgotten the proposed audition and this was to have been the big day. He tried to read a short story but his eyes stopped functioning after ten lines and he was looking clean through the book at the musty floor. Of course they'll be O.K.—I was the least important voice, anyway! They'll bloody well *have* to do without me—I don't belong to them any more!

The Lowland countryside was flat and unfriendly until Stirling, then at the extreme of one field of vision the Wallace Monument rose on its lovely green pedestal, noble and remote as the liberty its hero once promised to achieve. It vanished without protest behind more modest works of stone which housed the modern Scot; in their little rooms the men-of-the-houses turned their tired backs on the view, finding freedom from the real in the square shining faces of their new deliverers. Wallace had some good ideas for his time, but what's in an accent when you consider that Britain as an island could be wiped out in one big bang? Let's wait and see what the box says.

Stirling was south of them a few minutes later, and in the surrounding countryside they knew the first real breath of the North. From Johnny's seat it was just possible to see a rough, broken line of blue in the distance; the first chain of the Grampians, the hills of West Perth. He drew a long thankful breath inward.

They passed Callander, and he told her of the rich towns that the hillmen of these parts had plundered, fabricating his story as he went along and lying without shame. Soon they found the twisting serpent of Lubnaig, and the prolific foliage of summer swayed heavily on the hillside. Strathyre lay ahead, broad and bonnie.

Johnny pulled the window down. "D'you smell that," he gasped. "That's pine, real good Perthshire pine."

As they approached Balquhidder Junction, passing Kingshouse on the right, he remembered some true stories of the area, and he was still telling the tale of the young Lamont saved by his victim's father, when they drew into Lochearnhead.

"O.K. love, it's us," he almost sang, tumbling her out of the train. "This is the moment that the glens have waited for since the death of Deirdre—the coming of a Princess of Ireland!"

He scanned the horizon for his father's car. A man of middle height, built foursquare with a broad face that shone like a new brick, hailed them in a Donegal accent.

"My God," said Johnny. "It can't be—Con Gallacher?" It was; Con Gallacher squeezed his hand, kissed an astonished Nora, and inside a minute they were roaring round the lochside in the back of an old jeep.

"What the devil are you doing back here, you old scamp?" roared Johnny above the scream of the engine.

Con grimaced over his shoulder: beneath the heavy beer-jowl, belts of muscle clenched and relaxed. "They can't keep me away, Johnny. The Hydro boys made an awful mess after I left, and the girls in the village all signed a petition to get me back!

Your father's a bit tired tonight, so ould Con has been ordered to bring the prodigal home."

"That I can hardly believe," said Johnny. "Nora, this is my old boss from my days on the Hydro schemes, Con Gallacher. The devil incarnate himself—the man who taught me all the things a boy shouldn't know. There was a time my mother forbade me to speak to him, but he seems to have come up in the world."

"I'm surely pleased to meet you, Mr Gallacher," yelled Nora. "I've heard so much about you. The cherub here seems to think you're a great gale of a boyo."

"He's got good reason to," answered the Irishman. "When I knew him he was just a rough kid startin' University. I had to knock the ould rough corners off-a him."

"Rough corners?" shrieked Nora. "Thank goodness I didn't know him then!" She looked over at the still, clouded waters of Loch Earn—did it really mean the loch of Ireland?

They left the strath and climbed a narrow road studded with stone cottages, then roared around and through a small piece of wooded hill which fell sharply away from the new surface. The road hung precariously to the incline; a new slab of banking had been built on the underside. The forest opened, and the glen appeared before them in all its grandeur. From black rock and scree the mountains fell to green and growing purple, seeking the warmth and stillness of the riverside where the short rye grass was rich brown and the water glinted in a different spot every second.

"D'you remember what I used to say about this place?" called Con.

"Yes," said Johnny, half to himself. "Here there is calm, and a valleyful of quiet to love in; but only for a while."

"Who wrote that?" asked Nora.

"Con did," said Johnny. "Isn't it hellish?"

Glenellin's snug gardens were full of ripe lawns and straight trees and the green battlements above made a splendid backcloth. They drove through the straggling main street, turned right and crossed the Ellin by the white Parish Church.

"This is really just in the foothills of the Highlands," said Johnny. "But you get a bit of lushness round here that the wilder northern scenery doesn't. I wouldn't change this little glen for all of Wester Ross. You ought to lie out on the bank there, when there's a big harvest moon sitting on the hills and at first you can't tell the peaks from the teeth of the clouds—Nora, my heart's love, it's terrific."

"Johnny." She clutched his hand. "Darling, what if your mother doesn't like me?"

"She's bound to. And if she doesn't, she can go to hell—you're my first consideration from now on. Remember what Ruth said to Naomi—that's how I feel about you."

It was a good answer; she gave him one of her vintage smiles. "Thanks darling," she said. "I love you."

The road flexed fractionally left and on the flank of a small pine plantation two grey villas faced each other.

Johnny pointed to one. "That's the old homestead. Isn't she beautiful."

She was in fact about seventy years old, tall and square. She lay behind a large square lawn and in front of a small birch wood that climbed to deeper green further up the hill. Her path was grey gravel that made a satisfying crunch under the feet; her flower borders were weedy and undug.

Con stopped at the gate. "I've got to get back for me own tea," he said.

"Where are you staying?" said Johnny.

"Still at good old St Mungo's," said Con. "It's the roughest hotel in Scotland, but you won't find a better laugh anywhere—you remember it, Johnny."

"Indeed I do, boy. I'll try and come down tonight."

Con drove off in a cloud of dust, waving madly.

"He's great, isn't he?" said Johnny in his best ministerial voice.

They approached the porch, the sun-scorched brown door opened, and Nora conquered an urge to turn and run. Mrs Ferguson walked out to meet them, a small, thin woman with a narrow, lined face, rimless glasses and a halo of pure white hair. Behind the spectacles Nora saw the terrible strength of which Johnny had so often spoken; it thundered straight out of the close eyes that sat beneath pencil-straight eyebrows. But just now the eyes were smiling, and as the woman murmured a few words of welcome her voice was friendly and natural—her thin lips were dry and warm on Nora's cheek, utterly unexpected into the bargain.

Mrs Ferguson kissed Johnny, then drew back sharply; a dart of anger plummeted across the grey eyes. "John, you've been drinking—what a way to come home!" The look was indelible, and made Nora wonder just what would have been said had Johnny been alone. She felt criminally betrayed by his carelessness.

"He's had a row from me already, Mrs Ferguson," she said. "But he was saying goodbye to his friends. You know what they're like," she finished loyally.

"Don't tell me, Nora," said Mrs Ferguson with surprising kindness. She pointed to her hair. "You see this? There's the young man who changed it overnight." She shrugged almost without hope and waved them inside.

Nora's spirits were approaching zero as she crossed the threshold. For a minute she hated Johnny and his mother with a sudden release of outraged dignity, resenting the fact that she should be pulled into a family squabble at the front door. And the old man was still to come.

In the dark panelled hall she met him and forgot her fears. Andrew Ferguson was an older edition of Johnny, yet somehow every feature had been refined to create the difference between Johnny's attraction and his father's handsome nobility. The older man's smile was straight—there was no wicked crook here—and the fine lips and proud nose might have gleamed on an Italian fresco. He was about two inches taller than Johnny, still lean in the middle, and his straight hair was as grey as raw iron, but his eyes twinkled with the same humour that she had first loved in his son, and their liquid depths possessed a softening kindness. A burden of tension fell from her like a sack, and she went for the greeting handclasp as shyly and eagerly as he did.

"Welcome to Glenellin, my dear," he said in a soft, flat accent that contained just a crumb of the North. "You're just as lovely as Johnny said in his letter." Nora found herself inside a violent blush and was relieved when Mrs Ferguson pulled her upstairs to show her to her bedroom.

The room had plain lemon wallpaper, a white ceiling and a hideous splurge of old manse furniture, but there was a small window with lace curtains that faced the young birches, and summer filled the room with warm, heavy sweetness. Nora shut her eyes and found herself miles south of Dublin. This was a homecoming.

Mrs Ferguson eyed her appreciatively. "Just you take your time to freshen up, Nora." She gave the order in that strident voice which seemed so odd for a little woman. At the door she hesitated; one fell swoop noted costume, lipstick, nylons, unpainted nails and the pulsating white throat; she relaxed for the first time, and said: "Thank the good Lord you've come into his life, my dear. I hope you'll make a man of him; it's more than I can ever do."

Nora turned towards her in pity but before she could speak Johnny's mother had cocked her eyes to the white ceiling and stated histrionically: "You've no idea the number of nails that boy has driven in my coffin—children don't realise what sacrifices their parents have to make!" She closed the door behind her, leaving Nora simmering.

She changed into blouse and skirt and after a few minutes' uncertainty left her hair as it was. I suppose I am beautiful, she thought in front of the mirror, but I hope that's not what has always brought the men running. I don't think I'll ever lose the inferiority complex that started when the Belfast girls called me a bog-arab, and which Aunt Rose helped along in her bletherings about Irish country girls never settling properly outside their own backyard.

She descended the stair in trepidation, but the sight of Johnny and his father smoking comfortably on either side of the living-room fire dispelled her agitation. She accepted a comfortable red armchair and sat between them; as they engaged her in conversation the roaring grate of pine seared her cheeks in turn. Mr Ferguson questioned her with a quiet and sympathetic interest; she found herself expressing sentiments with indecent ease. They discussed the Church of Ireland, Partition, Gaelic football and stockbreeding; she was amazed by the Scottish minister's unexpected liberalism to things Catholic and Irish.

"Johnny tells me you're getting engaged in October," he said.

"Yes, we are," she replied jerkily. Behind her the clatter of cutlery ceased: Mrs Ferguson paused heavily for a minute, and gave Nora a thin smile. "How very nice, dear," she said, and now every cup and saucer seemed to hit the white cloth twice as hard.

The lady of the manse had anticipated their appetites, for a glorious stuffed leg of lamb lay hot, new and dripping from the oven before Mr Ferguson's place. He carved with the hand of a surgeon, and Nora's mouth watered when she looked down on thick brown slices of roasted meat, small golden garden potatoes that parted under the knife like butter, green peas, mint sauce and green chopped salad that was just sour enough to drag a world of flavour from the tiniest mouthful. Mrs Ferguson asked the odd judicious question; Nora attempted to denude her answers of the growing distaste she felt towards the woman. A Scotch trifle followed, topped with three inches of whipped cream, its jam sponge enriched with a dash of malt whisky.

"Come and have your tea by the fire," said the minister. They basked in the fierce red glow, drinking strong tea and eating round girdle scones with freshly-churned butter.

Nora rose to help Mrs Ferguson with the dishes, but was summarily waved away. The little woman worked tirelessly to the accompaniment of a loud selection of Moodie and Sankey hymns.

The doorbell rang.

"Here are the rest of the clan," said Johnny's father.

The new arrivals pulled their chairs to the fire, screaming for tea and ribbing Johnny without mercy. His married cousin Morag looked Nora up and down very rudely, and said: "She's no' bad, Johnny—I've seen you wi' a lot worse!"

"Aye," said her husband Davie, a big red Argyllshire man with an attractive ugly face: "He's done better than some of us here. You stick in, Johnny lad, and ye'll bring home the bonniest bride we've seen in years!"

The other cousin, Fergie, added to the fun. Nora took an especial liking to him: he was very much a Ferguson in his looks, and was reputed to have a baby in every village between Crieff and Crianlarich. Mrs Ferguson said least of all; her fingers worked quietly away at her knitting on the perimeter of the group, and a trace of tenderness was just discernible where the flickering firelight trysted with her mouth.

"I suppose you'll be having a reunion with all your old *squarejaw* pals," said Morag to Johnny.

"That's enough, Morag," said Mr Ferguson. "You're forgetting that Nora's Irish."

"Nora's respectable Irish," said Morag, wrinkling her plump

nose undeterred. "She's a whole world removed from the scum that's ruined this village."

Johnny turned to Nora. "Morag blames the Hydro-Electric workers for everything. It's the locals' way of excusing their own decadence."

"Decadence, nothing," snorted Morag. "When I was a kid this was a place for decent folk to live in. Now if you walk down the road at night you're lucky if you're not hit with a bottle, or dragged into the bushes."

Davie roared with amusement. "Who wad drag an old thing like you into the bushes?"

"That's quite enough!" Mrs Ferguson cut the laughter dead. "Remember that this is a manse, and that we have a guest here who's been living in my own native city, where Scots people are civilised."

"Scotland's better here than it ever was in any city," said Johnny. "But unfortunately, the people here are so very respectable getting, that they forget that these Irish boys are their blood brothers. By gum, I'll never forget their loyalty. They stood by me in one or two rough scraps."

Mr Ferguson's soft voice hushed the hubbub of argument. "The trouble is that you're both right, and you're both wrong. There was a time, when the language north of the Highland Line —and that means here—was roughly the same as that spoken in the hills of Ulster. But now the men of this village speak a dialect closer to that of Berwick than to Donegal, and to all intents and purposes the old language is gone. Our conversation is completely anglicised, and years of bitterness over politics and religion have made the people forget that they were once the cousins of old Ireland. Frankly, I don't think the Irish workers here have been very good ambassadors: I know Johnny developed an admiration for them, but one day he'll stop idolising brute force."

"Och well," said Fergie, "some of the girls here certainly like the old *squarejaws*. I could tell you a few tales."

"We'll do without your tales, Fergie Ferguson," said the minister's wife. "Nora hasn't come up here to listen to loose talk."

"You people make me sick," said Johnny. "These lads have built just about every decent bit of road in the country: you've no idea what good, simple chaps they are at heart, and they've got none of the evils of civilisation until they come over to our cities and become corrupted by them."

"Ye're havering, Ferguson," said Morag. "If Nora wasnae such a nice lassie I'd say ye were a traitor to yer own race." She winked at Mr Ferguson.

Nora was genuinely uncomfortable in the middle of all this, and was glad when Mr Ferguson switched the conversation to the coming grouse season. That little wisp of inferiority was challenging the composure of her fixed smile, and she also felt a grand and terrible concurrence of opinion with Johnny.

"Where are you going to settle when you're qualified?" Davie asked Johnny. "Here?"

"Well, in a way I'd like that," said Johnny. "It's what I've often dreamed of, working back here in the guts of my own people—the keepers and shepherds for instance. That's the sort of job that can make Medicine a really noble profession."

"It doesn't sound very noble, the way you describe it," sniffed his mother. "I thought you wanted to specialise in Surgery."

"Yes, that's another dream," said Johnny. "But it's no life for a married man; you never see your wife."

His mother rose. "I'll put on a wee cup of tea," she said.

"We could do with you here, Johnny," said Morag. "That old Dr Bruce gets more senile every day. I went to him last Christmas time—I had a sore ear, and he says: 'I'll write you a prescription for some drops, Mrs Shaw. By the way, how are your physical relations with your husband?' "

" 'What do you mean, Doctor?' says I."

" 'Mrs Shaw,' he says, 'do you realise the importance of the mental side of things? Most diseases are due to some mild disorder of the mind, and sometimes to unhappiness.' "

" 'Look, Dr Bruce,' I said. 'I don't blame you for thinkin' that anybody who marries the likes of Davie Shaw is a bit round the bend, but our physical relations have never touched my ears.' "

Nora looked rather shocked till she saw that Mr Ferguson was laughing with the chorus. It seemed that years of experience of the local earthiness of his parish had removed all pretence from his kindly personality.

"It would do us all proud to have Johnny here," he said. "And you, Nora."

Fergie's brilliant repartee finally silenced Morag's bluntness, and he delivered a series of impersonations for Nora's benefit. Under the dexterous rapier of his cynical tongue the flaws and petty jealousies of a small town sprang to life; his sly satire forced her to feel anger and injustice over things she knew nothing about: although terribly funny, it carried a poignancy that was scarcely deliberate. At twenty past ten he looked at his watch and said: "It's time we were home, folks. Johnny will be wantin' an early night."

Mr and Mrs Ferguson protested; Johnny grinned at the fire. The "Stag" public bar shut at half past nine, but at quarter past ten on the stroke Jock McVittie, the local policeman, always made for the dance at the far end of the village and the coast would be clear for a quick entrance through the back door.

They shouted cheerful farewells down the path, Fergie skelping Morag hard on the rump. As their silhouettes disappeared into the moonless night they left lusty quacks of laughter behind.

"What a wonderful family you all are," said Nora from her heart, sitting down again with Mr Ferguson.

"Aye," said the minister, "but we're getting fewer. There used to be four families of Fergusons, our Fergusons, in this village. But those rascals are all that's left, unless Johnny decides to come back." His eyes were old with meaning. Behind him Johnny gave a short grunt.

"Ah, here's the scamp," said his father proudly. "Nora, dear, would you mind if I borrowed Johnny for about ten minutes? There are one or two pearls of wisdom that I want to blow in his lug."

"On you go," said Nora, her voice low and rich in comfort. "I can think of nothing lovelier than dreaming by this gorgeous fire for a bit."

They walked to the door as if in ceremony; Johnny's father seemed to infuse in him a poise that came strangely close to dignity. She turned to the fragrant tongues of scarlet and welcomed them as friends.

He had awaited it for ten minutes, wrestling with a sense of foreboding: there was an ominous tenseness in the clumsy sentences with which his father laboured to the point.

"I had a small heart attack, Johnny. I was in Perth Royal Infirmary for four weeks."

"Oh, Dad!" This brand of cold sweat took him back ten years. He walked shakily round the desk; his hand fell awkwardly on the tweedy shoulder.

In the large bookcase the Family Bible nestled protectively against the German Higher Critics whom Mrs Ferguson was continually threatening with fiery extinction; on the lower shelves stood the morocco bindings of a lifetime's nostalgia. During his childhood the study was one of the few places where religion was sane, and God was always benevolent; God was still good, grey-haired, regal and kindly, but now He had a diseased heart.

A cold hand fell affectionately over his. "There's nothing to get worried about, son," said his father. "It wasn't really bad, and I made Dr Bruce promise not to write to you unless I became worse; as it happened I never looked back after the treatment started. You were better occupied in your studies."

"But *you* didn't write and tell me!"

"Johnny, we've written you faithfully for the past year. We've had one letter back."

Johnny recognised the slight shortness of breath. Why hadn't it struck him earlier? Fool!

"Hell"—he forgot himself completely—"to think I haven't even been home since last year."

His father was looking hard at him.

"It's time we got things straight," he said. "We've been a bit shy of each other in the past, son; I wish I had your mother's strong character, or yours—I think I've always said too little. Isn't that right?"

"Yes, Dad." The inescapable truth.

"I'm not really ill, Johnny, but health is an uncertain thing in my decade of life, and they won't let me preach yet. From now on you'll have to stand on your own feet. Are you really going to settle down to your Finals? If you start skipping your classes and fooling around again, there's not much I can do for you."

He tried to sound confident. "I'll be fine, Dad; things are different now."

"I can see why, Johnny. Nora's a delight, and the engagement has my blessing. You know, you don't believe it, but your mother is a wonderful woman too; she's shown a lot of strength and grace in these past weeks. I want to make sure that she's well looked-after in the future: you see why I'm so anxious about you, son?"

"Of course, Dad."

"All right. Can I ask for a promise that our worries regarding your wild behaviour are over?"

Johnny felt sorrowfully cheated; the situation was classical in its irony. Ninety per cent of him was ready to give the answer willed by this good and gentle face that was not without its weakness—and for the first time in his life they had reached a moment of potential honesty where he needed only to feel his father's reassurance integrating the reluctant ten. But the tiniest careless utterance that might lay another track of worry on the pale cheeks was the act for which the flames of Gehenna were devised. Small defeat was inevitable, be it as small as possible; remember Nora and recent successful endeavour, and forget ancient panicking doubts about staid professional existence and not being completely oneself.

He blew his nose and lost a small tear from his right eye in the process. "I've been a stinking, useless son," he said. "But I've got a wonderful girl now, I've broken my old wild ways, and I know I can make it easily. You wait until I'm in the money in a few years—I'll be looking after you and mother!"

His father smiled. "Thanks son, God bless you." His hand rested briefly on the young forehead. "Would you like a wee whisky?" he whispered secretively.

"No thanks, Dad. Would you mind if I take a stroll up the hill? I'd like to think about a few things."

"Slip out the back door, ye young rascal," said Mr Ferguson. "I'm glad to see you've got at least one of your father's traits. I like a breath of hill air last thing at night."

They clasped hands. "God bless you, son," Mr Ferguson repeated.

Johnny left him sitting at the desk. He prayed for the power to run to his father, to tear open his chest, rip out the old, diseased artery, and slam in a brand new one. He simply couldn't imagine life without the familiar smile and voice; they had always seemed as indestructible as the dusty old room.

He side-footed quietly down the stone passage towards the back door. From the kitchen he heard women's talk—his mother had relented and was allowing Nora to help her with the dishes.

Mrs Ferguson's voice rang hard above the clatter of plates. "I'm sure you'll be good for him, my dear." The scrape of a drawer, then: "It must sound awful to you, Nora, but he's drifted so far from us lately. It may have been my fault, but if you knew the nights of torture I had last winter staring into that fire, and seeing a little face all smeared with chocolate—oh, lassie, you'll know one day when you have your own."

Not any more, mother. Please, not now. He left the small door ajar and scuttled into the back garden. He did not seek the hill, however.

Snatches of song and laughter drifted toward him over the Ellin bridge. He leaned against its iron parapet and closed his eyes until the sound of running water washed him back through five crazy years of almost total exile.

On that night in his pre-University summer he had fought violently with his mother over his current girl-friend, a passionate little village brunette with the most provocative hands in Perthshire. He had left the manse in fury, signed on immediately as a chainman with the Hydro Board, and staggered along beside a bulging suitcase to St Mungo's Temperance Hotel, notorious for its limited cuisine—bacon and beans were served thrice daily—for the proprietrix's pink slacks and for its most noteworthy guest, the General Foreman of the Hydro Construction Company, Mr Con Gallacher, who had already outdrunk the "Stag" veterans to shamed defeat.

The thought of spending his summer among Mrs MacLaren's rough navvies, and the tales told in the village about these wild men had taxed his teenage courage and thrawnness, but when tubby Mrs McLaren escorted him cheerfully up to the bedroom he was to share with Mr Gallacher, he heard the rough music of Donegal voices and above them all a strange thin tuneful voice

—Con Gallacher with his masterpiece, "The Banks of the Foyle." They had all finished up good and drunk, and Johnny was one of them. It had been the start of a wonderful summer, and of a friendship rekindled on every visit home.

The wind-blown rain swirled him back into the present. St Mungo's front door was left open for him; most of the boys were seeking a fight or a fuck at the dance, and Mrs Mac. was off on her Saturday night pilgrimage to the cinema in Crieff, but Con was at home as he had promised, his feet baking on the rusty old stove in the kitchen.

He poured Johnny a long drink; there was usually more alcohol consumed in the kitchen of St Mungo's Temperance Hotel than in the three licensed cocktail bars of Glenellin.

"Well, Con, what's new in Glenellin?"

"You know what Glenellin is like, Johnny—it'll never change very much. I suppose you know about your father?"

He nodded. The cobweb hanging over the stewpot looked familiar; he was sure it had been there last year; at least it hadn't altered. But Glenellin *was* different—the wind of change had been buffeting his face all day, and him just home, damn it. Con had always said it was wrong to come back to a place and expect it to be the same, for the disappointment you felt could be disastrous. Johnny had an awful yearning to put the clock back five years.

"It's hellish about the old man," he said, refilling his glass. "The trouble is, for the first time in my life I was getting near real man-to-man stuff with him tonight, but when he told me I seemed to clam up."

"Aye," said Con. "And I suppose you've come down here to ruin my Saturday night with all your problems, just because I know more about life than any man you'll ever meet."

Johnny let his problem wait, however. There were too many precious moments to be remembered in a short space of time. They rolled the names of the leathery gangers and muscled navvies on the ends of their tongues; they recalled days of pick and shovel and nights of boring-hammer till he could smell the black Diesel fumes, feel the granite dust in his eyebrows, and hear the staccato bark of the "jelly" shredding the flesh of the tough old hills. There were the treasured hours of leisure too—necking with a dark girl in the back of Con's car, or sitting stupidly on his arse in the open fire of the "Stag," realising too late that a quick smash with the forehead was much quicker than a public school left-hook. Among those soft-voiced wandering Jews of the West he had been a man among men, fighting and conquering the elements at their worst—by God, that had been a time for men with fire in their hearts!

"Yes," said Con. "Old St Mungo's fairly made its name in those days. D'you remember, Johnny, when we used to come off our work on the day shift, and we had to wait till the night shift boys got out of our beds? Mrs Mac was fairly makin' her pile, b'jaisus!"

"What do you think of Nora?" Johnny asked.

"She's Irish," said Con. "But I want to see a bit more of her before I pass her fit to marry you. I remember a girl like her I used to know during the war, a nurse in Burma—" He rambled on, but Johnny was surveying the cobweb again.

"Con," he said a few minutes later, "d'you think I've changed much in the last few years?"

"You're older. But you're still the same old Johnny when you get with somebody who understands you, like me for instance." He scratched furiously at his crutch. "You know, when I was your age I was worryin' about stayin' alive, not about changin'—I was down in Uruguay at the time—"

Johnny's attention wandered. He said: "You're not in the mood for giving advice tonight, Con. What's wrong? Your opinion means a lot to me."

The big, brick-red face fixed him head-on, angry. "I'm tryin' not to give advice full of whisky," said the Irishman. "It's like drivin' a car when you're half-pissed—you go too far and fast before you slam on the anchors. No, m'son, she seems a wonderful lassie, but I'll wait a year before I say anything. But you know, Johnny, I get a queer feelin' when I'm tight these days. All of a sudden I get the message that there's somethin' wonderful inside me that's got to come out—you know, as if I knew the answer to everything. And then it passes, and I say nothin'. Johnny, d'you think that maybe I've drunk so much that I've jazzed up them dark areas of the brain that doctors talk about?"

"I don't think so," said Johnny with a hollow laugh. Con was changed as much as the village: he had always been a bit bombastic but his garrulous egotism was decidedly irritating tonight.

They finished the bottle in twenty minutes and Johnny buttoned up his jacket. "Good night, Con," he said dully.

Con put an arm around him at the top of the stairs. "We'll have a good night out next week. Look after yourself, Johnny; I'll look forward to seein' you again—and I don't say them words to many people." The red face ignited into a warm smile.

He gripped the big man's hand. "Till then."

At the door he found a figure sitting back to the wall. A strong stench of whisky rifted at him from the blurred Irish face. He lit a match. The eyes were utterly devoid of expression and a cut gaped above the left eyebrow.

"What's the matter, boy?" asked Johnny. "Had a fall?"

The Irishman muttered something quite unintelligible. Johnny was aware of shadowy figures on the far side of the road, moving around like ghosts against the wall of the Parish Church; suddenly, they clumped together and came across the road towards him—three of them. He could feel trouble freezing and stiffening the back of his neck.

"There's another o' the bastards," said a local voice which he recognised instantly. "Let's get him too."

Before he could move or shout, Con's figure filled the doorway. The clatter of footsteps slithered to a halt. "Back, for Christ's sake!" yelled the same voice. "It's Gallacher!" The three men turned and ran.

Con pulled the drunk to his feet. "I'll get him to bed—d'you want me to come down the road with you?"

"No," said Johnny, half-surprised. "I'll be O.K."

"Did you recognise any of these rats?"

"No," he lied. "I didn't."

Con looked through him. "That's a pity," he said. "If I were you, Johnny, I'd walk home in the middle of the road."

"I'll be O.K., Con. Good night."

Con Gallacher swung the babbling drunk over his left shoulder. Johnny heard his footsteps going clump, clump up the steps, then he crossed the road and rounded the corner. He was thankful that Con had appeared when he did, otherwise things would have proved unpleasant for him in more ways than one. Glenellin was still a place where you had to take sides: this was the sort of incident that Morag had been deploring, yet despite his trembling legs it had added a bit of excitement to an otherwise depressing evening.

He stood on the bridge again and gazed upstream towards the Ellin's rocky womb. He closed his eyes as before, for the moon was hiding and there was nothing much to see. But he saw himself five years ago and he saw himself five minutes ago, and for a second he realised without fear that in some ways he would never master the process that his father called growing up.

CHAPTER IX

"FOR GOD SO LOVED the world that he gave his only begotten Son, that whosoever believeth in Him should not perish but have everlasting life.

"For God sent not his Son into the world to condemn the world, but that the world through Him might be saved."

The Rev. William Cowan cleared his throat and adjusted his gown. His congregation, no more than a hundred in all, wriggled their posteriors into the tight pits of their pews, and settled down to enjoy or endure the ensuing twenty minutes. Sweet papers whispered furtively in a moment of sticky heresy; little dry mouths bulged with appeasement for the rest of the body's ordeal; Father gazed stolidly ahead and longed for a softer collar and a good deep drag of cigarette-smoke.

In the family pew, seven back from the front, the Ferguson clan supplied roughly one-twelfth of the congregation. In actual fact Fergie and Morag were spilling on to the John Drummonds' territory at the far end, but since Mrs Ferguson and Mrs Drummond had quarrelled at the Women's Guild last September the John Drummonds seldom came to church. Johnny's head ached abominably from last night's temperance session: his only comfort was that Fergie looked considerably more poisoned than himself.

The old Parish Church looked better outside than in. It had been rebuilt on conservative Gothic lines by the loving hands of Glenellin's stonemasons a hundred years ago, but despite its impressive physique dry rot had ruined much of the flooring, and a chilly damp flooded the throat and lungs at the start of every psalm and gnawed at the rheumaticky joints of the older worshippers. But it was an integral part of the Fergusons, and no matter how Johnny's religious temperature ebbed and flowed, his soul always assumed a cosy foetal position inside it.

Until the sermon.

Then he was at war again, bristling at every statement that appeared to be uncharitable and questioning every liberalism that was half-hearted. Preachers generally fell into two categories—

either they were soul-hungry fire-eaters with a subtle wealth of emotional offensive and no brains, or they were so tolerant in their rejection of such rubbish that their sermons were little more than fireside chats on morality which did not injure the spirit but left it ravenously hungry. His father was one of the few pulpit orators capable of holding him spellbound. Today he was being forced to listen to a fundamentalist whom his mother had dragged up from Glasgow; William Cowan was the son of one of her childhood friends.

"This is the crux of the Gospel message," he was saying. "In these two verses God has so providently supplied a compact little nutshell for the lost soul which is nevertheless strong enough to carry it through the roughest storms of life, that nobody who has come into his House of God today can dare to deny its offer.

"What can be simpler than that?—believe in Christ and have Everlasting Life. When you consider the enormity of your sins, my friend, and when you consider the terrible sacrifice that God himself paid at Golgotha that your crimes might be expiated, how can you fail to accept this free gift of His grace?

" 'How can I do this,' you say? Ah—here we have the simplest and most beautiful facet of the whole jewel—but first let me digress slightly."

Mr Cowan's digression used up ninety-five per cent of the sermon. He derided the wicked state of the world, the great fall in Britain's prestige because of her Godless leaders, the awful decline in the sexual behaviour of the young (Nora began to turn over pages in her Bible very rapidly) and finally told a gruesome tale of a young man who had rejected a Gospel appeal one Sunday night and had been knifed by an insane Chinese cook while walking home. Then the familiar recipe came to the boil. His voice rose to a most unmusical crescendo.

"Here is what you must do, my poor sin-sodden friend. Close your eyes and kneel at the foot of that blood-stained Cross of Calvary. Forget all your good works, for your righteousness is as filthy rags." His voice sobbed softer: " Look up at the Figure on that Cross and say: 'Come into my heart, Lord; be my personal Saviour, and live on in my heart for as long as it should continue to beat."

The Rev. Cowan asked the audience to bow their heads in prayer. Any poor sinner who felt ready to take the great offer of salvation, was to repeat silently after the minister the sentence about opening his heart. Then as a sign of his deliverance from the bondage of sin, he was to raise his right hand.

The Ferguson heads went forward. There was a look of infinite pain around Mr Ferguson's mouth, as if he had just swallowed a tin of baking soda, but Johnny's mother's face had a beatific smile plastered across it. Nora saw her lips move and an imp of amusement filter into Davie's rather puzzled frown; the soft utterance sounded very like "Hallelujah." At the other end of the pew Fergie, who was the only one amongst them with room to raise his right arm, had begun to snore with his mouth open and was in danger of losing his upper denture. Johnny was staring rather glassily at the large hat in front of him and biting his lower lip. Morag was shamelessly open-eyed, glancing over her shoulder to identify the contrite sinners.

Mr Cowan breathed a short prayer. Here in the stillness of this tranquil Sabbath morning the Holy Spirit was waiting to take over —how could you possibly refuse him, dear brother, sister? Silence reigned for two minutes; the congregation sat motionless. Mr Cowan and Morag were disappointed together.

"We shall sing the fortieth psalm," said the voice from the pulpit. A great energising bustle perfused the old pews; the Sunday roast was within smelling distance at last. There was no trace of defeat in the young preacher's face, however, for who can tell in how many aching hearts the Great Change is worked unseen?

Nora had not enjoyed the dissertation on sin. Well as she could have argued against it under fair conditions, to sit under the unopposed authority of that painfully sincere monotone had unaccountably upset her. When Mr Cowan had been ranting on about the loose morals of contemporary youth, she had been seized with a terrible, illogical sense of remorse and self-reproach. It had seemed as though every part of her that Johnny had touched was smouldering with an angry heat that threatened to erupt through her clothes and spell out her uncleanness in fiery letters. She was glad when the sermon closed, and resisted the temptation to throw up her right hand in moral self-defence, but when the heads snapped upright she found that Johnny was ashen and trembling beside her.

The organ swelled and the people rose to sing:

"I waited for the Lord my God—"

Johnny steeled his body against its desperation to crumple back in the pew. The Rev. William Cowan's thin, haunted expression was swimming in a flood of grey nausea; beside him Nora's face was thunderstruck, but she had placed a firm, stiffening arm behind his keeling back.

"What's wrong, darling?" she whispered.

"It's O.K., love," he managed faintly. "I'll be all right when we get outside."

They survived the psalm and an eternity of a Benediction; outside again in the relief of summer, she saw his pallor flood away, and as he moved her among new friends beside the cool worldly friendship of the old wall, the yew trees and the river, her heart rejoiced at the natural gallantry of countrymen, and she had little time to remember the most agonised expression she had ever seen on a young man's face.

But she wondered on the way to Morag's, and kept the query for later.

William Cowan had been invited to lunch at Morag's with the rest of the family. For such a spiritual young man he had produced a voracious appetite, but his blessing of the food had been mercifully brief. Now he sat beside the lady of the manse, who was obviously revelling in his presence; he had brought an air of sanctity and worship with him and this had been lacking in Morag's house for a long time.

"Aye," she said. "It's great to hear the Blood preached so faithfully by a young man, William. There's not many have the courage to do it nowadays."

Johnny cringed for his father. William Cowan looked even more uncomfortable: it was becoming increasingly obvious to him that apart from Mr and Mrs Ferguson, none of the people here were true, born-again-believers at all; there were times that the Glenellin minister himself seemed to have back-slidden into a rather modernistic outlook. What was worse, he could not take his eyes away from this lovely young Irish girl, and Morag, missing nothing, was staring at him with bad-mannered delight.

Stung by his sudden embarrassment, and seeing Johnny's shoulders shrug ever so slightly, he attacked. "I don't think Johnny would agree with you, Mrs Ferguson," he said. "Judging by his face he seemed to be suffering terrible anguish during the sermon this morning."

Johnny had a warning look from his father; his mother's eyes commanded "No blasphemy, John!" But this self-righteous little prig was beginning to annoy him, and he knew that his cousins were depending on him; their apostasy had the same domestic foundation as his.

"Your approach to the Scripture is far to dogmatic, William," he said. "I can find nothing in the Gospels about 'inviting Christ into your heart.' And what does 'personal Saviour' mean, anyway?"

William quoted: "Behold, I stand at the door . . ." and Johnny disputed his right to interpret "Revelation" literally; William postulated the historical facts of the Gospels, and Johnny maintained that the four writers had private axes to grind; why four Gospels, and what's the sense in the Christian doctrine of redemption, anyway?—in quick succession they said nothing new about Predestination and the Fall, the several Isaiahs, and the thorn in the Apostle's flesh.

Johnny sensed a flagging of his opponent's stamina, and filled his lungs for the final assault: "Belief in God is a personal attitude of mind, and with due respect to you and my father I don't think that any man has the right to stand up and tell other people what they should believe, at least, not unless the people are allowed to stand up and shout back at him. If that had been the case, Billy Graham wouldn't have had so many hypnotised people marching to the front of his meetings."

"You're an agnostic, then?" said William Cowan in triumph.

"If I am, then I obviously don't know what I am."

The air in the room was almost poisonous. Morag rose to open another window. Mrs Ferguson looked on the verge of a monumental stroke.

William Cowan was no fool. "We'll discuss it later this evening, Johnny," he suggested. "Then we can talk without boring anybody."

Hell, thought Johnny, if he doesn't have me saved before tomorrow's breakfast he won't eat it. "Fair enough," he said gratefully. "Come on, Nora, let's have a walk."

They wandered up and down the main street, past many old houses that were still old houses, and two old houses that were now cafes with juke-boxes blaring.

Johnny broke off their meaningless lovers' dialogue to remark: "This place is changing for the worse." She nodded absently, seeking a quiet way to question his strange discomfort of the morning.

About half-past four, in the full coming of the afternoon, they were lying on the right bank of the Ellin opposite the church. A large garden ran riot at their warm backs, scarlet and black-green with rhododendrons. Behind the bushes the bees had forgotten it was Sunday. Below them tiny trout-shadows flitted deep and swift.

Various people passed them and exchanged a soft greeting. Johnny lit a cigarette and exhaled a thin stream of blue smoke over the water. It was good to be home. He glanced up at the sound of approaching feet. Two tall young men came down off the bridge: they were friends of his childhood, two of the Murdoch brothers, the toughest family in Glenellin. They had guddled trout together in this very pool. Johnny waved cheerfully to them.

"Christ," said Hamish Murdoch loudly, "here's old Johnny Ferguson wi' a fuckin' nice tart." He was drunk.

Johnny's fists clenched angrily but Nora held his wrist. "Good afternoon," she said politely to the Murdochs. They leered at her and reeled past.

"Idiots!" said Johnny. "I apologise for this behaviour in my own town, Nora. We've got too many oafs left where there used to be men."

But she had already dismissed the insulting obscenity, for her own question could wait no longer. "What was bothering you in church, darling?"

"Oh, that." His breath hung heavily over the water. Reluctantly he said at length, "I know it's crazy, but those mad hot-gospel sermons always upset me a bit. It goes back a long way."

"But it was all evangelistic rubbish, Johnny. You know that."

"When I was thirteen, Nora, I heard a sermon in that same pew from William Cowan's father, when my own father was away at a Conference. It was the same stuff—literal, fallible interpretation of Scriptural imagery—the Blood, the Fall, and God help you if you don't accept what I say—the whole barbarous thing made me want to vomit, and I suddenly realised that I hated the sight of my mother's God."

She smiled tolerantly. "But we all have moments like that,

Johnny. For a moment I felt a bit queer this morning too. Come on, now, I bet it was Con's whisky that really made you ill."

"Balls!" His eyes were blazing with a deep, despairing fury. "If you haven't been raised in this sort of thing, you can't understand. I nearly drove myself crackers—I thought I must be an unbeliever bound for hell to feel as I did—it took me weeks to lose that part of it, then my father came back, and put a saner complexion on things for me. But I've never believed in any kind of God since."

"Poor old Johnny," she said. "You're a mixed-up kid all right. But I still think you're overplaying the dramatics."

"That may be," he said, mildly disappointed by her immediate dearth of perception. He remembered dusk on the relentless lemon walls of his bedroom, the mocking voices that squeaked damnation through his window in every animal pitch, the small frightened face in the mirror—"Except ye believe, except ye believe. . . ."

"It may be," he repeated. "But whenever I hear the bilge, it takes me back nine years, and I get a queer feeling that the air I breathe is flavoured with disaster."

She swivelled round, suddenly anxious to change the subject; the sun was gracefully stroking the purple pate of Beinn a' Chròin. "You must have fallen in love often," she said. "A young man couldn't help it in a place like this."

"Not really," he said. "Love's a thing I found not long ago."

Beyond the bushes a toilet flushed noisily through their thoughts.

He laughed softly. "Listen to that—the voice best-equipped to represent civilisation. I'm beginning to forget what a dry privy smells like."

CHAPTER X

GLENELLIN absorbed her in its own inimitable way. In ten carefree days of wandering the village, she was carefully inspected, then accepted; her beauty, her modesty and her spontaneous sense of humour seduced the native hearts completely. They were a virile, courageous, hot-tempered folk who inhabited this glen of grazing, shaggy beasts and the life-giving river, but they were lovable too, when one found their kindness, and their childish wonder at the happenings in and around the hills that were once so changeless. A border people originally, now they had no border to contend, but authority had always been suspect since the dark tartans took the lands of West Perth by guile, so the Nationalist Party was stronger hereabouts than in most places, although the God of Mammon received most supplication at the General Election as he did in Dorset and Pembroke.

Here, at any rate, was real character. Every villager had something quite unique to be sung or decried, and there was no trace of the self-effacing politeness which had become a form of suicidal treason further to the north and west.

Unfortunately, lost in the frantic number of calls they had made within the village, they had not made any incursions into the surrounding country. Then the wild called them.

Today bore comparison to the bard's fairest. After a three-mile tramp through heather and long grass that was scrumptious with mountain thyme, they followed the gleam of hot sun on water, crossed a little crooked back road and descended as close to the river as the thick tangle of thorn and bramble bushes allowed. Rabbits scurried across their path in unnecessary panic; from the hillside came the gurgle of grouse. Ten shades of green cushioned their feet and brushed their arms, and a concerto of traditional birdsong drowned the crooning coronach of the Ellin. Halfway down the glen the briars had been stolen by the fairies, and they were able to walk close to the water on the mossy bank.

Johnny stopped at an old wooden bridge that spanned a deeper pool. "This was one of my favourite spots," he said. "When I was a kid of about eighteen I used to lie here and dream about you. I used to write poetry too."

"I might have known," said Nora. "Can you remember anything of it?"

"Oh, yes. When the Hydro-Electric first came here I hated it. I remember lying here one day, almost in tears because of the racket they were making. Now, what was it I wrote?" His voice began to drone in harmony with the quiet murmurs of the valley:

> " 'The hills are still green in the evening
> As they were when my cheek was unrazored;
> A shadow of slope-side is falling,
> And the grope of the sun is delicious.
> Yet scenes that were seeded in childhood
> Are ghosts of a life that was lovely,
> A beauty whose birthright is buried
> In the corpse of a kindlier God' "

"That's lovely, Johnny. Is there any more?"

"Yes, but I can't remember it right now. Let's get further down."

Cruel barbs of fatigue were burrowing into her calves, but she did not demur. They were going fast downhill: about half a mile distant the Ellin appeared to lose itself in a strip of conifers. Johnny took her hand as the riverside path grew more and more rocky.

"Just think of the different people who must have used this path," he said. "Shepherds and milkmaids, Highland warriors, Redcoats, Bruce's soldiers, even Romans and the war-parties of Calgacus. For all we know we're stepping on ground that has shuddered under chariots and cavalry, that has seen lovers die because they found that love can be spoken in other tongues. This is a stirring country: who could slight a pretty girl when the valley is cool and fragrant with blackthorn in May, and who would refuse to fight for the continued rest of his fathers when he hears the storms of February galloping over the mountains at his back?"

Nora smiled rather breathlessly. "Go on, m'own little

warrior," she said. Her legs were aching atrociously with every step and the sun had given her a headache.

"Let's forget the past," said Johnny. "Here and now we have a man of the glen who has brought home a woman of his own blood from far across the sea. And the whole glen is welcoming her in sunshine, displaying its flowers and fruits, its perfumes and voices, that she may know it as a fitting place to delight with her fair face until the sun goes down."

"When will the sun go down?" she asked him. "When they've built a dam here you may not want to see another sunrise on your glen."

"Not really. Most of the Hydro people will go away again, and we'll have our old peace to sleep in. But don't talk about it, Nora; it makes me a wee bit frightened." He pulled her clumsily against him; for once his body lacked excitement: "*Here there is calm and a valleyful of quiet to love in—but only for a while.*" Damn Con for a sentimental old fool!

They were entering the woods, and the path made a detour from the river. The sound of water had risen to an angry battle-cry as it plunged headlong into the dell. They strode over the footway that was inches thick with dead beech leaves; she could see white glimpses of the waterfall through the dead and dying trunks that leaned askew on the soilless rocky slope. The thick healthy foliage above their right shoulders blotted out the sun completely; Nora shivered.

The path wound down to a large round pool that foamed at the foot of the fall. Johnny was impervious to her unhappy expression as he guided her through bracken and briar on to a large flat stone that stretched slippery and smooth far out into the churning brown water.

"Are you frightened?" he asked. She nodded with a lump in her throat. The river glowered at her angrily, growling deep in its murky belly.

"Close your eyes," said Johnny. "You'll feel better in a minute."

Strangely enough she did feel better. She opened her eyes to find that a single heroic sunbeam had carved a gap through the trees. The water had softened to a friendly gold and its voice was a gruff but pleasant greeting.

"This place has got something about it," he said. "A real

atmosphere. The old folk used to call this *'Lon an t-sagairt'*—the Priest's Pool. You get a lot of salmon resting here and lower down before they try the jump, but most old fishermen won't touch the river for a good two miles; there's a legend about this bit."

"What's the story?" she said absently, enjoying the relief in her tortured legs.

"Ah, you should hear my father tell it," said Johnny. "He sounds like a minstrel of Camelot. But the short of it is, that when Christianity first came to the glen about the time of St Fillan, a young monk built a little chapel down here, and devoted his life to good works—the whole glen loved him, even the animals, for he had the power of healing. But the former ruler of the glen, an evil fairy who lived on top of the hill there, resented his intrusion, and determined to destroy him. Eventually she seduced him in the guise of a woman as beautiful as Deirdre of the Sorrows, and after succumbing to her embraces he found that his powers of healing were gone. Broken-hearted he drowned himself in the pool. The tinkers say that sometimes you can hear his lost soul screaming in the night."

Brave in the sunshine she laughed away the spine-chilling of the tale.

"You're right to laugh," said Johnny. "Personally I think he was an idiot. What's religion against the soft arms of a beautiful woman? Come here, m' darlin', I haven't kissed you for an hour!"

He drew her gently to her feet and started to kiss her, softly at first, then with a fierce biting hunger. She responded violently, shaking in every limb. Then his caresses grew gentle again, and they stood motionless, giving.

The Ellin flowed on to the sea with the same indifference as it had felt beside the tramp of legions; the fish in its warming water lazed in their customary summer fashion as they had done yearly since the time of St Fillan. Things did not change very much here despite the occasional presence of monks and fairies, but today there was a special love on the edge of the water, which at least two people considered unique.

The sound of heavy engines and shouted commands glided through the trees. He pulled her behind a thick trunk.

"We'll stay here for a minute," he said. "The boys are blasting."

A few minutes later five explosions sounded close together and a pair of mighty unseen wings lashed the tree-tops. Hundreds of tiny stone splinters showered around them.

They came up to the road. One of the navvies was waving the traffic through from a sitting posture on the end of his red flag. Forty yards beyond him a gang of men were loading boulders of varying sizes onto the back of a large Bedford lorry, while a callow stripling with a fine fair down on his face was brushing the smaller bits and pieces off the road.

Johnny pointed. "It's my old mob—Billy Duffy's gang," and he fell to explaining the various techniques of drilling and packing. Several of the workers knew him and roared greeting. Their eyes devoured Nora with animal hunger.

"Let's move on," he said quickly, moving back into wooded twilight.

"This is wonderful," said Nora. "Johnny boy, every day with you lends some more excitement and glamour to life. It's great to think that I'll never be bored again."

"And it's great to know that from now on I'm loaded with good intent," said Johnny. "Every time I have an uncharitable thought I think of you."

"Rubbish," she laughed him down. "I've warned you before that I have my weaknesses. You know, until the last few weeks I didn't know what lust really was. I've always had this lovely starry-eyed feeling about you, but lately the sight of you makes me want to take my clothes off. Sheer ugly desire—aren't I dreadful?"

"Not on your life," he said. "We're getting so wrapped up in one another, my little soft fawn, that it's only natural you should feel like that. This little world of ours is idyllic, Nora—that's the only word for it."

"It's almost frightening," she said. "I feel as if I'm completely losing my character and taking on yours. You're so damnably strong, you little ancient warrior, that you pull every bit of affection out of me."

He took her into the wilds again. In the course of the next

two hours she staggered in and out of two small glens, through thickets and bogs that tore her skin and muddied her legs, but her body seemed to have assimilated some strange magic stamina from her sojourn at the Priest's Pool, and she bore the rigours of the march with cheerful equanimity.

They rounded a squat-shouldered hill and came into a valley not unlike Glenellin, though rather smaller and lacking in the same dramatic colour effect. The Lednock ran naked as far as the eye could strain, then, like the Ellin, vanished into a tidy forest that sloped upwards to a small hill, which instead of a fairy at its crest boasted a monument of stone whose rigid phallic tip was just discernible above the trees. Below them the road was pale and smooth; a few cars and trucks sped up and down.

The sloping sunlight was sheer joy to walk in; the evening was neither hot nor cool but occasionally both. Nora was listening to the local champion songthrush when they reached the little hill and saw a wooden pathway winding up through the branching shadows. He swung her up the first few steps.

"I suppose you intend to make love up here?" She was finding it hard to sound casual about this sort of thing. She would never again take worldly advice from any woman who had not been well loved and bedded—how could old maids understand the power that lived in the roaming hands of a boy?

"Yes, love," he said. "I've picked this place specially."

Ten minutes later they stood on the grassy summit and gazed on Strathearn. Against them on the far wall of the strath the Aberuchills flexed their dark-tinted ruggedness. Far to the west the loch lay black under cloud and curtained by a thin sheet of rain hung just distal to the spear of sunlight that shafted on to the early banks of the river. The Earn wound through the hillocky lowland into the drowsy town directly beneath them; men of old had named the latter after the confluence that it curled around. Then the water crept stealthily to the east and slowly, for the country was flat and ripe as the eyes turned from the sun, and the glens were gone behind a regiment of pine. On the near slopes the features of the North were soft in the shade—the greens, the purples, the mauves, the browns.

Nora swept the view from end to end till her vision clouded with black spots: I must keep this for when I'm old, she vowed.

Aloud she said: "Johnny, it's beautiful."

"Yes," he said. "You are now standing above the Highland Line; to the left of you lie the Lowlands of Scotland, to the right and behind you, the Highlands. What will you choose? Beauty and hardship or a flat, shoddy prosperity?"

"I don't know what I'd choose. I think I'd spend my life trying to unite the best of both."

His face beamed like a fed baby's and he clutched her happily from the ground. "That's the answer I'd give myself, Noreen Bawn," he said joyfully. "You're too perfect to be true."

She slid down his front, hooked her arms about his neck and kissed him with every fibre of her. The need in her had become a physical pain. "I can't wait, Johnny."

He found her a glade where the bracken was taller than young elder trees and the little animals of the hill could just be heard. There was no question of seduction; lip and fingertip were already superfluous. Burned near to madness by the flame of her kindling body he was forced to look on the splendid agony of her face to realise that she was something mortal. As their wild, wonderful love-song mounted in his ears and they bruised the juices from the grass beneath them, he capitulated to a throbbing power that was more than his own strength had ever been. The evening turned to a night that flashed with fire; the men of the plains ran in shrieking terror from the swords of the hills, and somewhere at the back of the screaming and roaring and the unbearable ecstasy of life and pain and death a woman's voice was louder than all. Goddess, harlot, mother, lover—laughing, crying, mocking, pleading—and without her there was still nothing. She shrieked.

The final consolidation. The plateau. Perfection.

She lay quivering and helpless beneath him now, who had made his spirit more than God and was rendering his flesh empty and less than water. There has never been This in life before, Johnny. Never, never—oh, Jesus, never!

The light came back to his eyes. He helped her up tenderly and they took a last look at the view. He stuffed two crumpled cigarettes in his mouth, lit them with the same breath, and gave her one. She accepted it with trembling fingers, but her eyes shone with nothing less than glory. She stamped it out after a few half-hearted puffs.

"You've been longing for a fag for days," he accused her.

She clenched her fist and thumped his chest. "Don't talk, Johnny," she said fiercely. "Just say nothing for a bit. I've discovered a wonderful new part of me, and I want to enjoy it. For a while I was wondering why people ever do anything else!"

He slipped an arm around her. "I've always wanted to love you somewhere near the graves of the heroes."

"The graves of the heroes?"

He pointed to the village. "Do you see that cluster of houses by the river, and the little mound beyond it? That's Dalchonzie—the hill of weeping, where the Caledonian women watched their men die at the battle of Mons Graupius. There are times when I can still hear those women."

Nora slipped her arm through his. "Darling, I think you're a throwback from somewhere. You don't deserve to exist among a people who bear the marks of defeat."

He yawned luxuriously. "Let's forget defeat for the moment. I'll start to cry."

"You're too sentimental," she said. "You and I could so easily finish up wallowing in the 'ifs' that bring tears to the eyes, that we'd never get anything worthwhile done."

He turned his cynical smile on her. "Cast your mind back five minutes," he said, "and then tell yourself to stop talkin' rubbish."

From below a bell pealed in agreement.

Glenellin was in dusk but the peaks opposite were still crowned by a spark of red sun. Where the village road left the hill in a horseshoe, a few fires were twinkling in the gloom of a small group of trees.

"Tinkers," he said. "Those are my friends the Stewarts; the last pure remnant of the '45."

"You know them?" she asked doubtfully. "They tell some awful tales about tinkers back home."

"You get that here too." Johnny waved a hand full of wisdom. "They're supposed to kill collies and steal kids, but it's all mythology—I've never found them anything other than courteous, in their own old-world way. Still, there is always just a tiny air of the sinister about the older tinkers. I'm sure they know things about this country that nobody on God's earth would dream about."

A scruffy little long-ribbed mongrel yapped at their heels as they crossed the road and entered the tinkers' camp. The tentage was a miscellaneous collection of army bivouacs, sail canvas and lorry tarpaulins stretched between trees. In the centre clearing the meal had just finished: the savoury aroma of rabbit stewed in herbs mingled with the smell of stale clothing and strong tobacco. Two long-haired women were washing a jangle of tin plates in a large enamel basin. On the far boundary of the firelight Nora saw a stack of bicycles, two handcarts and a small pony grazing.

A tall, spare man in shirt and trousers rose to welcome them, puffing easily at his pipe. Nora was surprised at the delicacy of the features—the high cheekbones, the long straight nose, and the hazel eyes crinkled up at the corners from looking far. He greeted Johnny in a Glenellin accent that was mixed with some indefinable softness. "Well Johnny, it's been a long time."

"It has indeed, Rory. Nora, this is Rory Stewart of Glenellin. No man knows this glen better than he does."

Rory Stewart welcomed her warmly. They sat by the fire on two rickety chairs; Rory's wife Ailie produced two steaming plates of stew and large mugs of tea. They found their appetites and ate heartily with huge old silver forks that scraped noisily on the tin amid the clipped chatter of the tinkers' bog-Latin. In the shadows an accordion proudly declared the artistry of an anonymous virtuoso; long fingers flitted deftly over the keys, full of wit and laughter, strong and brown as country ale. The women sang several songs of enchanting melody. Nora was astounded that completely untutored heads could produce an old ballad of 35 verses without a scrap of paper showing.

Ailie dumped a screaming bundle of shawl in Nora's lap; the peeling monkey face grinning up at her was scarcely a summer old; the tiny red mouth dribbled like a hole in an over-ripe apple.

"That's the latest," said Rory proudly. "He was born at Aberfeldy in March."

"He's a wee darling bundle," said Nora, stroking the little rough cheek. As she pulled the grubby shawl closer, an appalling stench of rancid faeces took her breath away.

"He's ayeways dirty," said Ailie apologetically. "I just canna keep him clean. I think my milk's ower strang."

Nora smiled and forgot the smell. Soon she herself would be changing a scruffy little Ferguson's nappy. She hugged the little crowing form to her: by her side Ailie rocked back and forward and hummed an old night-visiting song heavily embellished with grace notes. This was a day full of fresh experience, and when Johnny took his leave of the tinkers and she handed little Birky Stewart back to his mother there was a strange new sadness behind her eyes.

Rory walked with them to the roadside. "It's a pity that old Maggie Blair didna see ye," he said to Nora. "She'd hae read yer palm for ye."

"Is Maggie still with you?" said Johnny.

"Aye," said Rory. "She nearly died o' pneumonie last winter, but it'll tak' the de'il to kill her. She's still walkin' around, spittin' up brown stuff. She's out gatherin' herbs just now—she says they're better than any doctor's pills and it looks as if she's right."

Johnny gave him a rather brusque handshake. "We've got to go, Rory. Thanks for all your kindness."

Rory was chewing a twig of young gean. He nodded, and smiled; the brown face was a triangle of strength, the teeth white in the darkness. "Good rest to you," he said, then added something to Johnny in the strange dialect. Johnny forced a laugh, but he hurried her away.

"Is there something wrong, darling?" she asked.

"Of course not. But it's very late—we must get home." He took her hand and she felt a throb in his.

The wind was strong and playing an evil game with the moon. It hurled an endless succession of cannonburst clouds across the crescent face in an attempt to blot out its lucence; the little satellite was fighting valiantly, but had scant light to spare Glenellin. Nevertheless, they walked down the middle of the road without a faltering shoe. They had both been reared where the eye had little assistance on the dark side of the earth.

Nora was resentful and angry at she knew not what; somewhere in the past ten minutes something had crept between them and sprung a band of solid gold that had encircled them since Monument Hill.

They were less than 300 yards from the first house of the village when he gripped the flesh of her forearm. 'Listen," he whispered.

A scuffling noise came at her ears off the road. 'What is it?" She could scarcely speak; his anxiety was contagious.

"Someone coming," he whispered back. "They must be drunk judging by the way they're walking." The wind had loosed a barrage of opaque darkness on its noble little adversary and the road was now in complete blackout.

The scrape of worn leather grew louder. The shadow ahead grew very slowly towards them. Then the moon slipped the west wind's advance, and they saw her. She was old and pathetic, shambling and hooded, hith a shawl, and there was a basket on her arm. To Nora's surprise Johnny's pace quickened to Olympic tempo, but the old crone stumbled into their path, muttering to herself all the time.

"Good evening, young lady and young gentleman." Her voice was surprisingly deep and resonant, her words slow and distinct.

Nora pulled Johnny to a halt. "Good evening," she said politely.

"Hello, Maggie," he said with some reluctance.

"Well," said Maggie Blair with her face hidden in her shawl, "it's young John Ferguson home again and with his poor young lady. My tears for you, children, my tears for your sorrows. Ye're both so young."

"We're in a hurry Maggie," said Johnny, in a new, tense voice. He dragged Nora roughly on. "Good night, Maggie," he said, but she was already on her way, muttering as she went.

They were almost level with the gleaming white walls of the gamekeeper's cot before Nora had the courage to voice her disquietude. "Johnny," she said, "what's wrong with you, darling? You've been queer ever since Rory mentioned that old woman's name. She seems nice enough—but what did she mean?"

The whiplash cut of his retort almost bowled her over: "Don't be so bloody stupid, Nora. I couldn't give a curse about that old witch. She's as mad as a hatter. Now shut up about her, and let's get home!"

They walked up the main street in silence. He appeared to

relax as other human beings moved around them. Her spirits regrouped. It had been such a heavenly day, after all.

It was her turn to clutch his arm as they crossed the Ellin bridge. A paralysing scream shattered a lull in the wind's moaning, relegating it in comparison to a kitten's yawn. It rose to a pitch and intensity that belonged to the vocal cords of hell's legions and it hung above the water for a few seconds before it died a slow and defiant death that bequeathed its ugly echoing ghost to the hills.

"The lost soul," she gasped.

"It's a blasted wild cat," was his disparaging answer. "The glen's crawling with them."

Her laughter was the exaggerated mirth of relief. "I'm more superstitious than I thought, love," she said. "If you're not careful you'll find me traipsing up to old Maggie to have my hand read."

He wheeled on her and his tenderness was gone. "Nora, I've told you to forget that old cow. And don't you dare look near her; she'll fill your head full of nonsense. Now, shut up about her, I mean it!"

At the entrance to the manse drive he covered her face with kisses and asked forgiveness with a contrite voice. She leaned her head gratefully against his shoulder and squeezed his gentle hand, but she had left the supreme happiness of the afternoon fifty yards behind her, along with the few fallen tears that he had not seen.

CHAPTER XI

ON THE FOLLOWING morning he received a letter with a City postmark; the writing was Arnold's. He browsed over the pages of hospital notepaper for a full twenty minutes while his ham and eggs grew cold and congealed in their fat, and his father laughed at the vitriolic comments his bad manners extracted from Nora and his mother.

The most interesting and newsworthy paragraph concerned Nell, Stella and Ricky. Despite his absence at the audition, they had gone down extremely well with the American record agent, and were in the process of having an EP made; in addition to the record, Bernstein had promised them a tour of the South of England during the Christmas vacation.

Johnny felt betrayed. He had recognised their talents early, pulled them together against their will, and after many finger-aching, hoarse-voiced hours of practice had forged them into a weapon of powerful promise in the folk-entertainment world; he hated to see the result of so much sweat and tears (literally!) come to realisation without him. However, all good things come to an end, and he wished them luck.

Nell seemed to be settling down, according to Arnold. There was strong talk in the cocktail lounges of the West End that a certain eminent town councillor was soon to put a ring on her finger. Good luck to him, too!

Arnold had quite typically gone out of his way to glean the thicker ears of Connor's corn. Starkey Shearer had been barred by Stan for the seventy-fourth instance, this time for smashing the plate-glass front window; as Starkey had been propelled backwards through same by the violent hands of an outraged creditor, the consensus of Connor's opinion was strongly opposed to Stan's action, and considered it extremely unsporting.

Jimmy Anderson and Joe the Rat had enjoyed another minor brush with the High Street Teddy Boys; Colin was in the Lake District with Jean. Hector Gunn had been in Dublin for the past week, and was feeling awful. Pat Leitch was keeping a student clerkship open for Johnny during August and September in the Casualty department of The Royal City, and was ready to pay him a modest weekly sum from his own pocket.

Johnny needed the money badly—his grant would not be forthcoming for at least nine weeks—but in view of his father's precarious health he felt that he was duty-bound to remain at home a little longer. His father, surprisingly enough, made the decision for him.

"You'll go back, son, of course you will," he said. "If you can keep yourself over the next two months, it'll be a load off my shoulders."

His mother raised no objection. She had been at her best this past week. There had been no jarring notes in the sweet music of their stay; Johnny observed with particular approval that she and Nora were combining splendidly, and was at a loss to understand it.

One morning, quite early in the holiday, Nora and Mrs Ferguson were clearing the breakfast table.

"You think I'm a hard old nut, don't you, dear?" said Johnny's mother without emotion.

"Not really," said Nora, taken aback.

The older woman smiled grimly. "You know, dear, there's a wild, bad streak in the Ferguson family, and Johnny's father is the only one of them completely free of it—his elder brother died a drunkard. I thought if I raised Johnny rigidly in the fear of God I could mould him into the same shape as his father, but he's rebelled against everything. Perhaps my own Christian example was a failure."

Nora contented herself with the reply: "Johnny's got good stuff in him, Mrs Ferguson; he'll be all right. I'm sure that he's more fond of you than he pretends to be. I'll take good care of him, I promise you."

"Bless you, my dear," said Mrs Ferguson, and for the second time in a week Nora was on the receiving end of a dry kiss. From that moment their relationship had never looked backwards.

Johnny decided to leave for the City on Saturday afternoon. Thereafter Nora was to go home for eight weeks. He was dreading the parting; all of a sudden he realised that she had hardly been out of his sight since they had met, and his imagination was over-active in its fanciful production of sinister hazards.

"Please be good, darling," he pleaded. "For God's sake don't fall in love with Kevin all over again."

She scorned his fears. "You little idiot; I swear by all that's holy that you've got nothing to worry about. You be good yourself, ye divil-o—that's more the point!"

Johnny re-read Arnold's letter three times. He was constantly amused by the last paragraph: "In a way I'll be glad to get off to the army. The Newton has been a wonderful experience for me, and I'm getting to be quite a dab hand at the routine stuff; I can take out an appendix in fifteen minutes flat. What worries me is poor old Sister Glen—I think she's really a bit too fond of me."

Con Gallacher was invited to the manse for supper on Thursday; this was an occasion. The big Irishman behaved himself magnificently; he spoke not one word out of place, praised Mrs Ferguson's cooking with an admirable lack of slime, and discussed current affairs with a very atypical dearth of prejudice; his deference to Nora could not have been greater had he been courting her himself. Johnny saw with satisfaction that his parents were quite impressed.

"Do I have your permission to take these young lovebirds out tomorrow night?" Con asked the minister on leaving.

"Of course." Mr Ferguson squeezed the Irishman's shoulder. "Why don't you make a night of it at the dance with Morag and Company? It's time a truce was declared."

"A truce it is," said Con sincerely. "Johnny boy, we are livin' in momentous days—the old squabbles between the Scots and the Irish in Glenellin are comin' to an end."

The truce was begun in the lounge of the "Stag." The couch upholstery was deep and the walls were colourful with tartan plaids, claymores, and a fine royal stag's head over the porch. The night was oppressively dark and thundery. A sulky barmaid eavesdropped on them from behind the counter, but as the room filled up their voices assumed anonymity beneath a steady hum of chatter.

The drinking grew lively; at half-past ten it seemed that half of Glenellin had assembled round their table, and the "Stag" proprietor did them the honour of remaining open until Con and Morag waxed sentimental and sang "Bonnie Mary of Argyll" so well that he threw them out.

"To the dance!" shouted Fergie.

The sound of violin and accordion awakened an old smoulder in Johnny as they passed the churchyard gate and advanced on the village hall.

Morag led Nora through a floor packed with eightsome-reel sets to the little kitchen that served as a Ladies' Cloakroom. A few bare-legged girls stood around the small table where one of their number lay senseless on top of the ladies' coats. She looked about fifteen.

"Is Ireland like this?" said Morag pointedly.

"No," said Nora. "Not really."

"This town gets worse every week," said Morag. "If I'd been in that condition at her age, I'd have had my backside well scudded."

They threw themselves into the dance with vigour. Nora and Johnny danced a screaming quadrille with Morag and Fergie; the girls' shrieks drowned the music as their feet flew from the ground and their sharp heels jerked back the onlookers' heads.

Glenellin dancing was famous on a Friday night, and buses came from miles around. The hall was bursting at the seams with locals, roadworkers, bracken-cutters, and soldiers in battle-dress. The women represented a fair scoop of the barrel also; young village matrons like Morag and their brasher unmarried sisters rubbed shoulders with the henna-haired little women from Glasgow who donned powder, paint and ripped stockings every pay-night to tour the favourite haunts of the Hydro boys. These were everywhere; broad weather-beaten faces, gentle and savage, gleaming red above dark shabby suits and glaring ties, rejoicing in their whisky heat that softened the cool hostility of their hosts and brought desirability to the roughage of wasted, mincing faces that ogled them. There were more outlandish inflections to be heard than those of *Tir Conal*—Nora recognised German and Italian and made a fair guess at Polish and Ukrainian.

A progressive barn dance separated the Ferguson crew, and she found herself dancing with a strange variety of men. One or two made a rough pass at her in the brief twenty seconds allowed them, but most of the dam workers were too shy or too drunk to lay more than a flat foot on her toe—her one problem proved to be a thin, elderly Austrian who clasped her to him and tried to lick her face.

The music was calculated to make a Free Kirk minister dance; reels, quicksteps and waltzes followed one another in spirited procession, and the polished floor rocked and reeled under the careless feet that drummed on its yielding strength. This was the finest dance Nora had ever seen; it was wonderful to laugh among such a friendly convocation of nationalities; it was wonderful to see Con polka-stepping with Morag, each of them momently discarding distrust of the other's kind; it was most wonderful to whirl in the pulsating beat of a Highland Schottische with Johnny, and to feel his passion answering the thrilling screech of the fiddles. She stood after the dance between Con and Davie, an arm thrown round both of them, screaming her head off at a piece of Fergie's comicry. She loved the world tonight, but above all the world she loved Johnny, and above all the rest of him she loved the part that loved this wonderful place.

Then came a strip-the-willow. Davie and Morag led off to a chorus of eldritch howls; they whirled and twisted up the lines, and staggered panting into their new places. When Con and Nora took their turn the girls flew in all directions; the big Irishman pivoted and thrust, laughing like a boy.

Johnny saw the trouble first. In the group next to them a little Black Watch squaddie was partnering a tall, pretty Glenellin girl. Several Irishmen stood at the gate of their set; the tallest of these, a red-faced Mayo kid of about eighteen, was using foul words loudly, as if he had newly learned them. The little Scot told him to shut up, then was thrown back into the dance. Two other Irishmen lined up with the Mayo kid. As the Black Watch squaddie birled back towards him, the Mayo boy stepped forward. The Scot turned for his partner's arm to find her being spun round helplessly by the big navvy.

There was a slithering flurry of blows, and the two men grappled together, rolling to the floor with the heavier Irishman on top. He clawed for the soldier's throat, but the sandy head struck like a cobra's, and the Mayo kid screamed when his big red hand was viced by two rows of pitiless yellow teeth that burst the skin like paper and crunched deeper. It was then that one of his mates stepped forward and broke the squaddie's nose wih his right boot. Women screamed and ran for the walls; the corner of the hall erupted into a jungle of drink-maddened beasts clawing and swinging at each other. The Mayo kid lay groaning across the still form of his opponent, his fingers groping blindly for the five-inch gash on his crown where a webbing belt had struck. His two friends, outnumbered for the moment by the angry hornet's nest of soldiers and local men, struck out bravely with their backs to the wall before they went down under a pile of bodies.

Morag hurried Nora to the other side of the floor. "For heaven's sake stay here," she said. "Anybody's liable to get a belt if they stand too near. Just look at our stupid buggers—they're the worst of the lot." The band was playing "The White Cockade" with great gusto; finer incidental music could not have been devised in Hollywood. Most of the self-styled chuckers-out were too terrified to interfere, and Constable McVittie had taken the first flying fist as his cue for a walk in the churchyard.

It had resolved itself into a straight issue, Glenellin and the army united against the Hydro. With one minute gone the score in prostrate bodies was two-all; a curly-haired baker's boy was doubled up against the platform without a breath of wind left in his body, and the Mayo kid's hard-kicking colleague had received a taste of his own medicine; there was blood on the boots of the tall corporal who was helping his little mate from the floor.

Johnny found Hamish Murdoch and his old Irish ganger, Billy Duffy, trying to throttle each other in ludicrous tableau. He ducked between their arms and parted them with a twist of his shoulders; Duffy staggered against him and he grabbed him by the lapels. "Screw the nut, Billy—you'll get yourself the bloody sack," he gasped, but Duffy spat in his face and wriggled free, only to be imprisoned from behind in Fergie's massive bear-hug. Hamish grinned, and aimed a wide swing at Duffy's unprotected face; Johnny reacted automatically, and kicked his feet from under him. Hamish sat down heavily and looked up at him, utterly incredulous.

The fight was under control inside four minutes, thanks to the might of Con Gallacher. His initial momentum bowled three men over, and he was in the thick of it, his fury indiscriminate. A young soldier was lifted bodily by the hair, and flung ten feet. A little wiry Pole turned, presenting an ugly leer and a long sheath knife; both vanished as Con swept him to the floor with a contemptuous flourish of his open hand. He used fist and foot to break up a hard nucleus of scrappers; only the last Mayo man dared him in the end—Con closed his small, boxer's hand, and felled the man with a terrible right cross to the throat. A group of shamefaced torn-shirted men stood around him.

"That's all, boys," he said very quietly.

The band stopped playing. Murdoch rose slowly to his feet and dusted himself down. Johnny started to speak, then turned away. The bouncers had recovered their courage, and were escorting several of the young men to the door. The soldiers moved off in a welter of threats; their original champion appeared quite cheerful, despite his broken nose; his head leaned on the shoulder of his pretty dancing partner who was complaining violently about the "Irish Papes."

Con was sucking his right hand. "Let's get them bodies out of here," he said calmly. "You'd better have a look at them, Johnny, in case they need a doctor."

Con's victim managed to walk to the door, wheezing through his bruised windpipe, and the kicker staggered with him, his forehead swollen like a Martian's, bruised and bloody. They pushed Johnny aside with profane snarlings.

He found Nora standing outside the hall door, in the middle of a large crowd. The original Mayo kid was slumped on Con's knee, and they were trying to staunch the steady flow of blood from his scalp. He was weeping softly.

"This kid's hurt bad, Johnny. I think there's an artery pumping away," said Con. He looked at the wound by the light of Con's lighter. There was a small vessel spurting, bubbling merrily in the smooth edge of the cut. He pressed his thumbs on the occipital pressure-point, but the gouting red fountain continued to drench Con's handkerchief. He wrapped his other thumb in the handkerchief, and pressed on the wound. The Mayo kid screamed as he leaned his weight on the bleeding, greasy head for a full minute. The flow slowed to a tiny trickle.

"This wound needs a stitch," he said with certainty. "I'm going to walk this boy down to Dr Bruce."

"Nora's going home with me," said Morag. "And this is the last dance you'll see me at for a long time. This place is only fit for hooligans." She glared at Con, challenging him.

"You're runnin' away," he said. "Most o' them folk in there are decent people, an' if we're goin' to let a wee scrap ruin our evening, we're a shower o' bloody fools."

Johnny helped the injured boy to his feet; he was still crying. Then the throng parted, and the Murdochs came through. More trouble.

Hamish Murdoch stopped in front of Con, his three brothers behind him.

"We want this bastard, Gallacher," he said.

"Get lost," said Con. "This kid's half-dead already."

"We saw what happened," said big Hamish. "We don't like gangs of Irish hard men round here—we saw him pick on the wee Jock. It wisna fair at a'."

Con stood up slowly from the low wall. "I'll give ye ten seconds to clear out, or I'll belt ye."

A small spotty-faced bracken-cutter spoke from behind the Murdochs. "This is what we thought we'd get from you, Gallacher. But we've got a dozen men—we'll rush ye, if ye dinna gie us this big get." There were, in fact, about nine angry village men standing behind him.

Johnny stepped forward. "You mind your language, McEwen. An' if it's fair play you're talkin' about, I found an Irish boy done in last week when he was as drunk as an owl. The rats who did him were all for havin' a go at me in the dark outside St Mungo's—and then they saw Con, and they bolted like the yellow skunks they are. I'll tell you somethin' else—one o' them spoke wi' your voice."

"Ye're a bloody liar," piped the bracken-cutter.

Con moved ominously towards him, several Irishmen with him. "I was sure Johnny knew that voice," he said.

Nora stepped between them. "You ought to be ashamed of yourselves, the whole lot of you," she shouted. "There's a boy needing a doctor, and you're ready to start fighting again. Can't you see sense?"

The two factions fell back, looking stupidly at the lovely girl with the long red hair and furious green eyes.

"Let's go, boys," said one of the Murdochs. "There'll be another time!"

"There will," Con promised grimly.

"Just a minute." Hamish Murdoch glared fire. "Whose side are *you* on, Johnny? We used to be pals at school, and tonight you raised your boot to stop me hittin' a *squarejaw*—are you a Glenellin man, or what the hell are ye?"

"I'll always be a Glenellin man," he answered. "You and I have changed a lot since school, Hamish." He remembered last Sunday. "I'm Glenellin the same as you, but I won't fight against my friends, an' I don't like to see a man hit when his arms are held."

"*You're* not a Glenellin man," said Hamish, smiling without humour. "You're not one of us, and ye don't belong here."

A mad voice screeched in his ears, telling him to kill. "Don't say that, Hamish," he warned.

Of course ye're not a Glenellin man," piped the spotty little McEwen. "Ye've turned into a wee posh University bastard!"

Johnny hurled himself at him, screaming insanity. Con and his cousins were forced into using an agonising rough-house grip to pull him away. "You putrid scum of hell's gutters," he sobbed. "I'll kill you."

A van screamed round the corner fifty yards away. The cohorts of law and order had arrived from Crieff to reinforce Jock McVittie.

"Over the wall, all of ye," said Con.

The opposing battle orders melted into the night, their feet pounding on the churchyard turf. When the sergeant and his men arrived in the hall they got little response from a masque of bland, innocent faces, and left in a cloud of blue curses.

Johnny stumbled towards the surgery with an arm round his woeful patient. The head was bleeding again. "One of these days," he muttered venomously, "somebody is going to suffer for what I've just been through!"

He followed Dr Bruce into the comfortable sitting-room. The cut had required nine stitches; it had been difficult to hold the patient down.

"I've been looking out for you Johnny," said the doctor. "You've only one more year to go? What sort of career do you fancy?"

"I've often dreamed of Surgery, Doctor. But you know how tough the Fellowship is—competition's terrible these days. What are my chances of General Practice here?"

The village physician leaned back opposite him: a heavy man, his huge bald head gleaming like a polished igloo before his lamp standard. "I'd have you here with pleasure, Johnny, but if you're sensible you'll leave G.P. work alone. Is my advice still worth something?"

"Of course it is. You advised me into Medicine in the first place. I used to treat your opinion as the last word in common-sense."

"I thought that your crusading fire should be used on people, although you were so strong in the Arts, Johnny." The doctor's genial, obvious features wore a reminiscent smile. "You were going to alleviate the suffering of the world on your own—you made me quite ashamed of myself. But during the past few years I've heard some pretty hairy stories of your felonies; I've been terrified that my advice was wrong, for the wisdom of Solomon can't fathom the workings of a young mind. But I've got some advice now that I know is good."

Johnny waited in meek assenting silence.

"Listen, Johnny. This new Health Service has produced a mass of truculent morons who are just intelligent enough to realise their rights, and nothing else. In the old way, when a doctor had some proper standing, he could get up every morning in Glenellin and look forward to an interesting day's work. Now there are at least five bitches in this place who call me out repeatedly; when I go to them they'll be gossiping with their next-door neighbour, and not a thing wrong with them. But I don't ignore them; for if by any chance something did go wrong, they'd scream for the Executive Council to trample on me. I still have some patients whom I'd sweat my body dry for, but they're getting older and fewer all the time. Socialism and democracy—tripe!"

"I don't think I'd like that sort of Medicine," said Johnny. "Why d'you want me to do Surgery?"

"You've got a nature that demands a bit of drama," said the doctor. "And there's a wee touch of obsessional ambition about you too; you've always liked the limelight, Johnny. In Surgery at least you deal with young folk who come in very ill and go out very well, instead of prolonging old age in progressive stages of discomfort."

Johnny paled. "About my father, Dr Bruce?"

James Bruce slapped his forehead angrily. "I'm frightening you with my stupid talk," he said. "The electrocardiograph looks quite reasonable. With a bit of luck he'll be with us for a long time to come."

"Thank God." Johnny looked at the tired widower's face, pleasant and full-coloured, with the tracery of prominent venules round the nostrils. What have you to look forward to?

It was well after midnight when he left.

"Come in and see me whenever you're home," said Dr Bruce. "And try not to worry about your father."

"Thanks, sir," he said. "I suppose you'll have a busy day tomorrow?"

"Yes," said Dr Bruce wearily. "I shouldn't complain, Johnny; my job isn't all that bad, but stupidity is such a difficult disease to treat."

"This talk has been invaluable to me," said Johnny. "I'm sure you're right."

Despite his love of Glenellin, he could not see himself on a daily round packed with smokers' coughs and hangovers. He was not destined to practise Medicine in his native hills, and his surgical pipe-dream was to become reality. As he walked home a small voice told him that the doctor's advice had been sharpened by Hamish Murdoch and the spotty-faced McEwen, but this was quite ridiculous.

It began to rain heavily.

They left Glenellin on the first morning of August, and the heavens wept to see them go. Thick banks of cloud had sliced away the hilltops, and remained brooding over the bedraggled glen. The Ellin was turning from grey to the colour of army tea as it rose steadily, gnawing remorselessly at its soft banks, growing in voice and volume.

Johnny found his farewells surprisingly painless, although he kissed his mother in a way that she had not seen since he wore shorts. He wrung his father's hand, kissed Morag, slapped Davie and Fergie on the shoulder without any of his younger melancholy; as Con drove them slowly away it was Nora who returned their final salute.

She, in fact, felt the parting much more keenly than he did, and promised herself to return to Glenellin as soon as possible. Nothing could ever destroy her feeling for this town and its people, despite their propensity for melodrama.

Johnny was not unhappy but was paradoxically apprehensive because of this. The day did not make for bitter-sweet regret, but before he had always been a bit emotional on the drive out of the valley; now he was almost indifferent. He felt a deep sense of accomplishment as far as Nora was concerned: he had made her into a round peg in the family scheme of things, and despite his atrocious behaviour on the night of the dance and the night of Maggie Blair, she had surmounted the obstacles coolly and cleanly in her competent, thoroughbred way. He was also thankful for his discussion with Dr Bruce, and proud of his new single purpose, although he regretted that he had not taken the trouble to accompany the doctor on his visits and make his own criticisms. As for the rest of the holiday—well, there were always things which you could and should have done, but he had changed more than he realised, and had grown away so far from the wall that it would not be good or comfortable to tie himself back, and he would have to live with a moderate homesickness for the rest of his life. So much for home.

They drove to Lochearnhead in a heavy silence. They left Glenellin to the mist and Nora looked eastward to where she had walked four days before, and had been loved in Lednock; she felt a fleeting exhilaration.

They had seventeen minutes to wait for their train. Johnny left them briefly to visit an old friend in the hotel.

She sat with Con in the waggon, waiting. "Con," she said suddenly, "do you know that old tinker woman, Maggie Blair?"

"Yes," he said. "I know everybody in Glenellin."

"What's she like? I think Johnny's a little frightened of her."

"She's a queer old stick," said Con. "They say she's a bit fey. Johnny used to tease her a lot when he was working on the road. I seem to remember that they had a real barney once, but it can't have been very important. Have you met her?"

"Only just," she said.

"She's really a poor old soul," he said. "I've heard it said that she was the loveliest thing you ever saw when she was young—can you believe it?"

"No," she said firmly. "I can't."

The train moved southward out of the rain and Nora stared regretfully at the receding hills. On the journey up she had been rather nervous while he had been full of the glories of Glenellin. Now their feelings were almost exactly reversed.

"Next stop Finals," he said with an air of bravado.

III

THE CITY

End of a Year and More

CHAPTER XII

SEPTEMBER WAS a warm red-gold in the City this year; after the wet misery of August he felt a comforting matriarchal protection in the lanes of dry, peeling leaves and the crisp, autumnal lines of the grey buildings.

And he was further compensated for the heart's cold rapier-point of loneliness in Nora's absence by the vibrant canvas of life he saw daily in and around the Royal City Hospital.

Pat Leitch, the famous Connor's man, supervised the Casualty Department with minimum fuss and maximum efficiency. Despite the nuclear blast of gin and tonic that he breathed round the treatment rooms he was a better doctor outside four doubles than many of his superiors were when sober. Johnny's insignia as the lowliest member of the staff was a white theatre gown; he envied the S.H.O. and the two housemen in their laundered white coats. He was enjoying casualty work tremendously; each day was spiced with a variety of admissions. On Monday and Thursday afternoon Pat took him into the adjacent Out-Patients' Surgery, where he assisted the chiefs in the long lists of varicose veins; on Wednesday afternoon he helped in the ano-rectal clinic, clerking the engorged condition of the City's back-passages.

Another lovely afternoon. He changed into his voluminous gown, gleaming transparent in white light. Pat gave him a stitching case to do; a young grocer's apprentice who had nearly decapitated the pulp of his finger on a bacon-slicer. From this he graduated to a badly torn shin and a cut eyebrow; suturing skin was a wonderful business once you realised that it was not so much like digging a ditch as it first seemed; he was becoming justly proud of his tidy scars with their balanced tension of stitches.

In the late afternoons and evenings most of the admissions came through Casualty. An elderly woman came in with a stroke, and died just inside the door. A scrawny old tramp, crawling with lice, was borne in in a delirious, febrile condition, coughing filthy brown sputum and clutching the left side of his chest. The

S.H.O. and Johnny went over him together; he had a lobar pneumonia with pleurisy; they referred him quickly to the waiting medical ward.

He saw an epileptic, a boy with a crushed foot, and a successful suicide before he had time for a glass of milk in the Scala and a ribald ten minutes with Maria; she was apparently enjoying more leisure-time now, for her neck was radiant with love-bites.

When he returned to the hospital the "nights" houseman was coming on duty. Pat and the S.H.O. discussed orthopaedics in the doctors' duty-room while Johnny drank coffee and read Nora's latest letter; she loved him more than ever, she said, and was getting the key of her hormone-box ready for her return to the City. He read suspiciously, seeking the unconscious innuendo that spelt deceit and disaster, but was forced to a final thankful admission that it appeared heartfelt.

After seven-thirty the traffic picked up a bit, and Johnny stayed in his favourite little stitching-room, repairing the wounds that Pat selected for him. He revelled in the quick bite of his needle in strong tissue, the gaping slashes that shut their red mouths so meekly under the black silk, and the mystic passes that his slick wrist made round his needleholder; motions that looked so devastating and were in fact so simple.

He was called along to "A" Treatment. Pat was setting up a cut-down transfusion on a very ill young woman. Beside the trolley lay a pair of pink pyjamas, drenched crimson in their lower half.

"Criminal abortion," he said flatly, working quickly beside the staff-nurse. "She won't say who did it—they rarely do."

"Are you sending her over to Gynae?" asked Johnny. He looked at the drowsy ashen face, and the little rough hand that gripped his; the girl was about eighteen, and still alive enough to be frightened.

"You bet," said Pat, as he tied his last stitch. "She'll have to be scraped immediately. This smells like a Dettol job, probably done about three days ago. She's come away tonight in about a dozen pieces, and there's a lot left in, poor kid."

"I wonder who the bastard was who did that job," said Johnny, as she was wheeled away. "He's nearly killed the poor lassie."

"Why bastard?" asked Pat.

"God, it's obvious why," he said heatedly. "You can't go around killing what is potentially a human life."

"Uh-huh," said Pat sardonically. "If that's your line, then you shouldn't eat fish, and then where would the Papes be on a Friday? I suppose you do believe in evolution?"

"Don't be silly," said Johnny. "It's not the same thing at all."

"With apologies for my crude speech," said Pat, "have you ever had a woman up the stick?"

"No, I haven't," said Johnny.

"Then don't judge your brother till you've lost some sweat in his moccasins," said Pat.

"I've seen lots of abortions done," said the S.H.O. "When I was working with Mungo Blaeney he had no compunction about it—many of his scrapes were young girls in trouble."

"That's another story," said Pat. "His kind are rare, but I'm sure he did what he thought right. Let's be thankful that we're not gynaecologists."

"Would you do it, Pat?" said Johnny.

"No," said Pat Leitch. "I've seen too many hysterical tears afterwards."

In the next hour they had little of vital interest. Pat looked at Johnny over a sprained finger. "You've been looking a bit tired tonight, youngster. On you go up to Connor's and have a pint." In Pat's big, injected face the massive bone structure radiated boozy health.

"I think I will, Pat—I've been missing the boys."

He wandered into the chilly open, tired round the eyes, but walking with the spring of high morale. Since three o'clock he had been working in the seam of life and it left him not only contented but with a bellyful of elation. A good day in Casualty made the body weary, but the mind boasting that its home was Mount Olympus.

He entered Connor's. The Moonshiners were sitting just inside the door. Three open mouths.

Johnny recovered first. "Congratulations to one and all," he said shakily.

Ricky and Stella held hands and said nothing. Nell was looking attractive and she was sober.

He smiled at her. "That's a lovely tan you've got, Nell. Have you been to Monte Carlo?"

She turned away from the others. "I got it about two miles away," she said quietly. "I've been sunbathing on the balcony of a friend's flat all summer. I feel a new woman."

"You look it," said Johnny. "I can guess who the friend is, and I'm glad that he's doing you some good. Funnily enough I don't feel jealous."

"And I don't want you to be jealous any more," she said blithely. "I've found a sweet old man of forty-five who's obscenely rich and famous, and the thought of marrying him fills me with nothing but happiness. You know, Johnny, he likes our singing!"

"Good for you, old girl," he said. "We're friends again. This calls for a drink!"

"Are you coming to hear our Festival Concert on Friday?" said Nell.

"You bet," he said. "I'm anxious to hear the new blend."

"You're a doll," she said. "I was wrong about Nora. She's done a wonderful bit of lifeline-throwing."

"Well, well," he said, surprised. "I can't get over this change of heart, Nell; I'm not altogether sure that I trust it."

She laughed—low, throatily, and it could still heat a man's blood. It was the sound that drove a good king mad on the roofs of Jerusalem, and the evil resonance that tolled over the crackling walls of Troy.

"That's enough from you, Ferguson," she said. "I'm old enough not to trust myself at all, but so far I'm doing fine. You leave me alone, you brat!"

He finished his beer. "No sooner said than done, madam. I'll be cheering like hell on Friday night."

He left the Moonshiners and walked across towards a slim, familiar back. Torquil McLelland was having an angry political discussion with Jehosaphat.

"I don't know how you tolerate this gargoyle," said Torquil McLelland. "He knows less about politics than you do."

Jehosaphat sniffed. "He's bloody crackers. He's all for gettin' out the guns, the way the Irish did. I'd like to see him if the D.L.I. got their bayonets near his backside." He strode up the counter, to where a reinstated Starkey Shearer was liquidating the last pound of Ellen's pay.

"What's up, Torquil?" said Johnny.

"Things are really moving," said Torquil. "We've got the Party on its feet at last."

"I see," said Johnny. "Has your membership reached double figures?"

"Don't be facetious," snapped the economist. "We've got some really good young lads now. We've painted a lot of slogans lately, and an E II R sign was torn off a lamp-post on Sunday night. Did you not read it in the papers?"

Johnny shook his head. "I only have time for the headlines. There's a lot of trouble in Cyprus."

"Aye," said Torquil. "I wish we had a few Cypriots in Scotland; EOKA are a great bunch."

"They certainly seem to be adept at shooting people in the back," said Johnny. "They'll be killing women before long."

"Nonsense," said the Secretary of the Scottish Free Party. "You get more unsound every day—decrying EOKA and consorting with that sort of rubbish." He pointed up the bar.

Johnny blew a smoke ring at Lizzie's left ear. "I'm sick of telling you that I'm a better Nationalist than you," he said cheerfully. "But if you want me to follow a brand of Nationalism that precludes me from liking a crazy old devil like Jehosaphat, you can stick it up the dirtiest orifice in town."

"You should see some of the young boys I've got now," said McLelland. "They're real Nationalists. We've got a new young speaker, a Glasgow Irishman; his father's an old I.R.A. man. We've not had his like since the days of John MacLean."

"I don't know what John MacLean would think of your new Party," he answered. "Anyway, what do you want me to do?"

"Come in and lead our commando squad," said McLelland. "We need somebody who knows the old ropes—and somebody who knows where to get gelignite! An extremist body in Glasgow has promised us support. Three letter men!"

"Oh, for God's sake, Torquil," he answered. "I never did anything more dangerous than painting walls. In any case you've tried all this before; it's got no relation to reality at all. No—I'm a coward, Torquil. I want to qualify next year, and I'm not losing my degree for any of your mad dreams."

"Will you come to our open-air meetings occasionally?" said McLelland, as a poor last resort. "They may change your mind."

"I will," said Johnny. "And I'll join the party as a sleeping member, and I'll pay you my subscription faithfully. I still have a weakness for lost causes, especially Scotland."

"Why?" said Torquil angrily.

"If I told you," said Johnny, grinning, "you'd have me rubbed out. I wouldn't like that." Torquil walked out, slamming the door in fury.

The Moonshiners were taking their time to finish drinking. Ricky and Stella were still holding hands, and Nell was rudely powdering her nose. Joe the Rat had taken off his jacket, and was threatening to fight a wizened old charwoman in the corner; she in turn was directing a scalding stream of vituperation at his tiny frame. Jimmy Anderson and Murdo were flirting with two little Scala waitresses; Jehosaphat was sitting on the floor debating existentialism with Lizzie's fox terrier. There were at least a dozen other regulars present who were beginning to exhibit their particular symptoms of inebriation. This could have been a night of last year; the maelstrom of change and decay that hovered around the lives of these characters could not touch Connor's; at ten o'clock you were still twice the man you were at five, despite the increasing presence of grey hairs, and the swelling, softening paunch.

He looked hard at Nell. A year ago he would have been sitting beside her, relishing the thought of the hours that lay ahead. She looked bloody beautiful now—just look at those lovely long legs.

He saw her face light up as a man's head screwed round the open door. The cool, distinguished well-fed smile was not a Connor's face; the black homburg was not a Connor's hat. He had seen that smile often before in newsprint grey; Nell's ambitions were certainly climbing an expensive ladder. The head disappeared; Nell said something to her friends and followed. At the door she turned, gave a shining toss of her black head, and dropped her left eyelid straight at Johnny. He winked back, forgetting to close his mouth.

You big smooth Judas, what d'you mean by coming in here and taking one of our girls? She doesn't belong in your glib world of legalised half-truths. If I didn't have a better girl, I'd bloody well take her off you—you smooth pimp!

"Come and have a coffee with me, Johnny," said Starkey beside him. "I need a friend to pay for mine."

Arm-in-arm they sauntered to the Scala.

He had ten more days to survive without Nora.

The concert proved to be a great financial success, but the discerning critics gave the new Moonshiners a terrible sherracking. Although he could not be truly objective in his opinions, Johnny agreed with the sarcasm in their columns, and was not a little ashamed of the smug feeling their acid gave him.

While the packed City audience were generous in their novice applause, the row packed with Connor's men (the most fanatical connoisseurs of folk-music in urban Scotland, thanks to Hector Gunn) was moved very little.

Ricky was now leading the group, and was too gentlemanly for the job. Stella's arrangements had always tended to be a bit ornate; Johnny had bludgeoned her into tearful defeat when she had overstepped herself, but now she was making chorales out of bothy ballads, and turning modal mountain blues into church-song.

What was worse, others of their songs were tasteless compromises with pop-music; they were received with great enthusiasm by the greater part of the hall, but a low rift of contempt swept along the Connor's rank; Starkey blew a drunken raspberry on his programme at the end of a jangling "Beautiful Brown Eyes." Nell tried hard, but the old edge was gone. Johnny sunned himself in the realisation that he could have organised a much better performance.

He did not go back-stage after the performance, but he could not avoid Hector Gunn at the door.

"What did you think of it?" said Hector pleasantly.

"It seemed to please the audience," he said, avoiding the issue.

"It's not as good as it should be, is it?"

"No."

Hector rubbed his moustache with the back of his hand, a sure sign that he was annoyed. "You know why, Johnny. You should be there. If you were still teaching that group they'd be the most promising folksingers in the world; as it is, they're utterly chord-bound to the noise of their instruments. It'll take some hard work to straighten them."

Johnny looked for an avenue of escape, but Hector handed him a half-bottle from his large sporran. He took a small swig.

"You know," said Hector, "you let us down badly in the summer, when you didn't turn up for the audition. It was touch-and-go before Bernstein agreed to give the Moonshiners a run, and it took a lot of Connor's whisky to convince him. At one time I thought I'd never forgive you."

"I'm sorry," he said lamely.

"Thats good of you," said Hector. "I must go and tell some lies to the gentlemen of the Press."

The ensuing ten days passed all too slowly. He left Casualty at the end of the week, and informed his landlady that he had found "digs" nearer to the University; Nora's landlord, a Pole, had leased her the flat for another year. She had no objection, she wrote, to Johnny's living with her; she was now more intent on giving him decent surroundings for the grinding hours of study that lay ahead, than worrying about her reputation; he, on the other hand, had no intention of making their cohabitation a source of speculation in the University—his virtue was rewarded and the problem neatly packaged when Colin Morrison found a tiny flat for the two of them less than a mile from Nora's.

The dragging, tantalising days were partially redeemed by one incident.

Jehosaphat failed his "re-sit" as most of the bookmakers in his year had hoped, for he was utterly unpredictable, and carried long odds. He passed Physiology easily, and scraped through Biochemistry on the strength of his broad, verbose County Durham answers; little of these were intelligible to his oral examiner, but they were too lengthy to appear less than erudite. Anatomy, however, could not be passed by gamesmanship, and here he was found wanting. His paper was a tragedy, though it contrived to include a paragraph on Descartes, and his practical examination in the pungent formaldehyde atmosphere of the Dissecting Room gave the tough old external Professor his first real insight into the aetiology of a nervous breakdown.

On the night of the results the luckless candidates stayed well away from their joyful brethren—all but one. If he could not celebrate success, there was always the fact that the army dared not claim him until he had failed once again, and he was assured of at least six more months of state-subsidised wantonness.

He sang more loudly than any of his fellows in Connor's that night, set fire to the newspaper that Starkey Shearer was reading, and kissed Lizzie four times to the intense chagrin of her fox terrier. He met Johnny just before closing time, and they had a quick concentrated session.

At ten o'clock they staggered into the Scala. At half-past ten Maria's brother Franco ejected them when Jehosaphat stood on a table and called upon all medical students present to toast the coming wedding of the Anatomy Professor's parents.

Jehosaphat struck off for his "digs," leaning heavily on Johnny. As they passed the main gate of the Medical Quad, he stopped. "Let's go and see if my name's on the list," he said thickly.

"Don't be damn silly," Johnny replied. "You know very well it's not."

"Life is relative,' said Jehosaphat. "My state is now relative to what it was this afternoon; perhaps the notice board will be relative too."

He entered the Quad, and ran his finger up and down the list of names.

"Come on," said Johnny, "your name's not there, you idiot."

Jehosaphat jumped from foot to foot, shouting at the top of his voice. "I've been bludy well victimised," he screamed. "I demand another trial."

A voice issued angrily from the little porter's box inside the gate: "You'll get a trial a'richt, if ye dinnae beat it double quick!"

They went over to him. "Would you please be a little more civil—peasant!" said Jehosaphat acidly.

The little porter pushed his shoulders through the box window. "Less o' that, ye hairy gowk. If ye're no' oot o' here in ten seconds I'm phonin' for the polis."

Jehosaphat stood back and bared his watch from his sleeve with a great flourish. He counted up to ten slowly. "Now try it, ye little flapper-mouth!"

Johnny made a rapid decision: "Good night, Jehosaphat."

"Certainly," said the porter cheerfully. He thrust his

shoulders through the opening, and stuck his dried raisin face against Jehosaphat's. "I've had enough trouble wi' you kids; I suppose this is what ye get lernt from yer teachers!"

He withdrew his head, reaching for the telephone at his left hand, but this queer-looking student with the retarded expression moved with surprising swiftness. Jehosaphat seized the cable with his left hand and ripped it from the 'phone a split second before he grabbed the slide window and slammed it downwards. The porter's roar of fury climbed to a piercing screech of pain as the heavy wooden sill smacked him squarely on his withering head.

Jehosaphat began a Highland Fling of triumph, but in turning round he struck a pillar which seemed to have moved six feet. When he got up, he saw that the pillar was pot-bellied and clad in blue.

The bench of his High Street cell was quite comfortable, although his reflection in the toilet bowl at its end gave him a fright first thing in the morning. He sat placidly in the Burgh Court awaiting judgment at ten o'clock, convinced that here was an experience that no citizen should miss. His phlegm wavered during the judgment of the two citizens preceding him—an anaemic little prostitute who received three months, and a petty thief who was given four.

His charge was read.

"Have you anything to say?" asked the short-sighted, plump old Baillie.

Trembling, Jehosaphat assumed his orator's stance: "There was a man of ancient times, who when foully and wrongfully accused of sodomy, stood lone before his countrymen, and—"

The Baillie put on his spectacles. "Fined two pounds," he interrupted incredulously.

CHAPTER XIII

THE PERITONEUM LAY glistening in the natural light of noon, suggesting moisture that was yet beyond it. Beneath it something writhed and twisted with the anguish of a gut-shot rabbit.

Arnold's palm snapped shut over the forceps that came to him from his right. 'Thank you, staff. Right, sister; pick up peritoneum with me." The four blades clicked together as two; Sister Glen required no instructions.

The glistening bag was cut open, and the self-retaining retractor tested the elasticity of the abdominal wall. He slipped his rubber hand into the wound, seeking the organs of the pelvis.

"Nothing's wrong here," he informed the theatre quietly. "I thought she might be an ectopic, with her period being slightly overdue."

At the head of the table, Dr Menzies stopped reading *The Scotsman* to remark: "I'll bet you a dollar you'll find the appendix inflamed; she's got a typical appendix breath."

"Could be," said Arnold. He flipped the long coils of intestine on to the skin of the belly with contemptuous confidence and slid them through his fingers. Sister Glen worked unobtrusively opposite him, swabbing automatically, gently adjusting the big retractor, and adding a small copper one.

Arnold turned to the old anaesthetist. "You're right as usual," he said; "she's not terribly inflamed, but there's a blockage. It's one of these long thin appendices, lying well up behind the caecum."

He paused for a minute, looking down on the sight that he had come to love like home—the living, squirming bowel, and the smoothly-painted triangle of red skin within the perimeter of the neat green towels.

"It's a bit soft, sister," he said. "We'll have to be careful. Just have a pack ready."

On with the small clamp across the tip, then. Gently with the meso-appendix, lengthways your big clamp—"Thank you, sister" —and get your vessels one by one. So far, so good. There's your appendicular artery nicely dissected out. Ligature now—"Thank you, sister"—that's sorted the bleeding points nicely, we're doing fine. Pick up by the tip, clamp on the base—"How's she doing, sir? Thank you, sister. Knife, please, sister—knife and phenol." Gently does it, away she goes—appendix removed. "Nurse, for heaven's sake, stop dreaming and get that filthy thing out of here at once."

Let's wash our hands again, then a careful minute for the purse-string. "Right sister, continuous for peritoneum—hold your forceps up a wee bit." Through and through, through and through, "Damn it, there's a knuckle of omentum coming—oh, well done, sister." Through and through—cut. On with the sewing up—what a great thrill it is to work with a pair of hands like she's got. It's just about as close as you can ever get to a woman without—"Right, sister, give me a few interrupteds; she's got a lot of dead space."

Continuous for skin now—edge to edge, edge to edge, edge to edge—back through again, tie and cut. Nice little job, though I say it myself. "Thank you, sister."

Dr Menzies slipped his fingers on the temporal pulse. "You're getting really expert, Arnold," he said. "It's a pity you're leaving us."

"It's a great pity," said Arnold. "But it's a good way to finish; I still get a kick out of appendices."

He stripped off cap, mask, gown and gloves for the last time in Newton Hospital, and walked slowly into the doctors' room. Mr Rutherford had just changed—six feet four and built in proportion. Arnold poured out three cups, and sat down, sipping his tea without milk or sugar.

"Well," said Mr Rutherford, "that's the end of your Surgery, and you've done pretty reasonably. Most of my housemen have been decidedly more idiotic than you. What are you going to do when you're finished with the army?"

"General Practice is for me," said Arnold.

"Good luck to you, said the surgeon. "I don't know how anybody who's had a taste of General Surgery can stomach General Practice."

Dr Menzies crunched a biscuit. "I dunno," he drawled in his rough Queensland. "Surgery seems to do funny things to some men."

"Maybe," said Mr Rutherford, rising, "I've yet to see it. We'll all meet at the Clarendon at eight, then. You'd both better be in good form; this is my first night out for three weeks."

"Yes, sir," said Arnold. "It's very kind of you."

"Kind be damned," said the anaesthetist as the door closed. "We'll have to spend the evening listening to tales of Hammersmith and McGill. That man can talk about two things—Surgery and Austin Rutherford."

"He's taught me a hell of a lot," said Arnold. "He has his faults, I know, but I'd forgive the man murder purely because of his ability."

"I won't deny that," said Dr Menzies. "But he doesn't know his own limitations and that's dangerous. The houseman before you used to tell the old story about Sir Neville Stott, the psychiatrist, being summoned to Heaven to deal with an emergency. When he got to the gate St Peter told him that God was suffering from delusions of grandeur. He thought that He was Austin Rutherford!"

Arnold laughed. "Never mind, we'll get a good dinner tonight."

"I'm sure he'll do us well," said Menzies. "You know, I'm a bit sorry for him. He'll kill himself if he's not careful; quite apart from operating in three hospitals, he's on every committee in town. Thank God I'm not ambitious, Arnold. I'm a broken old vessel leaking whisky, but I'm as happy as a king."

"I wish I could say that," said Arnold thoughtfully, thinking of the dreadful scene that Betty had created the night before. Her ring was in his pocket. He changed and went back into the wards. The new houseman had already appeared; the handover was brisk and pleasant. Arnold shook hands with his ward staff, feeling strangely detached from the whole thing; it seemed ridiculous to suggest that he would not be back on duty tomorrow as usual. He had a pleasant farewell chat with matron over a glass of Benedictine, then he packed his suitcase and took it into the theatre to say goodbye to Sister Glen. He hoped that she wouldn't break down, poor old soul.

She was writing her report in her beautiful flowing script. He stood looking down at her for a long time before she looked up and reached for her cigarettes. He took one, and flopped down by her table.

"Well," he said, after three long puffs and blows, "this is it, sister."

She smiled, still writing. "Don't sound so final, doctor. You'll be back to see us sometime, no doubt."

"Of course I will, sister. But I want to get away for a bit. I'd like to get to Hong Kong or Singapore."

"I hope you do get out there," she said. "You don't regret not marrying Betty?"

"Truthfully, no," he said. "I'm glad she made the final decision herself. I feel a bit guilty about the whole thing."

"You have a good time in the army," said Sister Glen. "If I know anything about it, you'll have a load of nurses falling for you before you know it."

Arnold looked at her carefully. She was smoking quickly, otherwise she was surprisingly composed.

"I've a lot to thank you for, sister," he said. "You've been a pleasure to work with."

"Nonsense," she said, flaring crimson. "You're the first person I've been at home with for a long time, and it means a lot."

He waited for her to continue, but to his surprise she stood up and held out her hand. "Goodbye, Dr Ayton, and all the very best. I'll be thinking about you—and we'll miss you."

He held her hand, fighting for words that eluded him. He picked his suitcase up and turned to go. "Don't go marrying an old man while I'm gone or I'll be damned cross."

"Of course not," she said cheerfully. "When I do, I'll make sure that you're around. I've got nobody else to give me away."

"Of course," he said, feeling grossly unsatisfied. He stopped at the door, and looked her up and down rather rudely. She must have been beautiful twenty years ago.

"Goodbye, Sister Glen."

"Goodbye, Dr Ayton."

She listened to his footsteps muffle with distance. The theatre door closed slowly, relinquishing with regret the young hands that had served it. She walked over to the sink, and stood gazing down at the devitalized tissue that had fallen to his knife. In some ways life would never be the same again. In peculiar fashion he had become hers for the past six months; with the bitter honesty of forty years she knew what she could have done, had she been willing to give a hearing to the voices of her weaker moments. As it was, she would see him again sometime, and would probably hate his wife like poison without showing it. She picked up the lonely little diseased organ, and smiled. She had seen perhaps two thousand of these, and somewhere after the first five hundred she had realised that nothing lasted for ever.

Arnold walked slowly to the bus stop. He was still amazed by her nonchalance. She would probably be having a good weep right now, poor old soul. By God, but she was full of guts.

In an odd way, he would miss the hospital—those early morning rounds with sunshine blessing the white sheets, the hours that passed like minutes over the table, the duty-room talks with Rutherford that turned you into a fact-absorbing blotting-paper, the light-hearted sessions with dear old Menzies—and Sister Glen: big, handsome, lonely and incomparable.

Two young nurses swung by him in blue capes, singing a popular song softly, their personal hymn to three hours of freedom. He turned his face hurriedly away from them, for the pain of his eyes was spilling treacherous and hot over his cheeks.

CHAPTER XIV

TERM STARTED early in October with the usual flourish. The S.R.C. representatives spent a full week escorting bands of rapturous freshers around the University buildings and dances; talent was good this year, said the veterans of the Medical Faculty, and admirably reinforced from the U.S.A.

By the following Monday the Final Year had more to think about. Lectures and cliniques missed fewer renegades than ever before, and beneath the *joie de vivre* of the talk that swerved around the nauseous steam of Union food the thought of nine-months-hence prepared to raise its ugly head and come into its own.

In the second week of term Johnny's grant arrived and he bought Nora a neat little engagement ring in rubies and diamonds that cost him £20. They had a small, select celebration party in her flat. Nobody was terribly drunk, and they all agreed that it was very nice.

The nights darkened steadily, and the misty yellow of the lamplit quad was raw and cold on the skin. The squadrons of fur-booted naiads hastening into the Union of a Saturday night became ever more wrapped and shapeless; aged lungs were no match for the sudden drop in temperature and put their trust in God and penicillin. The trees lining the Middle Meadow Walk faced the breath of the east in hapless skeleton order; already the vanguard of the cold season had lowered the pennants of autumn. Johnny and his comrades rose gingerly in the chilly hours of morning, and were glad to seek the comforts of the warm lecture theatres.

His first term cliniques were surgical: he found that his knowledge was adequate, thanks to his hours in Casualty and the Newton. The bookmakers listened carefully, and noted that Ferguson should have shortened odds; he had obviously been banging the books. Many students were learning avidly, as if time were already too short, but Johnny showed a more leisurely interest. He skipped one clinique per week and treated himself to a pleasant few hours with Murdo in the Folklore Department, listening to the latest collections of songs and folk-tales.

The lectures were merely a way of passing the time. A few were interesting but he had always found it difficult to concentrate amid the scratching of obedient ballpoints and the wooden faces that lost all initiative to the lecturer's voice; he claimed that his refusal to take notes was on principle. For *his* hour was still months ahead; about six weeks from the start of Finals he would be seized as he had been before by a mighty, all-compelling urge to scan textbook print for hour after hour, at a pace that few of his fellows could stand. For any examination 40 days' hard labour was more than enough, and in the meantime he was content to absorb only what he found interesting.

His discomfort was increased by the proximity of certain sections of the class which bored him to distraction. People whom he had successfully avoided for years made a habit of joining his Union table and discussing Coming Events in funereal undertones; they rarely took offence when he told them to fuck off. Some considered him too far behind in theory to have any chance at all, and they were reasonably pleasant; others were not so sure, and eyed him with suspicion, graphing desperately his present understanding against his ability and the time left for him to use it—Johnny sniggered to himself and aggravated their neuroses by his invention of tremendously convincing data. But with his real friends, Jimmy, Colin and Martin Clark, a young East Lothian High School product, he found a reasonable attitude towards the Thing; they discussed it when its relevance was unavoidable; otherwise there were other subjects to sweeten the bitter taste of Union coffee, and one could still pretend to forget that for the next stretch of life's pilgrimage a narrow gorge must be traversed with a hideous, inescapable cave at the end of it, the darkest midnight of the medical soul. One could only hope that the momentum of one's guts and *savoir faire* could smash through the dark brain-trap and gain the brilliance of the qualified City of Gold on the other side. Johnny did not resent the apprehensive bungaloid mentalities who were secretly praying for his downfall. In many ways his past negligence merited it, and they had all worked their middle-of-the-class intelligence to the cores of their bony skulls; furthermore, there was no one ordeal in the academic world which stimulated the instinct of self-preservation more than the final M.B., Ch.B.

He dabbled with his books most nights in Nora's flat. She tried to be a hard taskmaster, and to drive both herself and Johnny relentlessly, but he found it easy to deceive her. Their social evenings were regular and chosen; every second Friday night Johnny was allowed to go on his own to Connor's and the "Folk-song" while Nora attended the Celtic Society. He slept most nights in his own flat; on Saturdays, when they all invaded The Union, Colin entertained Jean at home afterwards and Johnny moved over to Nora's. At the weekend conviviality reigned supreme; it was a damn shame that Finals lay ahead of all this.

The Moonshiners practised quietly and waited for their Christmas tour of the South with great excitement. On their few appearances in Connor's they gave some impromptu performances which showed distinct improvement from their September debacle; Hector had talked to Stella with short and angry words. There was no sign of an engagement ring on Nell's left hand as yet, but the eminent personage was still to be seen in her company. Of Johnny Ferguson she saw little, apart from a few fleeting moments at the Folksong Society; he sang occasionally, but without his old gusto, and members heard the comment passed that perhaps his leaving the group had not been a bad thing. He always seemed vaguely uncomfortable now, and his old stage personality had faded. With his decline the late-night parties were becoming fewer and fewer; the Society remained but the Institution was gone.

In Connor's Jimmy Anderson remained the fulcrum: his class-marks were shocking and his drunken bouts increasing; he ceased to talk of Finals seriously, but dulled the haunted defeat behind his eyes with beer and whisky.

Behind the counter Stan observed the disorder of pickled individuals uneasily. From other bar proprietors he had heard unpleasant mention of the new Teddyboid gang boss who called himself King Bobo, and who had vowed to clear Woods Street of students. Already the University had been forced to withdraw from further down the road, and many of the scarves using Connor's at week-ends hung around polite young men who drank sparingly. They were obviously refugees.

But Torquil McLelland was ecstatic. The Scottish Free Party now had several hundred members, and several branches throughout the country, while their Sunday night meetings in the orators' square by the Art Gallery drew large crowds. Early in October a Molotov Cocktail was thrown into an empty T.A. Mess, severely damaging three square feet of hideous wallpaper. The City took little notice, but in London questions were asked in the House. Real violence at last! Torquil diverted all enquiries with a shrug and a sly wink, and thrilled at the sight of tall men in belted raincoats moving in and out of the large, heckling Sunday crowds. We've got the buggers worried again!

November was a month of gloom, shrouded in a filthy wet mist that sat heavily on the breath and clothing. Pavements were dangerous with dead leaves and slime; the streets cringed beneath the dripping, phantom trees and buildings that loomed darkly over them. In Cyprus soldiers and Cypriots continued to die, and women were no longer safe; the British Government stressed the need to preserve her strategic bases, probably because there was not a decent harbour on the island. Her young khaki-clad emissaries stood in the sun and suffered provocation beyond the limits of human endurance; their vengeance occasionally licked the innocent, and at home they were rightly condemned by hairy, squeaky little men who would have done the same and worse in their position.

In the City the Sixth Year medics plodded slowly towards Christmas. Midnight oil was burned in varying quantities; already a fortunate minority felt assured of a place in the sun, and read the small print in their tomes with new-found relish. At the other end of the scale a few cried to themselves that eternal hope was a myth, and wished that they had been kicked out of the Faculty earlier. Somewhere in the middle Johnny trotted along steadily, loving Nora with the greatest steadiness of all. Most of their evenings together were placid lagoons of contentment in which they alluded to Finals with modest expectancy, and looked beyond with immodest faith, but Nora took good care that Johnny was never far removed from her sphere of influence, and blew up on him one Friday night when he lapsed and drank too long and freely in Connor's. He was having odd restive moments in the middle of his bookwork; he would slam the book shut, pick up his guitar, and crash out a few angry chords; then the mood would pass, and the evening would proceed in a quiet pageant of turning pages, cups of tea, and long warm kissing.

Towards the end of the month Johnny received a long account of his basic training in Hampshire and London; Arnold was bound for Hong Kong early in the new year. A few days later Betty Warren was seen in the company of a large fat Indian registrar with an extremely fast reputation.

Still the Scottish Free Party grew in strength, and still the Teds filtered into Woods Street. Torquil McLelland's ulcer was giving him less trouble these days; Stan was suffering hellfire with his, and kept a milk bottle below the counter.

In the November Finals "re-sit" Professor Price and his colleagues passed twenty-four candidates out of thirty-five. One of the failures gassed himself.

As a final treat to end the term the clinique was allowed to watch the chief commence a bilateral adrenalectomy as a last resort on the remains of what had been a woman. They stood and watched with contemptuous, critical eyes, for the chief was an old man, and his hands were bunches of seaweed. For ten minutes they heard the assisting houseman receive the blame for the several things that went wrong, then they filed out. The veiled irony in the registrar's comments concealed thoughts they guessed—here am I with better hands than him slaving my guts out for a pittance, and what ruddy chance have I of promotion as long as people like him can still lift a scalpel?

"So much for modern Surgery," said Colin to Johnny.

"It's not all like that," he said. "You should see Austin Rutherford."

There were a number of strangers round their usual table in the snack-bar, including the American, Huxtable J. Peterson, who was normally to be found with the public school cliques, or offering scented cigarettes to the medallists. Johnny normally ignored him; Huxtable's middle name was Jonas, and should have been slightly different.

Huxtable was holding the floor. "My Gawd, the thought of Finals is a pain up my ass just now. I've just been talkin' to a friend of mine who failed last June. The poor guy crammed like mad for his whole Final Year, then they gave him a weird case of scleroderma in his Medicine Clinical. He hadn't a chance, poor bastard."

Johnny's gut gurgled uncomfortably. "So what?" he sneered at the American. "Any friend of yours is bound to be a bit dumb."

Huxtable was picking his nose in nervous anger. He attempted to combine the gesture successfully with a look of sly superiority. "That's not funny, Ferguson. The guy hadn't done enough work in former years, and the examiners were after him—they're experts at smelling out the careless characters. If you haven't got the basics at your fingertips already, you might as well join the Salvation Army."

"I find all this hard to believe," said Johnny bluntly. "If a chap has the ability to do work in a short time, why shouldn't he pass? He'll probably make a better doctor than the bone-headed robot who's studied every night for six years."

"I don't believe it, Ferguson," said Huxtable smugly. "You can't make up for all the general knowledge you've missed. We'll probably see a lot of failures this year."

Colin looked sideways at the American. "It's time you consulted your psycho-analyst, Huxtable. You get more bloody neurotic every day."

"I take exception to that,' said Huxtable, wiping his fingers furiously on his lapel. "I'm as well-adjusted a personality as you'll see in the class. I haven't been a crammer by any means; there aren't many men around who've had the number of screws that I've had."

Colin guffawed across the table. "I've seen them—the half-crown tarts from Rose Street. Come off it, old boy; with a face like yours you'd have to pay a camel."

Huxtable snorted, and got up angrily. "Some of us won't be feeling so clever in the summer." He lurched flabbily toward the Reading Room.

Martin Clark looked up from his lecture notes. "Well done, Colin," he said. "We've got some beauties with us."

"I wonder what part luck plays in Finals," said Johnny.

"You need luck in any exam," said Colin. "But the more reasonable boys will tell you that Finals is probably the easiest Professional you sit. They all say that they wouldn't go through it again for the world, but in the end the stuff you're asked is pretty fair and basic; they want to know if you're safe or lethal. The real hell of it is its large scale; it's a ruddy great endurance test."

"To hell with it," said Johnny. "I'm sick of this place—you just can't get away from the subject. Let's go down to the Arts Common Room and have lunch with Nora."

The Old Quad Common Room was not patronised by many medical students, although the girls of the Arts Faculty were many and pretty. Bad blood still existed as a result of last year's catastrophic Rectorial when the more intrepid disciples of the medical candidate had assaulted the place on numerous occasions, breaking furniture and skin in a joyous exhibition of hooliganism. Johnny had been a ringleader of the band, and had received most of the blame for his candidate's eventual defeat, for despite the dearth of warrior blood in the large *impis* of the Old Quad, the havoc wreaked by the medics on the Common Room had turned the neutral departments solidly against them; not only had the medical vote been disappointing, but in the traditional final battle fought in the Arts quadrangle Johnny and his desperadoes had found themselves facing the standards of old friends—the dentists, the chemists, and worst of all, the real *samurai* of the classroom, the vets. It was a bitter memory.

With the passage of a year most of the blows and blood were forgotten, and nobody paid much attention to the four scarlet and gold ties that pushed their way through the cramped lunchers towards the large circle of students round Nora.

Johnny noted jealously that she had a young man on either side of her; she held out both hands. "Hello, ye young rascal, I hope you're not skipping a class?"

He wagged his finger. "That's enough of the bossing, teacher. just because you're top of your Latin class. Any more cheek and I'll have your pants off in public."

The two Arts boys rose and left, their expressions screaming distaste.

"There are too many gentlemen round here," said Jimmy.

"That's enough, you lot," said Nora. "These are decent girls here. Try and behave like what you're soon going to be."

The thought occurred to Johnny that as a Final Year medic he added some lustre to Nora's position among her female colleagues, who were all eyeing him very appraisingly. Nora herself was not unaware of this, and the thought amused him greatly.

She handed him a copy of the latest edition of "Halcyon." "There's something here that'll interest you," she said. Her friends smirked: he thumbed the pages and found the reason.

On the last page was an article by Allan Prentice entitled 'Portrait of a Future Life-Saver'; the sketched figure at its head was an unflattering caricature of himself. Prentice's artist had accentuated his untidy hair, the triangular hatchet of his chin and the length of his nose. The first three columns of print were devoted to his past piratical exploits in the University, and the latter thrusts dealt cynically with his rumoured change of heart since he had found salvation in Nora's saintliness.

Johnny seethed as he read. The description of himself started with a heavy-handed lampoon, then the prose began:

"The face is Satan's with a hangover, the body is short—a Bechuanaland baboon's straightened by the grace of a jesting God; the mind resurrects an old dialectical problem—can one define or describe nothing?"

A murderously compact narrative of his misdemeanours followed, including The Rectorial campaign, then the article concluded:

"That the villain is now hallowed in the big, soft eyes of his adoring bloodhounds, we cannot deny, but thank our blessed stars that nothing more sordid than alcohol drools from their savage jowls; victims are few this year. The black centaur has knelt over a woman of innocence, yet in return for his evil advance she has awakened smiling to return good for evil. She has sweetened the stale smell of his hairy body, and clothed him with her decency. We await the *coup de grace* with baited breath when by their combined efforts the time will come for him to don the white coat of honour in the service of our suffering—God speed the day! In short, Mr Ferguson, please pass your Finals. Otherwise we shall have to look at you for a space longer and the strain is telling!"

Johnny crumpled the magazine into a ragged ball. "I'll kill Prentice for this."

Nora put a hand on his arm. "Darling, you'll only get yourself into trouble. Please, Johnny, for my sake treat it with the contempt it deserves. He *wants* to provoke you."

"O.K.," he said quietly, throttling the explosive temper in his hands. Then loudly to the whole table: "Ladies and gentlemen, you see before you the power of true love. Thanks to my lady's intercession Prentice has escaped instant death."

The girls giggled in disappointment, viewing his tacit adoration with envy.

"I don't know," said Colin, "I think Prentice needs another little lesson. He's got a long memory, the swine."

Johnny gazed worriedly round the pleasant leisure-space. A few couples necked expertly on the red leather couches round the walls. The old piano against the grubby mock-Grecian pillar was suffering Jehosaphat Smith and "Basin Street Blues."

His wandering thoughts glazed the scene from his eyes; Prentice certainly *did* have a long memory. He was now an implacable enemy, in whom vengeance waited thirstily for a day of retribution.

To hell with it—words can't hurt me.

They had a quiet beer with Jimmy, Martin and Colin, who toasted Johnny's impending visit to Ireland.

Back in her flat he drank a gallon of tea, loving the sweetened tannic bite of his milkless cup after beer, and gorged himself on new white bread and a can of baked beans. Nora admonished him as they lay snugly on her sofa: "You're getting a pot on you, *a bhuachaleen*."

He pulled her on top of him, unfastened her upper garments, and laid his head between her white pouting breasts. She hummed a little air softly to herself over the strong male perfume of his hair.

He propped himself on one elbow and kissed her throat. "Art thou cold or false or dead, Iseult of Ireland?" he quoted.

"Anything but," she said, warming with the heat of his skin. "I was just thinking."

"What were you thinking?"

"Oh, several things. What a hard term it's been and how well you've studied. How I'm looking forward to seeing you capped in July. How I'd love to have a big fat baby of yours. You know, just—several things."

"Why are you so keen for me to be a doctor? Is that the special attraction,"

"You'll get your face slapped. I'll love you as long as you're Johnny Ferguson—and that's always." They kissed long and hard, teeth on teeth.

"What if I decided to throw up my studies and become a writer of pornographic literature?" he asked her somewhat breathlessly.

"I'd still love you. But you wouldn't do it anyway, love. Despite your tough guy performances you'll never be happy if you're not doing somebody some good."

"Nora," he said. "What's the most important thing you've discovered about me?"

"There are so many things, Johnny. Your dramatic energy, your idealism, and your loving, when you make me all creepy and helpless. You've actually taught me humility, and I think a good woman should be humble."

"What's the most important thing you've learned about yourself, Nora?"

She loosed a lovely sound, a tinkling thrill of laughter-drops, the difference between this and Nell's laugh the line between love and lust. "I'll tell you, Johnny-o," she whispered. "I never cease to wonder that I can wash your awful shirt-tails and love you all the more."

He exploded with mirth and turned her against the back of the couch. His hands burrowed deep to where her flesh was warm and wanting him.

He found Nora's people full of the grace and goodwill of their race. He had been prepared to dislike the three maiden aunts who reinforced the matriarchal atmosphere of the family, but he found their charm so devastating that he forgave them in the space of five minutes for all the early prudery he had encountered in Nora. The North Cork countryside was lovely even in winter, but his heart sank as he searched in vain for the young faces that it deserved; this was the tragedy of the Scottish Highlands all over again.

But he saw one young face which disturbed him greatly. Kevin Corcoran came down to the O'Briens' dairy for a packet of cigarettes two days after Christmas, and Mrs O'Brien asked him into the house for a seasonal refreshment. What amazed Johnny was the beauty of the young man's face. It was broad, and bright with health and humour; from the wide expanse of weatherbeaten forehead the lines of strength fell to the small, gentle mouth; the chin was jutting and strong. The eyes were that especially dark blue that belonged to the old mating of Irish and Viking blood. The hair was blacker than a panther's, but greying discreetly at the temples. Combined with his long, powerful body this was a magnetic masculine force and Johnny wondered even more that Nora could forsake such a man for himself.

Nora, ever the mistress of circumstance, kept a steady stream of inconsequential subjects on their lips while they pretended not to weigh each other up over their glasses of stout. She seemed so much at ease with Kevin present that Johnny had no doubt that her old passion was well and truly buried; he was not so sure about the young Irishman. Although the latter's talk was never more personal than that of a good neighbour, there was that in his fierce blue eyes and mellow voice that was more than pain whenever she glanced his way. He stayed for less than ten minutes, and left wishing them luck in slow, courteous tones. His farewell handshake was pulverising.

Johnny made a few pioneering remarks about their wedding. Nora's parents welcomed the idea of a match in the following year, but Mrs O'Brien insisted that no definite arrangement should be made until he was done with his examinations. "I won't have you tyin' yourself up when you've more important things to think about," she said with a wink, but she sat down the same night and wrote a long letter to Mrs Ferguson.

On the return journey they spent the best part of a day in Dublin, and Johnny renewed his worship of the most hospitable city in Western Europe. He accompanied Nora on a shopping trip in the morning, ate a large fry-up lunch in Leeson Street, and spent the hiatus between Holy Hour and their train departure over pints of the best draught Guinness.

"It's a heavenly place, Dublin," said Nora. "If it wasn't for you I'd be dyin' to get back here."

"Wait till you have a New Year in Scotland," he said. "That'll sort your home-sickness."

The crossing from Belfast to Glasgow was one of the roughest in years. Johnny's stomach was never at its best with so much water around, and he was losing his Guinness in stages before the lights of Antrim had receded. Nora managed to gain the Broomielaw without a trace of salivation, but her sympathy for him was great; he had been sick twenty-six times, and they thought that this must be a record.

CHAPTER XV

HOGMANAY WAS always celebrated on a grandiose scale by Connor's, and was not to be missed at any price. This year a rather special problem presented itself, for no appropriate venue could be found. Starkey was the only member of the gang with enough courage and idiocy to place his abode at the disposal of his friends on the 31st of December, and had religiously provided them with various flats, usually leaving them the following week under legal duress. This year, however, Starkey was living in a tiny flat off the High Street which even Connor's considered most unsuitable for a party. There were eleven separate families and two small toilets in the rickety building, and the stairs smelled of a thousand cats; moreover, Starkey's next door neighbour was an irascible coalman with seven screaming children and a pair of shoulders wider than the Bosphorus. The man had been quite sociable when Starkey first moved in, and had offered him a half-drunk bottle of whisky for a night with Ellen, but when she refused to comply his friendship curdled and he had broken up a recent revel in a manner that brooked no interference.

Baliol Strachan finally provided the answer. He was a long, asthenic individual with an interest in Nationalism and a large personal income. He was also the ever-willing prey of scavengers, for he had a gregarious heart of gold that needed friendship and usually had to buy it. On hearing that the annual festal celebration was still without the promise of a roof, he offered his sumptuous West End basement flat to Connor's on the condition that he and Torquil McLelland would be allowed to make political speeches. Connor's agreed to this without a thought. Every political creed had its representative in the place: left-wing Nationalists like Hector Gunn, right-wingers like McLelland, rabid true-blue anti-Nationalists like Jimmy Anderson and independent anarchists like Starkey, but the communal sense of values was very enlightened, and there was never any question of a drinking party coming second to a political.

The last day of the old year was wet and cold; the hordes

streamed in out of the spluttering night. Hector led the singing—the Moonshiners were just pulling out of York on their return from London—the boys gathered round him, roaring out their bawdy war-whoop on the months to come. The old campaigners drank their whisky slowly and without water, for the night would be long and rugged; tired faces assumed a bland indifference to the world outside the door and beyond the morning. There were no fights or threats of fights, not even from the Rat. At twenty past ten Stan had little bother in clearing the bar, and the jolly circus of revellers headed for the West End.

Nora and Johnny arrived after the main body was already safely esconced. Their host was absent: Baliol and Torquil McLelland were not yet returned from Derek Paton's house, where a small political pentecost was being sponsored, and Strachan's guests were doing full justice to the contents of his cellar and refrigerator. In the tiled kitchen Murdo and Lizzie were heating a pile of hamburgers in a large oven, and Starkey was rapidly demolishing a pound of beef sausages in the frying pan, wolfing the long mincemeats with knife and fork as they browned. The cocktail cabinet in the large contemporary lounge boasted seven varieties of whisky, numerous expensive liqueurs and wines, and the floor at least two hundred bottles of beer; in addition the mantelpiece sported an ocean of drink that had been brought from Connor's in bulging hip pockets and paper bags. The large armchairs were groaning under the weight of loving couples who flirted merrily on top of them and already the first body of the evening stretched across the white Persian rug before the fire.

Most of the company were still in a condition that could tolerate a little exercise and the large radiogram added an afterthought of normality to the room. They jived to Chris Barber, smooched under dimmed lights to Julie London; they danced a reel to Jimmy Shand which ended in fisticuffs when the Rat was tripped by Starkey and landed among the beer. Order was restored by Jimmy Anderson, the finest fistfighter present; Starkey was relegated to the corner with a hamburger and the Rat sentenced to twenty minutes' detention in the coal cellar.

Johnny moved around, talking with countless old allies, and realised with a mixture of pride and regret that their attitude to him was different now; they spoke to him with a new, grudging respect, but without the old intimacy that had trusted him with their darkest demerits.

The only regrettable feature was the lack of unattached females; this was rectified when Hector Gunn appeared escorting eight very attractive members of a visiting Viennese girls' choir. Two seconds after they had removed their coats they were under heavy attack; Hector stood over them, a tall, handsome pontifex in a kilt, until they had been paired off to his satisfaction and dragged in a state of uncomprehending anxiety to various dark corners of the house.

Johnny sought Hector out at the cabinet. "Are the Moonshiners coming tonight, Hector?"

Hector emptied a pint glass of pale ale. "Oh, by the Lord Harry, I needed that," he gasped, wiping the froth from his moustache. "Yes, Johnny, they'll be here after twelve o'clock. And when they come, by the saints, they will sing the music of the People until this bloody bourgeois mausoleum shudders with terror." Johnny grinned, thinking that if the mausoleum could remain standing after the past hour, it would take more than a tribe of mastodons to disturb it.

Baliol Strachan and Torquil McLelland appeared just before midnight, full of the fire of their previous sortie. The host's ardour was curbed somewhat by the unrecognisable state of his home, and he made a few puny attempts to clear the noisy bowers of Venus upstairs, but finding the doors locked on the inside he turned his back on the plaintive appeals in broken English and German which came shrilly through the keyholes. Baliol then tried to quieten the howling throng in the lounge. He delivered a short, and not unintelligent speech on Scotland's problems, which was received with polite disinterest, but when he called upon McLelland to rouse the Scottish hearts of the international assembly, the hour struck, and a mad spate of kissing and handshaking ensued. "Auld Lang Syne" was sung and danced by a huge circle; glasses were charged to the brim and the usual Burns toasts rebounded from the mausoleum walls.

"I wish they wouldn't insist on making speeches to this mob," said Johnny to Pat Leitch. "It's degrading."

"Nobody takes Nationalism seriously," said Pat laughing. "What does it matter?"

The first-foot was the tall, dark Franco from the Scala. In the next five minutes everybody associated with Connor's piled into the room. Torquil McLelland, in Periclean form, made a vain attempt to deliver a carefully-rehearsed oration, but when he came out with an ill-advised anti-Hamitic statement, an outraged Hector Gunn picked up the gauntlet on behalf of all oppressed peoples and began to sing "The Ball of Kirriemuir." The party lost all assumption of order, and disintegrated into sheer confusion.

The Moonshiners made their entrance quietly, and Nell was upon Johnny and Nora before they had time to pull out of a very protracted kiss behind the lounge door.

He turned to his ex-mistress with heavy eyelids and no loss of composure: "You know Nora, don't you?"

"We've met once before. A long time ago." She was not at all glamorous tonight; the long journey had deepened the pits beneath her eyes and she was wearing conventional folksinger's dress, an old sweater and jeans. She looked absolutely dull beside Nora's fine skin and hair and bright lemon taffeta dress; there were a few streaks of grey crawling back into her bun. Her face was deathly menstrual pale.

Here goes. "I think it's time you two girls got to know one another."

Nell watched him thread an unsteady path across the room. "He's a bastard, isn't he," she said to Nora. "He's always been a bit of a coward."

The lovely face flashed lightning. "I don't think so. He's giving me a chance to say a few things that are overdue."

"Have you got a fag, dear?" said Nell wearily. Nora gave her cigarette and flame. "I know what you want to say," Nell continued, "and I'm not interested. You want to tell me how sorry you are for pinching my man. Well, you can go to hell: you took him because you wanted him, and if you want somebody like Johnny badly, anything's fair."

"What I wanted to say," said Nora evenly, "is that I'm sorry you were hurt. I've always hated hurting people, and I've had you on my conscience for a long time. If you can find it in your heart to be friends with me, I'd welcome it."

Nell made a sarcastic gesture with her glass of gin. "I might have known. You're the youthful angel all right, but you know as much about real emotion as a pig's arse. Have you the slightest idea what I went through? You've never had to fight—men only need to look at you with their stupid, half-blind eyes. Christ—you've hated hurting people!"

Nora twisted the stem of her glass with shaking fingers. She was controlling her temper with difficulty. "Don't cast my youth up to me," she said, not without malice. "I don't blame you for being bitter. But don't tell me that I don't know what hurt is. He can still hurt people, Nell."

Nell surveyed her frankly. "I know what you mean, Nora. Look, dear," she patted the milky shoulder gently, "I shouldn't have blown my top like that. I had a hell of a time getting over Johnny, but I'm over him good and proper now. I don't particularly want to be friends with you, simply because we haven't got much in common. But I bear you no illwill at all; inasmuch as that's worth a damn, we're friends of a kind."

Nora felt queerly outplayed. She had always thought of Nell as a rather talented sex-machine without much brain, but there was more than music to this handsome woman, much more. She felt desperately in need of something clever to say, to wind up the cat-fight on top but with no talons showing. "I'm glad you've found somebody nice," she said.

"Yes," said Nell. "He's nice. It's a nice word. Don't kid yourself, dear. He's longer in the tooth than yours by a long way, and dare I offend your sense of decorum by saying that he makes a woman pant and squeal much more than Johnny? You know what I mean, don't you?"

"Should I?" They both laughed uneasily.

Nell snatched a bottle of gin and filled her glass. "Does Johnny still play his guitar a lot?" she asked.

"Yes," said Nora. "He finds it a wonderful way of letting off steam when he's studying."

"Do you think he should have left the Moonshiners—quite apart from me?"

"Yes. Frankly, he had talent of a kind, but so have at least twenty people like him in Scotland alone. If he'd stayed with you, he'd have neglected his studies and gained little in the long run. As it is he's going to achieve something that's really worthy of him and Lord, I'm proud of him."

"I hope you're right," said Nell. "I just can't imagine him as a doctor."

"He's basically an idealist, that's why Medicine suits him," said Nora. "Your form of entertainment is becoming another part of show business with all its lack of scruple."

Nell laughed. "You're much more perceptive than I thought. So you're feeling quite pleased with yourself, are you, dear?"

She looked over her shoulder to where Johnny was standing with Hector. His face was wearing one of its cardinal expressions, the one that always reminded her of the little Knave of Hearts, for he was singing a naughty ditty in front of Ellen. His hair was hanging well below his right eye; he had a beer bottle in his hand and his foot was beating out a tattoo on the thick carpet. She was tempted to tell Nora that she had been with him last Hogmanay, and that the only renovation she could see tonight was his smart new suit. Instead she said: "I suppose he is better off now. I can't really judge him any more."

Nora lit a cigarette coolly, watching the other woman with steady eyes; there was a slight jerk in the tired voice.

"You're *sure* that you're safely over Johnny?" she said.

"You'd make a regular little knife-twister if you got the chance, wouldn't you?" said Nell. "I've been wondering when the real woman was going to emerge."

"You're wrong again," said Nora. "I'm being horribly sensible. If by any chance you're not telling the truth, I'm going to make very sure that he doesn't see you again."

"Very sweet of you, dear," said Nell. "For the last time I no longer love your young Mr Ferguson. You could maroon him with me on a desert island and I'd be quite happy to spend the evenings taming monkeys. Are you quite sure that you trust him, Nora?"

"I *do* trust him. Johnny's pretty honest with people. Let's stop sparring, Nell. In ten years' time when we're both loaded with kids we'll look back on this conversation and pretend that we were drunk."

"Maybe," said Nell. "But I don't want any kids at the moment. I loathe the little bastards. I have few tender feelings, Nora. I love to chew my way into a man who can master me; you know, Carmen all over again. If you take my advice you'll try an affair with a middle-aged man when Johnny begins to bore you. The men in Scotland are like the bloody weather—they don't heat up until late in the year."

Nora put down her glass. "As you said, my dear, we haven't really much in common. I'll stick to Johnny, if you don't mind."

Nora stalked away and Nell settled back against the wall

sipping her neat gin. Jehosaphat sidled over to her. "What are you up to now? I'm pretty sure it's nothing commendable."

"Jehosaphat," said Nell, "what do *you* think of Johnny's queen?"

"I think she is superlative. She makes the dramatist in me cast Lucretia and Dido as comic charwomen."

"Cut the crap. What do you really think?"

"I love her. I love her slightly less than I love Johnny."

Nell made a face. "You get crazier all the time. Don't tell me you're turning queer."

"No," said Jehosaphat. "I'm not. But was I hearing right when I heard you say you had no hard feelings left?"

There was an ugly suggestion of triumph around the corners of her large mouth. "What d'you mean?"

Jehosaphat took her glass and drank deeply. "The Lord has laid a heavy sorrow on me," he answered. "He has given me the lust of Don Juan and the face of the Black Plague. But while he torments me, and forces the exotic women I desire to run from me in horror, he gives me a small consolation. I have the power to read their minds."

Nell's laughter was too loud. "You're a card," she said. "And you're damn right. I didn't mean a word of it. Let me tell you something, Jehosaphat. Until tonight I was almost resigned to marrying old you-know-who."

"I've heard he's the biggest scoundrel in the City," said Jehoshaphat piously.

"Of course he is," said Nell. "But what the hell? This is the first time I've had a chance to talk to little Miss Celtic Twilight, and she's not half the woman I hoped she wasn't."

He shook his head. "I don't see it, Nell. You're trying to convince yourself."

"Listen to me," she said. The gin was passing into her head and speech. "I know Johnny bloody well. She was bragging tonight about his honesty. My God—in his few honest moments Johnny's at his worst—he can't stand himself. She hasn't a clue! I now have the belief that one day he'll see her for the little slush-pedlar that she is. Jehosaphat, my boy, again there is hope in the world."

"You're bletherin', Nell. But I'd better go and tell Johnny what you said."

She gripped his arm painfully. "You'll shut your mouth. This Yankee gin has a helluva kick. But I nearly laughed in her face —you think I'm wrong, Sir Philosopher?"

"You're all wrong," he said. "You're a bad bitch, Nell, but you're a damned sexy one. I despise myself for the evil thoughts that gather whenever I survey your lovely fat arse."

She went away suppressing her laughter and gathered the Moonshiners together. Soon the room resounded with blues and Glasgow street-songs, Australian bush-ballads and ribald student parodies.

The songs finished, and Nell shouted: "Come on, Johnny, give us a treat. Let's hear 'Arlin's Fine Braes'."

He made a meagre pretence of unwillingness, but Ricky thrust a guitar into his hand. He commenced softly, picking out a harmony to his voice with inverted shapes on the treble strings, sliding back up to the top fret on the last line, and finishing with a minor run that echoed resonantly on the bass E. It was a fine little song, capricious yet melancholy, and Johnny's north-east accent would have fooled a Buchan carthorse. He handed back the guitar, longing for the duration of a bar to carry on singing for ever.

A few people began to collapse where they drank, others rejoined the party from upstairs; these last had spent the early hours of morning striving with the choir girls' Teutonic fitness and propriety. A tall buxom blonde collected the Austrian maidens, went to Hector and thanked him loudly for introducing them to a completely unique folk-custom, then as he bent to kiss her she drove her flock speedily to the door. Most of the girls looked as if they had just been on a day trip to Dante's Inferno. They chatted noisily as they retreated, comparing sordid notes.

Gradually the gaiety ran down; Johnny decided to storm the Doctors' Residency of the Royal City with Jimmy and Lizzie. He was seeking a taxi at the telephone when he heard a spine-chilling shriek in the bathroom on his left. Starkey and Jimmy emerged from the cool recluse, pulling the source of the noise behind them —the Rat, with his trousers round his ankles.

Johnny put the 'phone back on the receiver. "What the hell's going on here?"

Jimmy tumbled the Rat to the ground. "We found him in there with two bottles of whisky, and the party's getting short. The crafty wee reptile—he's goin' into the lounge with his trousers off."

Johnny's sense of fair play was injured, but it seemed right that the Rat's greed should not go unpunished. He watched them through a haze as they stumbled across the floor, pulling the Rat by his hairy little legs. While he pondered with his waning powers of logic which side to take, the Rat brought the parade to a halt by lashing out wildly with his foot. It broke Jimmy's grip and the next thrash struck Starkey above the knees, bowling him over forwards against the lower stairs. His head struck the edge of the bottom step, and he lay still. They ran to him as the Rat struggled to hoist his fallen colours. Starkey was snoring loudly: a cursory inspection showed that there was nothing much wrong. A great crowd gathered around him; the Rat began to whisper apologies.

"It's O.K.," Ellen reassured him. "I've never seen him look so peaceful."

Unfortunately, a ragged cut had appeared above Starkey's right eye, and a small pool of blood was welling up on the floor beside his face. Baliol Strachan pushed to the front, saw the pool of blood, and his squeamish system turned somersaults. "Oh my God," he said. "Who did this?"

Somebody said it was the Rat's work.

"Oh my God," said Baliol, and shot through the front door.

Starkey revived after some very strange methods of resuscitation had been applied. He shook hands with a very relieved Rat, and began to tease him again, holding a strip of Ellen's underskirt to his damaged head. The merrymakers were back to the vine and the barley when the host walked in the front door with two police uniforms behind him.

The next half-hour should have produced a glut of coronary thromboses. The policemen were rather overwhelmed by the fantastic sight that greeted them in the lounge, and their interrogation was influenced by this. The bigger uniform belonged to a plump, sweating sergeant who was in the state of mind that can be expected of any Scottish policeman on duty on Hogmanay, and called from a winning poker hand.

"Where is the victim of the assault?" said the sergeant, and Starkey stood up smartly. "I thought ye said he was bloody near deid," the sergeant said to Baliol with disappointment.

Baliol pouted righteously. "So he was. And there's the attacker," pointing to a visibly shrinking Rat.

The police were not at all impressed by Starkey's injury, but the sergeant insisted on taking statements, and here the witnesses encountered trouble. No two accounts tallied; not only were Johnny and Co. intent on clearing the Rat, but they were also too fuddled to recount minor detail correctly, and the consequent contradictions in their statements drove the lawman to the erroneous and unwelcome conclusion that they were concealing a crime of greater magnitude. The constable made a sly, unwarranted search of the house. His chief finds were several bedded couples making winter hay with gay abandon; on hearing this report the sergeant looked at Strachan with suspicion and asked him what he did for a living. His further interrogations proved fruitless, however, and a very profane Starkey refused to prefer charges against his assailant.

The sergeant's temper was not improved by his examination of Hector and Torquil McLelland; the former informed him that he was a parasitic slave of English imperialism, and was solemnly warned to watch his fuckin' language. Torquil drew himself up and looked scornfully at the policeman. "I am the right-hand man of the saviour of Scotland," he said with very slurred speech. "I command two full companies of the S.R.A.—beware their vengeance."

The sergeant looked at his subordinate. "This is either a brothel or a nuthouse," he growled. "I'll let yez off this time, but if this wasnae Hogmanay there would be a few of you comin' wi' me to answer questions, and you, sir," turning to Strachan, "would be of considerable interest to the magistrates."

Hector gave a roar of approval. "By the Gods of war," he thundered, "you have been bitterly misjudged, sergeant. Listen to me, all of you! This man is a nobleman, and whoever dares annoy him will answer to me!"

The astonished policemen found themselves plied with pint glasses of beer and cigars. With happy resignation they removed their helmets and sat down. Baliol Strachan held his head sorrowfully in his hands. Never again!

They rolled up at the Royal gate and tipped the taxi driver with a slug of rum. The Residency was one of the old isolation wards; a squat red building set apart from the main block. They were welcomed loudly at the door and Nora and Lizzie were kissed by at least seven white-clad housemen. Johnny and Jimmy observed with a mixture of amusement and jealousy. There was still a great quantity of liquor to be killed. Johnny found a bowl of delicious rum punch and drank three large glasses.

And after the meeting with the punch his memory remained a blank, apart from a few impressions of people and voices that his anoxic brain contrived to rescue for the following morning. He vaguely remembered pulling Nora away from a tall, slim doctor who had been dancing with her for far too long; there was something said about him having to watch his girl, she was far too pretty for him, and there was something said about the chap having to watch his teeth, they were far too pretty for him. There were brief trailer snapshots of Jimmy having angry words with some supercilious registrar; there was the recollection of vainly pinioning Jimmy's broad shoulders and receiving a sickening elbow in the stomach as they were all pushed through the door. Then the night was a ghoulish torment of retching and throwing up bitter stuff with Jimmy and Nora rubbing his back, and a bed that swung from floor to ceiling with awful simple harmonic motion and squeezed his pleading stomach into a thimble of painful muscle; noises came from his throat that belonged to a dying man, and in his waterlogged ears Nora's voice floated to and fro, now cool and motherly, now bitterly acid. The touch of her hand on his brow was the last thing he remembered before he fell asleep.

He awoke about ten o'clock, and was awake for two full minutes before he realised where he was. He was lying on Nora's bed, undressed down to his vest. He sat up and the vengeance of heaven fell on his head. He lay down again; the pillow smelt of his stomach. He sat up and looked at it; there was a brown stain in the middle, the size and shape of a negro's head. He threw the pillow angrily to the floor, and it landed with a wet slapping sound. He looked fearfully over the edge of the bed and saw it nestling in the chamber pot that Nora had providently left beneath him. His mouth felt like the darkest recess of a sex-maniac's intelligence, and his raw throat was screaming that thirst can kill.

He swung his legs gingerly over the edge of the bed and walked unsteadily to the door. When he opened it, he heard Nora singing in the kitchen; the sickening smell of frying bacon bathed him in an icy sweat. He ran for the toilet.

Shaving and dressing were acts of raw courage for which there was no medal. He looked at himself in the mirror: the whole face appeared swollen and utterly devoid of colour; most of the blood vessels had migrated to his eyeballs. He offered a short prayer and drank a glass of cold water; it stayed down. He drank another, and prepared to face Nora.

She looked up cheerfully from the stove. "Well, well. A Happy New Year to you, my prince. Don't you look fit to tear the future apart?"

"Drop it, dear," he said. "I've said before that I'd never drink again, but this time I mean it. Oh, Christ!"

"Would you like some breakfast?" she enquired, face innocent of guile.

Johnny clutched his stomach. "Give me a cup of coffee."

"You certainly distinguished yourself last night, didn't you," she said, pouring a strong black cup. "I don't suppose you can remember much about it."

"Nonsense." He sipped the scalding fluid slowly, still feeling decidedly queasy. "I can remember everything, apart from little bits in the Royal."

"Do you recall that we were *thrown* out of the Royal?"

"No. Why were we thrown out? Jimmy was scrapping with somebody, wasn't he?"

"Jimmy was going to hit that registrar," said Nora testily, "because you told him that the poor bloke said that Lizzie looked like a you-know-what."

"Did he?" said Johnny.

"No," she said with a mirthless smile. "He didn't. You seemed to be in a seditious mood after that nice doctor danced with me."

"Nice doctor!" he sneered. "I know him. He boasts about how easily he makes women. If it hadn't been for me you'd have played right into his dirty great hands."

"That's nonsense," she said. She forked a large piece of egg and ate it with relish. Johnny looked away. "What is more," she went on, "after you were put outside you started shouting and swearing—we couldn't shut you up. D'you remember the porters?"

"What porters?"

"Two of them. They'd been bringing a drunk into the Casualty Department, and they heard the awful racket you were making outside the Residency. They wanted to send for the police—as if we hadn't seen enough of the police force already!"

The scene floated painfully back to him. "I'd completely forgotten that. What happened next?"

Nora banged her knife down. "Lizzie and I had to do something. We kissed them a Happy New Year, and Jimmy got you into a taxi by the gate. It was a good job that he came back for us; they were all for taking us into the trees." She shuddered. "They were a pair of blighters."

Johnny found a teaspoon bending between his fingers. "Is that all?" he said quietly.

"Then," she said, "you passed out in the taxi, and that idiot, Jimmy, tried to waken you by pouring whisky all over your face. You were sick—all over my shoes, and then in the stair again, and then several times in bed."

He filled the cup again. "I'm hellish sorry, darling. I had no right to let you in for all that. The way I feel right now, I'd like to drink nothing but cool clear water for the rest of my life."

"I want no apologies, Johnny," she said with a tiny echo of a conscious sigh. "But I do want something a little more concrete. I'd like your assurance that you'll not go through that performance again. I cried myself to sleep last night; I can't bear to see you like that."

"You've got it, Nora," he answered with a penitent nod. "Not only a resolution but a promise. You won't have to put up with that again—ever."

"I had my doubts about going to a Connor's party," she said. "Lunatics like Jimmy seem to bring out the worst in you. Why must a talented wretch like you insist on mixing with all those half-witted people? I've got nothing against characters like Starkey and The Rat but you can't say that they're normal. They're miserable unless they've got a pool of drink inside them, and then they go completely mad. Look at last night in poor Strachan's house. Why must you waste yourself among them?"

"I'm not wasting myself," he cried. "Och, I don't know, Nora. I suppose I wanted to be with them at Hogmanay for old times' sake. But you're right—they're not normal. They'll see damn little of me in future."

"Just think," she said. "Imagine our own house in the future; we'll have plenty of nice parties with the young doctors from your own hospital. Can't you see yourself being just as happy?"

"Of course I can. I'll have to leave Connor's completely alone. They're a savage lot for drinking, and I'm too weak to say 'no'."

"You won't regret it," she said. "I'm going to make you the happiest man on earth. I must go and freshen up now. By the way, I'll bet you five bob that the boys in green win today."

"Done," he said. Nora lit a cigarette and left him.

He looked at the half-naked blonde on the calendar above the table. "I wouldn't mind a slice of you," he muttered. "Just look at the tears in my eyes, you big blonde bitch—I'm saying my final farewells to Connor's. I don't suppose you ever knew any Italians, did you, blondie? They're great people, the Italians; they've got some wonderful proverbs. One of them says that every time you say goodbye you die a little."

IV

THE CITY

Winter, Toil and Sunset

CHAPTER XVI

THERE WAS A DAY late in the following February when it snowed for eight hours on end. That afternoon Nora sat in her favourite horse-box in the Scala talking to a small, pale girl with a pleasant snub-nosed face. They were both drinking hot chocolate; large fat puddles of melted slush sat around their fur-lined boots.

"Life's going to be a bit tough," said Mrs Jean Morrison. "But I think we can hold out till Colin qualifies."

Nora looked past her at the swirl of woolly flakes outlined against the sombre grey of Woods Street. "You're a hero, Jean," she said. "I don't know how you went through with it."

Little Jean stirred her chocolate. "I wouldn't like to go through it again. I was nearly out of my mind. The worst bit was telling the old folks. Mum was awfully good about it; she didn't cry much, but Dad said nothing right up to the wedding."

"You'll be all right," said Nora. "People will forget all about their stuffy morals when the baby comes along."

"Yes," said Jean. "Even the matron at the Royal was quite reasonable, but there was one nurse who kept dropping dirty remarks about girls who have to trap men into marriage. And that damn Nurses' Chaplain was worse; he kept insisting that no matter what people said he would never judge a girl in trouble. He had a queer sort of excited look about him."

"He probably thrives on tears," said Nora grimly. "Johnny always goes wild with such people."

Jean laughed. "Trust Johnny. I don't regret anything we did; not even that first night in your flat when I blubbed for hours afterwards. But if you take my advice, Nora, you'll get married in white, and you'll have a nice respectable gap between your trip down the aisle and your first baby. What I dread is our first real fight. If Colin casts anything up to me, I don't think I can stand it."

Nora flushed. "I'll be married in white," she said.

"Oh look, Nora," said Jean in confusion, "I wasn't suggesting anything."

"I know you weren't." She laid a motherly hand over the little wet glove. "But I can handle Johnny, don't you worry." She drummed her fingers on the table.

"You don't mind him having to leave the flat?"

Nora smiled in magnanimity. "Of course not. You and Colin will need all the room you've got soon. He can live with me quite easily—I'm past caring what people think."

Voices rose over by the door. Maria had Jehosaphat by the scruff of the neck and Franco was pulling a bar of chocolate from his pocket.

"You lose this-a time, Mr Smith," said a jubilant Maria. "I saw ye stickin' yer-a paw behind the counter, ye bad-a bugger. When are you gonna pay your bill?" she added.

Jehosaphat straightened up. "By the end of April, when my paper is accepted, I shall be rolling in money. Then you'll be your sweet mercenary selves again, won't you, Maria?"

"What sort-a paper are you tryin' to write?" asked Franco.

Jehosaphat's lower lip twisted. "I am doing a paper on the incidence of incest in Calabria."

Mercifully Maria misunderstood him. "You be careful what-a you say about Calabria," she said with dignity. "We got-a no insects like you there. You better pay your bill, Mr Smith—I ken a man who knows Professor Price."

Jehosaphat passed on, and saw the girls. He stood to attention, placed a forefinger in his mouth, and uttered a prolonged Indian war-cry.

"What's that in aid of?" said Nora.

"Today is the anniversary of Sitting Bull's wedding," said Jehosaphat. "And who should we find here but little squaw Morrison?"

"Dry up," said Jean. "You should be working for your exam or you'll find yourself singing your Indian love-call in the army." She stood up and reached for her shoulder-bag. "I must go, Nora—give my love to Johnny."

Jehosaphat watched her go. "Ah, there but for the grace of God go I," he announced in sonorous tones.

"Hardly," said Nora.

"When's the baby due?" he asked.

"September," said Nora.

"I wonder if it was the night of the End of Term Revels," he said, blinking in the poor light.

"Jehosaphat," said Nora. "That isn't the remark you should pass in front of a lady."

"Deepest apologies, Lady Nora," said Jehosaphat. He had found an empty cigarette packet in the ashtray, and was chewing it hungrily. "No offence to your maidenly modesty—I am your devoted slave, and your No. 1 spy."

Nora cocked a perfect eyebrow. "Who d'you spy on for me?" she asked.

"Nell, of course."

"Oh, for God's sake, Jehosaphat. You don't have to spy on Nell. Leave the poor girl alone."

Jehosaphat wagged his scrubby head. "Not on your life, Nora. I don't trust that hellcat one inch. She'd take Johnny back off you at the slightest opportunity."

"I'm not so sure," said Nora. "She seems fairly well wrapped up in her councillor."

Jehosaphat gestured with his dirty, open palm. "That's what I mean," he said. "You *do* need an undercover agent to keep you informed. Nell has forsaken her paramour, and denied him before the faces of men."

Nora was lighting a cigarette, and she looked up, eyes narrowing and glinting, pools of greeny gold behind the flame. "What do you mean?" she said carefully. She cut the flame with a firm hand.

"There was a scene in a certain cocktail bar last night," said Jehosaphat. "I have a full eye-witness account. The old boy was a bit tight—and he got amorous in public. She took a dim view of this, an' it developed into a very degradin' slanging match. Nell finished up by clatterin' 'im across the face, and walking out."

"That's nasty," said Nora. "But it doesn't necessarily mean that they're breaking up."

"What d'you bet?" he offered.

Nora shook her head.

"Watch her," said Jehosaphat. "I'm warning you, Nora, watch her."

"I will," she said. "Thanks."

Tea in the flat was one of her specialities today: a good fat hunk of ham with cabbage and onions.

"Nell's broken up," she told him casually. "She's left her old big-noise."

He showed no emotion, and did not answer till his mouth was empty. "I'm not surprised," he said. "That fellow wasn't her type at all."

"Are you glad?" she asked.

"No. If you're thinking things, you can forget them. I couldn't care less what she does, darling, but I'd like to see her happy."

"I saw Jean today," she said with a quick glance at him. "She's really a brick, the way she's come through it all."

"She has indeed. I've been thinking a lot about Jean and Colin."

She waited for an explanation, but he continued to attack his heaped plate. She let it lie for the moment. "How are you enjoying your cliniques this term?" she said.

"Much better than I believed possible," he answered. "I've never been terribly partial to the physician's side of things, but I'm enjoying Doctor North's wards tremendously: there's something absolutely fascinating about chests." He leaned back replenished.

"Come on, now, Johnny," she said, "down to the books. We're both slipping this term; there's far too little studying being done."

"Let me finish the song I'm composing, Nora." He went over to his guitar and sat with it across his knees, drawing his fingers across the strings until their sound filled the room. "This is in your honour," he said. "The finest I've written yet; it's even better than 'Connor's Farewell'."

"Look," she said. "This is all very well, but I'm worried about you not working; you've done precious little since New Year. Do you realise that Finals are exactly seventeen weeks away?"

"Nora sweet," he said, without missing a note, "I know how much stuff I've still got to cover, and believe me, there's ample time. I've always worked this way—let's have a wee lull this term, then we'll crack it open in May and June."

"No," she said. She picked up a thick textbook from the table, and flipped the pages. "Here's a chapter on the Rhesus Factor in pregnancy. I'm going to do the dishes, and have a bath, then I'll question you on it. One of us must be sensible."

He snuggled resignedly into the kitchen's single comfortable chair, and placed his guitar against the wall. He forced the print into his head, and for half an hour reading was easy. But the haunting refrain of his "Irish Lovesong" began to invade the territory of Landsteiner and Wiener; scientific data were absorbed between flashes of creative inspiration, and Nora flitted in and out of the big, bare words. He shook his head, angrily, and bored deeper into the pages: "In Erythroblastosis immature red cells are present in the blood as a counter-measure" . . . "where is my love, but in fields of spring, warm in the smile of the South" . . . "In Icterus Gravis Neonatorum jaundice and anaemia are present together. . . ." "the stars they have stolen her eyes to smile, the thrush the song of her mouth" . . . "Neurological symptoms may persist permanently in Kernicterus" . . . "what is she now but a memory, sweet as the kiss of the sea" . . . "the baby is born dead or dies shortly after birth" . . . "leaving a desert where grasses grew and an age of pain that was me." He closed the book hopelessly.

Words and music came together in an instant flash of perception. He played the complete song through, and sat back with great satisfaction, smoking a cigarette. I must go and tell Nora—she'll love it.

When he entered the bathroom she was already drying herself in a large white bathtowel: her back was to him, and the death-rattle of the scented water in the plug-hole muffled the opening door. The heat had reddened her in patches, accentuating the round ripe peaches of her buttocks and the slender girdle of her waist. Her feet were smaller when she was naked, and the curve of her calf was throbbing with healthy shape; not a tiny roll of fat clung to the lean cylinders of her thighs; the deceptively broad white back was innocent of blemish, and gleamed smoothly beneath the thick tangle of her hair.

Johnny thrust his hands into his pockets. She turned to pick up a tin from the shelf, and saw him. At first she blushed with the vestigial guilt of her childhood, then with a gesture that spread coquetry to her fingernails she slipped the towel to the floor and placed her hands on her hips. "How's the Rhesus Factor?" she asked.

He shook his clammy head, unable to speak. Her flushed face was honest with desire above her naked body. Beneath there was a hot expectancy heating in the centre of her soft throat, and the long slim nipples that thrust forward and upward from the deft craftsmanship of her conical breasts were moist and quivering, demanding the benediction of his hands. The white belly that encircled her small navel boasted the slightest inkling of fullness before it dropped to the triangle of shade where the wavy down of her body was softer and more golden than the fire of her hair.

She came towards him. "Let's go into the bedroom, love," she said. "The Rhesus Factor can wait for a few minutes."

He picked her up, and held her warm wetness against his shirt. The door swung wide as he booted it. The bedroom was chilly; she slipped quickly between the sheets.

Then she saw his face. The mask of desire had fallen; in its place was a very pensive expression. "Is something wrong?" she asked.

He walked to the empty fireplace, and stood looking into it in one of his characteristic poses, with one arm resting on the mantelshelf. "Nora, there's something that's got me worried just now."

She took a quick breath: "Nell?"

"No," he said quietly. "It's Colin and Jean."

"Oh," she whispered. "You're frightened, then."

"Yes," he said. "I'm scared to death. You don't realise just how lucky we've been."

"I never thought much about it," she replied truthfully.

"I know," he said, nodding into the grate. "That's the damn trouble; you really don't know much about the other side, do you? I don't want to betray your trust, Nora."

Her body rustled beneath the linen. "There are ways and means, Johnny; I'm not all that green. Don't try and tell me you can stop as easily as all that."

He came back to her, and sat on the bed, stroking her shoulder gently. "That's the damn trouble, Nora—I can't. But I'm goin' to make sure that nothing goes wrong before we get married. I heard the remarks that people dropped behind Jean's back, and if they said similar things about you I'd bloody well kill them. So from now on, I'm afraid, things will be a wee bit calculated."

"I don't know," she said. "I can't imagine it, but I'm sure I won't mind, darling. Oh, Lord, I want you, Johnny—come on in!"

He pursed his lips. "I'm afraid I hadn't thought about tonight."

"Tonight's all right, little man," she whispered. "We're as safe now as we'll ever be."

He tore off the remainder of his clothing as she deliberately drew the top sheet down to her waist. They lay close together for a minute before his hands moved; the alarm clock ticked away on Nora's locker. It was hot and noisy, but there was somethink lacking. Beneath his apparent physical ardour there was a deep reluctance somewhere that knocked them awry, and she felt a sorrow of emptiness and frustration when it was all over.

Johnny looked stonily over her head at the pillow. This was only one colour in the painting, and for the moment her flesh had lost its subtlest bouquet. It's fantastic how the blood can change —in five minutes a lovely marble nude can drop in price fantastically, no matter how much you love the things that go with it. Strange what a different world it is, just because a little moves a little. Where's that guitar? You can change a woman with what you do to her; back to the old, faithful companion.

She lay staring at the ceiling as he dressed carelessly, and listened to the strains of the "Irish Lovesong" that seemed to filter through the door for endless hours. It was her song; it was beautiful; and she never told him how much she hated it.

In the many nights that followed, after they had been careful, she would hear it hammering in her brain, and curse it for easing a part of herself out of Johnny Ferguson. Monument Hill never came to her again except in dreams that made the light of morning unwelcome; and though she continued to bask in his worship she felt the thorn of the small loss within her, and bemoaned the day she had first clapped eyes on Colin and Jean Morrison.

CHAPTER XVII

DR NORTH HAD the kindest pair of blue eyes in the City. There was a warmth in them that one rarely saw in a staunch church elder; although he saved his preaching for the Sunday School class that he ran in his fashionable South Side parish, his best sermons were the fragments of bedside humanity that he dropped on frightened faces: it was impossible to watch the light in his patients' eyes without being impressed, and the tough young gentlemen of his Final Year Clinique whose shoe-leather clattered from bed to bed were forced to think in terms other than the possible respiratory questions in the Medicine paper when they saw the heavy, sweating faces of cor pulmonale come alive with fighting courage, and the hollow cheeks of bronchogenic carcinoma flare with colour. The doctor's words were the best sedative Johnny had ever encountered; he watched from deep in the ranks and his heart applauded wildly.

When Walter Petrie, Dr North's senior registrar, offered him the houseman's locum during the first two weeks of March he was surprised and elated; he accepted it eagerly, for Nora was becoming irritable as her own term exams approached, and was cajoling him more than ever because of his lack of effort—a busy fortnight in the Royal would surely mollify her, and temporarily remove the temptations of darkness that he was beginning to fear.

March was little milder than February, and the wards seldom possessed a cold sheet. Patients were admitted officially on Thursday, but the Bed Bureau were well aware of Dr North's reluctance to waste an empty bed and admissions rolled in on all sides. Johnny slept by his 'phone in the Residency and appeared on duty before 8.30 a.m. He collected his blood specimens quickly, for slickness with a hollow needle had always been a natural art of his, then he would accompany Walter round the beds. The big handsome Rugger Blue was a younger edition of Dr North, and his conversations with his patients were the same painstaking words of comfort; he treated his housemen with a mixture of impeccable manners and good humour, but imparted the message quite clearly that he would stand no carelessness.

Johnny was amazed at the speed with which knowledge was disseminated here. There was an almost surgical urgency about the place—at least two patients always lay in the new polythene oxygen tents that were the unit's pride and joy, and the resistant staphylococcus required an impressive barrage of antibiotic artillery to keep it quiet. When on call he sat up till late talking to the pretty night nurse: frequently, Walter paid a late visit to the ward and dissected the cases over coffee and biscuits. Nora seemed to appreciate him all the more on his nights off, which did not make for sleep, but under this rigorous programme his grizzly-bear constitution bloomed defiantly. There was a great satisfaction in standing by the teaching chief in the morning clinique, listening with a supercilious grin to the mistakes of his fellows. To be on the inside of a unit like this gave one a curious sense of one-upmanship.

At twenty-past eight of a cruel, crystal Friday morning he was sitting by the outstretched arm of a wiry old school janitor who smoked sixty cigarettes a day and had been admitted coughing blood.

Johnny watched the rich, dark fluid pour into his syringe. I wonder what's wrong here. He's never had a day's illness in his life. We've certainly had our fair share of excitement this week.

The staff nurse appeared at his elbow. "Telephone, Mr Ferguson."

"O.K., staff, I'll be right there."

The line crackled. On the far end the G.P.'s voice was fruity public school: "Sorry to trouble you, old boy, but I've got something here I can't handle. A widow of thirty-five; a chronic depressive. She's gone into acute bronchospasm without any evidence of infection—her daughter says she's had it twice before. Can you take her in?"

Johnny spoke into the mouthpiece, imitating the other end of the line. "O.K., old thing. Just send the jolly old merchandise up."

The patient arrived an hour later. She was one of a thousand City women, crowned with the thorns of middle age before her time. The stairs of her tenement home had given her a puffy pair of housemaid's knees, and her hands were red and chapped from wringing her dirty cloth in hot, soapy water and frosty morning air. Her truculent, unattractive eyes fixed Johnny with a beady stare as he and Walter bent over her: Walter prescribed the magic injection. Her breathing eased considerably.

They walked slowly to the door. "I think we've broken her spasm, but there's something about her I don't like," said the registrar. "She doesn't intend to help us much, and cases like this are always dangerous. Her trouble is starting somewhere upstairs."

"Still," said Johnny. "People don't die from this?"

"Don't you believe it," said Walter, wagging his forefinger. "I want you to watch her like a hawk."

The woman seemed to improve under Dr Petrie's sedation. Johnny required to give her only one more injection that evening and she slept reasonably well. By eleven o'clock the following morning her breath had reverted to short, painful whoops and the tip of her nose was as blue as German cabbage. A double dose of the magic liquid relieved her for a brief hour, then the noise from her corner rose again and her nervous neighbours gripped their sheets. Sister shifted her into the side-ward. Modern Medicine switched its attack: subcutaneous adrenaline and intramuscular hydrocortisone succeeded aminophylline; again she gained a brief respite and again she relapsed into a hideous state of breathlessness; the agony of her failing bronchial tree shrieked into the corridor. Johnny and Sister hovered near to her room; Walter and the chiefs came and went. By four o'clock the woman was on a steroid drip. Already her heart was showing signs of stress in the unequal struggle against the mounting resistance of her lungs.

Johnny's case was the centre of the tea-time conversation in the residency. Various housemen gave their opinion as to what should be done next. Pat Leitch winked at him above his *Sporting Times* and made faces at them. Johnny felt very important.

On his return to the ward he heard the noise twenty yards from the big glass doors; it chilled the swagger out of him. Walter was with her, ringing the changes yet again. They bound her legs and elevated the bed; Walter had a new little phial ready for the drip.

Johnny and Sister flattened her and were smoothing her pillows when she had a brief remission. She fixed them with that awful serpent's look. "Ye'll . . . no . . . take the mickey . . . oot o' me," she gasped.

"Now, now, my dear," said Sister soothingly. "We're no' trying to take the mickey out of you. Just you try and help us a wee bit."

The wet grey locks twisted savagely away from the gentle white hand. "Ye'll no' . . . take the . . . mickey . . . oot o' me," the cracked little voice repeated.

"What does she mean, Walter?" Johnny asked in the corridor.

Walter scratched his cheek. "Don't ask me, Johnny. I think there's a subconscious resentment in a lot of those cases; if you don't hit them early, they get a mental block somewhere, and you can do your damndest without getting any results at all."

Dr North came an hour later and immediately added his own brand of calm to the proceedings. But even he had an edge to his voice when the nurses came back noisily from supper; at 6.45 p.m. he called in the consultant thoracic surgeon and his anaesthetist. Tracheotomy was discussed and discarded.

She was now semi-comatose; her rough blue cheeks and pallid forehead were lathered in sweat and her special nurse was never still. Johnny stood looking down at her. Why the hell are you so determined to beat us? Surely there's something worth living for? Is this what years of charring does to a woman? Think of your daughter—the kid's only fifteen and she needs her mother. Come on, lass. Give us half a chance and we'll have you back to your pail and chamois in no time!

Moisture slithered forlorn down the transparent tube, and still the wild primordial howl of triumphant destruction issued from her open mouth. At 10 p.m. they wheeled her along to theatre. They took a calculated chance and gave her a general anaesthetic. She eased for a few minutes then the spasm returned; only the new hypertensive in the drip was keeping her pressure at a respectable level.

Dr North looked at his team. "It makes you humble, doesn't it? Here we have all the drugs and techniques at our command, and this poor girl is going down in spite of them."

Walter was listening to her back. "She can't stand much more of this," he said. Have you thought of trying hypnotism, sir? Her state of consciousness has come up a wee bit and it may go for good quite soon."

Dr North pondered for a minute. "All right, Walter. Let's have a go at the witch-doctoring." His eyes twinkled. "Johnny, go and ring the psychiatrist, and see if Sister's found her next-of-kin yet."

The psychiatrist was a little, bony man in a shabby brown suit. He looked vaguely like Adolf Hitler. Shortly after his arrival the daughter appeared, a frightened ordinary face thickly creamed with cheap make-up, a tight black skirt, pink ankle socks and black flats. The psychiatrist went to the patient, Johnny to the daughter.

"How's my mammy?" she asked. There were no tears yet. The truth had not yet penetrated her more personal horror of the sounds and smells of the hospital.

"She's very ill," said Johnny. "But we're all doing our best. She couldn't be in better hands," he finished lamely, realising the hellish limitation of words. The lower lip trembled and he flung an arm around her shoulder. "Buck up, sweetie," he said softly. "I know this is tough, but we'll make out somehow. I'm going to take you along to night nurse; she'll give you a cup of coffee and look after you properly."

At the duty room door she directed a wan little smile at him. "Thanks awfy much, doctor. Ye've been super to me."

He puffed out his chest. "Don't you worry, wee yin," he reassured her. "We'll no' let you down—but your mammy is very ill."

He walked back to theatre with another burst of importance. The psychiatrist was sitting before a fully conscious patient, swinging his key ring before her. "You feel very drowsy," he droned. "You're forgetting all your cares, you are forgetting that awful chest of yours, you are going to sleep . . . sleep. . . ."

The patient looked at him with contempt. "Ye'll no' take the bloody mickey oot o' me."

Patiently he repeated the performance: time after time the scientific blessing of his voice grappled with the evil spirit inside her. Presently she slid slowly and jerkily into a slumber, and her chest moved with a slower, smoother roll. Dr North slapped the psychiatrist on the back. "We've done it, I think." He became the director again. "Now—she'll stay in the ante-room till morning. I want her specialled by a staff nurse all night. And I'd like a doctor on the spot too."

"I'm pretty fresh, sir," offered Johnny. "I'll stay with her."

He settled down to sleep in the theatre sister's armchair while the special nurse moved around the bed without a sound. He seemed to have been asleep for mere seconds when a hand pulled at his shoulder. "The drip's stopped, Mr Ferguson. Her pressure's dropping again."

He sat up stupidly, shaking the drowsiness from his head. Damn the woman. "How did it happen—were you changing the bottle?"

The girl looked at him as though he had crawled out of a dead cat. "The bottle's not empty yet,' 'she said icily. "I've changed drips before, you know."

"What time is it?"

"Half-past five."

With a pained, superior expression he told the staff nurse to prepare a new transfusion set. When he searched for a new vein, however, it was his turn to feel humiliation; the vessels had shrunk in calibre enormously; after five unsuccessful stabbings he threw back his forelock and grinned apologetically at the tall girl. "I'm sorry, staff. I seem to be all thumbs." He saw to his horror that he had wasted an hour.

"Don't you worry, lad, it's not easy," she said kindly. "I think you should ring Dr Petrie—cutting down won't be easy."

His pride battled with his better judgment; in the end he rang the registrar. Walter was on the spot in half an hour, and ten minutes later the cannula was firmly tied in the skinny right ankle. Fluid poured in. The blood pressure rose shakily, but her respiration was becoming stressed again.

"Well done, young man," said Walter. "Let's have a fag and we'll see how she goes. I'd like to speak to her daughter."

"She's dozing in the duty room," said Johnny. "I spoke to her last night." He remembered his enjoyment of the conversation. You were in your element, you bastard!

The woman's condition worsened from then on, and her exhausted machinery screamed ever louder. Walter and Johnny had a quick breakfast together then returned to watch her, utterly helpless and perplexed. Dr North forsook his Sunday School to be with his team; the anaesthetist missed his Sunday golf. At ten o'clock, despite further extreme measures, the racket became ominously quiet and her chest came very nearly to rest. "She's going, damn it," said the anaesthetist, turning to Johnny. "Get me an airway—quick!"

He sprinted into theatre and yelled for an airway. When he returned the woman was dead, and Walter was injecting her heart with adrenaline and talking of cardiac massage. But Dr North held up his hand. "There's nothing more to be done," he said. "Any more interference on our part is pure exercise. Thank you all very much for what you've done."

Johnny walked back to the ward with Walter. "That was grim," he said. "If only we could have done something more." Inside he was secretly glad that it was all over; he felt all-in.

"Forget it," said Walter. "And then remember it whenever you see an early case, and attack it hammer and tongs."

"Who's going to tell her kid?"

"Leave it to the chief," said Walter. "He's the best man for the really dirty work."

Johnny wondered what Dr North would say. How could you make it sound anything but shit, knowing that the girl would want to see her mother, would have to look at that bloated, purple face and the swollen neck?

When he finished in the ward two days later he took with him the sincere thanks of Dr North, but also the persistent, disconcerting image of a frightened little teenager from whom he had reaped a moment of conceit when she had the ignorance to call him "Doctor."

You an idealist, Ferguson—Jesus Christ!

Nora watched his moody progress during her last week of term with growing concern. It was not merely that their physical love was poorer and less spontaneous. She missed the sun of paradise in her loins and the miracle of the strangled pagan scream, but worse now was his reticence to talk to her. He told her about the woman and her daughter when she was packing her suitcase.

"Now, love, you mustn't be silly about it," she said. "You'll have hundreds of cases like this in the next 30 years."

"Sure," he said. "Hundreds."

She finished packing. "I'll miss you, darling. Try and do a little work while I'm away, please."

"O.K., sweet, I'll try."

"It's a pity you can't work a bit more evenly," she said. "You were doing quite well last term."

"People who work regularly are of no importance," he answered. "A man's soul is small who can study for studying's sake. But when the end is in sight, and the prizes displayed, the Ferguson will come into his own."

He saw her off from the station on a wet, drizzling Monday. She broke down as usual, and he regretted his gruff behaviour in recent weeks. "Come back safely, love," he whispered. "You're my whole bloody life." He felt a very meagre size walking back into the Old Town.

He passed Connor's quickly looking straight ahead. On the corner of Woods Street Willie the tramp was selling newspapers. "Errly news . . . errly news . . . read aboot the fight last night . . . errly news. . . ."

Johnny felt in his pocket among the shafts of broken matches and cigarette ends. He handed the tramp twopence. "Here, Willie."

"Aye," said Willie. "They've done your boys this time, Johnny. It's they English, they're a' aroond us, a' aroond us. Cut their heids off, that's what I say. What a way to treat Jesus' children, Johnny, what a way!"

He walked into the shelter of the Quad and unfolded the morning edition of the *Evening News*. The headlines stretched his eyelids:

DISGRACEFUL SCENES AT NATIONALIST RALLY

Fists Fly as Soldiers Fight Back

One of the worst brawls ever seen locally occurred last night at the rally organised by the Scottish Free Party. Tempers were flaring early when strong statements were made from the platform, but things came to a head when Mr Derek Paton, the President, directed some offensive remarks at members of Her Majesty's Forces who had been heckling him. Blows were struck in all sections of the large crowd as Nationalists clashed with hecklers.

Plain-clothes policemen present in the crowd helped their uniformed colleagues to restore order, but several people required medical treatment for minor injuries. One young man was detained in the Royal City Hospital. Several arrests were made. . . .

The bus journey was slow during the rush hour. He sat upstairs immersed in unhappy thought as the seat beside him changed buttocks four times in twenty minutes.

There was no answer when he rang Torquil's bell. He repeated the movement vigorously and shuffling footsteps sounded down the hallway. The door opened and he gaped at the sight of his friend. The swollen black eye, the dishevelled clothing, the suffused, stupefied face. McLelland's normally tidy hair was spewed all over his head as if he had been nuzzling a Medusa.

Torquil swayed, supporting himself on the door. "Come in, Johnny," he said in a hoarse voice. "I'm afraid I'm slightly pissed."

Johnny followed him into the spacious living room. It stank of whisky. On the small round table a bottle stood three-quarters empty.

He sat down opposite the lean economist. "What's wrong, Torquil?"

"Have you read the papers?" McLelland reached for the bottle and upset his glass.

Johnny wiped the table with his handkerchief. "Yes, I have. What the hell happened?"

McLelland bit his lip with nicotined teeth. He sat frowning for a long time with his mouth hanging open and stupid, struggling with its whisky impediment. "It was very nearly the best meeting we ever had. You should have seen the crowd, Johnny. I spoke first. God, boy, I was in good form: I think I was inspired by the sight of those big plain-clothes traitors down in the crowd. I gave the crowd a few facts: our cultural and economic crises, Clydeside and The Highlands. Then I reminded them of what Scotland once was, and what she is now. I appealed to them as Scotsmen to cast aside the sort of comfortable protection that a helpless litle child occasionally gets from a bullying big brother. I told them to get off their knees and let the world see that they still cared to see their country's name revered, not numbered spuriously as a quaint and interesting appendage of England. In short, I appealed to them simply as Scotsmen to come to the aid of Scotland."

"How did it go down, Torquil?"

"Not badly at all. There were a few hecklers, but our pickets kept them quiet."

"Yes," said Johnny. "Not a very democratic procedure."

"Och, to hell with democracy—what a stupid idea it is," said Torquil. "You know, I used to have a pal, a bit of a queer chap, and every now and again I would find him laughing to himself. When I asked him what it was all about, he would tell me he was thinking about democracy—all those stupid people in tenements and bungalows taking part in the ruining of a country."

"Go on, anyway," said Johnny.

"After that good, sensible foundation, we called on this young Glasgow boy I told you about—he's a great little firebrand. He stood up and gave us ten minutes on the Irish Rebellion."

"Isn't the Irish Rebellion a little bit out of place nowadays?" said Johnny.

"Not on your life," said McLelland, his forehead throbbing. "Our present situation is directly analogous. This young chap gave us some terrific fire and the crowds grew and grew till they stretched right across the Square. There seemed to be a lot of Limeys present, and then those soldiers started up. I was chairman, so I pulled the young fellow down—we had a thousand ears straining ready for Paton's eloquence."

Johnny winced. "And then Paton went too far?"

"Yes," said Torquil in a low voice. "I've never been so embarrassed. He started making quotations from Hitler and Grivas and promised the people that if they would rise with him he would deal with every English settler in Scotland as the Nazis did with the Jews—all hell broke loose. One of the soldiers pushed his way to the front and grabbed him by the kilt. He fell off the platform backwards on top of me. When I got up off the ground the boys had pulled the soldier on to the deck and his pals were trying to rescue him. It was terrifying. All the other meetings broke up and joined in the free-for-all. The Young Protestant League joined the soldiers—half the crowd seemed to be against us. Then the police joined in, droves of them, but the meeting was finished."

"You weren't arrested?" asked Johnny.

"No. I was only attacked once—by that old meth-drinker—the one who's always giving her testimony for the holy-rollers. She called me a son of Satan and banged me on the eye with her bottle before I got away. But that little Glasgow kid was fined this morning for a breach of the peace. He thinks he'll lose his job."

"Poor little chap," said Johnny. "Torquil, you should have more sense than to follow people like Paton. They howl from their pedestals and let others pay the penalty."

"Don't talk nonsense," McLelland shouted in fury. "Paton has his faults, but he was the bravest man there. While the fighting was going on he ran up the steps of the Art Gallery and burned a paper Union Jack. The soldiers went after him, but he made a bolt for the street and jumped on a passing bus."

"How very fucking brave." Johnny was shouting too. "I'll bet he ran like a nun from a nigger, the little skunk."

Torquil poured the last of the bottle slowly with a trembling hand. "Leave off the indictments, Johnny. I'm heart-sick of politics."

"Come off it, you've got the whisky blues. What you need to do is to kick some of the worst cranks right out of the Party and get some good stuff in. Once we've had a few good meetings people will forget last night. Listen, I'll cheer you up a bit. I've been sitting on the fence too long. As soon as my Finals are over, you'll see me on the platform alongside you."

Torquil's head dropped. A strange artificial sound came from his direction; Johnny could have sworn he was sobbing. It came again, and again. Torquil *was* sobbing.

"Bloody hell, Torquil, what's the matter?"

Torquil looked at him with a painful, level regard. "I'm out, Johnny. They've sacked me."

"Sacked you? Who?."

Torquil brushed his tired eyes with the nervous gesture of a thrashed child. "The Committee called a special emergency meeting after the fuss was over. I'm afraid the axe fell on my scrawny neck. They decided that the organisation for the meeting was faulty and I was voted out in five minutes."

Johnny sat back flabbergasted. When he found his voice he lashed the room with every piece of filth that his roughnecked personality had absorbed since school. Torquil McLelland watched in owlish wonder. Johnny stood up, hurling his empty cigarette packet into the fireplace. "The slimy guttershits! God, if anybody's worked hard for the Cause, you have. And they'd use this as an excuse to throw a blanket over their puny little integrities and their stinking lack of guts. To hell with the Scottish Free Party, or any bunch of cannibalistic Scotsmen who'll tear the arse out of other Scotsmen to keep their own feet dry!" He picked up Torquil's glass and drank it at a swallow.

Torquil spread his shaking hands. "I'll be all right," he said brokenly. "I'll go into the political wilderness for a spell, and no doubt the devil will come and tempt me with thoughts of respectability to keep me out of Nationalism. But I'll come again, Johnny. As sure as God gave me breath, I'll come again."

Johnny lit a cigarette. His first puff reached nearly to the window. "Quit pretending, Torquil—you're finished. I'll tell you something else; unless a miracle happens Scottish Nationalism is finished. You know why?

"Our patriotism has been represented primarily as a negative, as a hatred of the outsider; if love for the virtues of one's country is not its prime motivation, then patriotism itself can't be a virtue. I only hope our Nationalism can recover from betrayals like yours—if we let Fascists represent us, we deserve the horrible fate of finishing up just another English county.

"We've been betrayed, Torquil. Bitterly betrayed, and the people who have betrayed us are the people who should have known better. We've had Parties for years but they've never worked as a single arm because their bosses were fighting with one another—Highlanders, Lowlanders, Catholics and Protestants —the Cause inevitably came second. And we've been stabbed in the back by too many Scottish pens, people who called themselves Nationalists with a little smirk to their friends: they played at it for a bit then they went off and wrote funny books about Scotland. Listen to me, Torquil. I hate intolerance, and quite frankly, you've got cranky things about you. But—at least you take your country seriously, and I love you for it. And I wouldn't clean my backside on Paton, Torquil. I think he's a filthy bag of Fascism, but you know who I hate worse? Those respectable Scottish bastards who picked up the paper this morning and laughed their respectable heads off because a man in a kilt was pulled off a Nationalist platform. Scotland has been betrayed by her own; I don't think she deserved it."

"God," said Torquil. "I've never seen you so moved."

"I could go on for hours. But it's just hopeless. We should have sense and forget it."

"I won't forget it," said Torquil. "Maybe I am a bit cranky, but I can't forget. I don't believe we're finished yet. We may see a strong personality emerge who will unite us." His head was sinking lower.

Johnny removed the cigarette that was blistering his limp fingers. "Can I do anything more for you?"

"No," said Torquil. "You can't. Bugger off."

He did as he was told.

He walked angrily about the streets for the duration of the afternoon, and by half-past five he knew where he was going.

Connor's was very quiet for the first two hours, and he drank himself easily to a loss of pain. Lizzie watched him quietly with her old-fashioned look and when he worked away stupidly in his pockets after five pints, she slipped him a half-note across the counter. The old-timers present left him alone—even Jimmy Anderson forsook his normal toast: "Here's to the red, white and blue, and the everlasting health of Good King Billy, who saved us from Popery, knavery, slavery—" tonight it didn't seem quite so funny.

Pat Leitch leaned to his elbow, in a drastic state of drink. "Hail Leitch, Thane of Burnside," said Johnny.

Pat mumbled over the counter, and Lizzie mixed a couple of large gins. Johnny sucked his straight down, neither tasting nor feeling a drop. Pat giggled, and bought two more.

"Be my saviour, Pat," he said. "Make me laugh, for God's sake."

Leitch shook his red retriever's head. "Mush shay few things t'you, Johnny . . . do y' shome good."

"Shoot," said Johnny.

"I wash talking t'Walter Petrie t'day . . . he tol' me 'bout your locum with North."

Johnny shifted his eyes uncomfortably to the feathery wart on Pat's chin. "I was absolutely useless," he said dishonestly. The red hair dazzled his paralysed pupils.

"—Walter wash talkin' 'bout the woman that died. . . ."

"Forget it, Pat."

"N'no . . . you 'njoyed it. Don' pr'tend y' didn't. . . ."

"How d'you know?"

"Walter shaw it 'n your face . . . never seen a young houshe-man so 'nthralled. . . ."

Johnny was feeling a little sick now. He took a very small sip of gin. "I suppose I was excited a bit."

"Yesh, but wha' 'bout th' times he used to go over the cases? . . . he'sh quite a gen-kiddo on Auerbach . . . you ushed to be bored stiff . . . that's what I've noticed 'n Cashulty . . . you loved abo'tionsh 'n cut throats, but discussin' cold theory with you wash li'e 'xplainin' contracepshun t' the Pope."

"That's balls," said Johnny hotly.

"Oh, no." Pat swayed near to his face. "I've come t' simple conclushion . . . you're 'n thish game for the wrong reashons . . . you wanna be surgeon . . . workin' up t' th' elbows in blood—doin' wonnerful op'rationsh all-a time . . . an' you haven' th' bashic interes' t' read a texshtbook f'r ten minutsh . . . y' haven't a hope, Johnny . . . two thingsh go hand-in-hand . . ."

"Nonsense." He was feeling very ill now; the temperature of his face was arctic.

"I'm right, Johnny . . . wouldn' shay thish if washn't pished, but I'm right . . . get out 'f Medshine, Johnny . . . get out b'fore it 'sh too late!" His legs gave way under him and he hit the floor like a belch of thunder. Lizzie took a sedate promenade round the bar and propped his lolling head against it. "Third one tonight," she observed. "That till's never been quiet."

Johnny was in the toilet. After he had vomited and flushed he sank to his knees again, gazing through tears at the little round mirror of water. His own reflection was indistinct; he half-closed his eyes and saw Pat Leitch; saw the uncut beetroot face, the suet nose, the hairy warts, and the wild red hair. Pat Leitch, my old pal—"Et tu, bloody Brute!"

CHAPTER XVIII

JOHNNY WAS IN Glenellin for ten days of the spring vacation, during which time his relatives found his demeanour very morbid. His father, in apparently splendid health, blamed Nora's absence, his mother the approaching ordeal of his Finals.

Somehow his conversations with McLelland and Pat Leitch had combined to produce an anxiety state whose resilience he had never imagined possible; fight as he did, life had developed a new plane of uncertainty that squatted heavily on his upthrusting courage; nor could he dismiss the strange insidious voice that declared the sun would never shine so brightly again. Nora's letters, ever tender, loyal and loving, became objects of suspicion —Corcoran must be hanging around somewhere.

A cold, showery April evening found him back in Connor's beside Murdo Macauley, fairly drunk on Murdo's money, frantically deflecting the conversation from the subject of the Meeting and Torquil lest he should go berserk—in his present mood he could have derived satisfaction from torturing a helpless cripple.

Murdo was describing in his usual polished style the peerless Gaelic saga of "Shehan"; the godmoving lines rolled smooth as gold off his sibilant tongue: ". . . Cha torainn do Iosa Criosd thu. . . ."

"Yes," he said, "I don't think I've ever heard that sentiment quite equalled in English poetry."

Then Hector Gunn came in with Nell. She was like a rubber doll, the damned woman; the last time she had been motheaten and sloppy, but now she had bounced back again, titivated anew by fresh make-up and hair-do, and that lovely big bust trying to drag your hands inside her raincoat.

Johnny scowled at her: "To what do we owe the honour tonight?"

She smiled lazily; the violet orbs vamped through him. "We heard you were back in your old haunts again. Does Nora know?"

"Shut up, Nell," said Murdo.

"Let's have a drink, by Jesus," said Hector. "Enough of this idle talk."

"How's the group?" Johnny asked by way of arbitrary pleasantry.

Hector indicated the poster on the arch pillar that advertised their next concert. "You'd better come to this one, boys; it's the last chance you'll have of hearing the Moonshiners for a long time. After this they're on a six-week contract with the Irish Radio. By the saints, but the Lord has been good to us."

"If it's anything like the last Moonshiners' concert," said Johnny, "it won't be worth a damn."

The nape of Hector's neck sprang sudden red. "Enough of your sneering, John Ferguson; the Moonshiners are singin' like the nightingales of Persia. By the saints, you're a sour character these days, Johnny, a sour character."

Nell slapped two pink squares on the counter. "Of course they'll come. Those are first row tickets, boys—a worm's eye view of my ankles."

Johnny sniffed. "There was a time—" he said maliciously, then he saw Hector's face and stopped. Instead he said, "Why the V.I.P. treatment, Nell? Will we be sitting beside your old fancy man?"

"No," she said gravely, "I doubt if we'll see him again. But shut up about him, poor devil."

"Johnny," said Hector, "I must ask you to moderate your talk. You are not the nobleman you were, not by any means."

He sensed a foreboding in the cool atmosphere of the fine Friday evening. People were pouring into the Free Gardeners' Hall half an hour before the scheduled start. Murdo and Johnny found themselves in a packed front row beside Jehosaphat, whose character now bore the twin stigmata of failed medic and private soldier, R.A.O.C., discharged from service on psychiatric grounds.

"It's good to see you back, you old bugger," said Johnny. "What are you going to do?"

"I've got the chance of a job at Dalneer Atomic Research Station," said Jehosaphat. "With a bit of luck I can put an end to this sorry scheme of things. I've got references from Hector and Starkey."

"That's enough to get you a life sentence," said Murdo.

The hall was looking very elegant; the stage was adorned with a fragrant braid of flower pots and greenery. Johnny looked around. There were a surprising number of well-cut suits for a folk-song audience. The Moonshiners, his Moonshiners, were becoming fashionable entertainment. He felt violated, prayed that they wouldn't be too good, waited with mounting apprehension for their appearance.

They came with smooth confidence, and he knew that it was going to be very good. There was one change obvious from the inception; Nell was leading, and leading with a snap which made all the difference; she had copied his old stance, the bitch, facing the group from the left, rapping her left foot on the stage, only she looked better than he ever did with her sweater almost indecently low and her face carefully powdered and pencilled back a few years.

They began by rousing hearts and feet with the chuckling bravado of "Turra Market," then Nell drove laughter from the earth with "Every Night when the Sun goes in": her regal melancholy floated from behind the tasteful, plaintive sympathy of Ricky's banjo; the splendid white walls of the South were distorted through a broken woman's tears, the heavy sweetness of magnolia was ravaged sour with treachery, the mocking-bird had a new lyric to jest, and a noble heart was moving without self-pity towards the Home and Death that waited under the green grasses of Marble-town. Deep inside Johnny Ferguson a newly discovered crevice of compassion was writhing in agony.

Murdo leaned over: "By God, they've improved."

"Yes," he said grudgingly, "by God, they are." He felt a spasm of hatred towards the Highlander. The praise savoured of treason.

The Moonshiners went from triumph to triumph; occasionally Nell would glance down at the huddled figure in the foremost row, and it snarled and cringed away from her victory. And yet, who could blame her?—he knew her exultation only too well. When you're up there on the platform, harmonising your voice with voices slaked and sweeetened by the same fountain, tripping in and out of the inimitable love-call of folk-strings, feeling the same rush of blood to the head as you tell the world how happy and sad a place it is, then you're on a hilltop, and you can see things that the people in the town down there can never see, for they can't hear the song of the gypsy laddies above the clink of their money-bags, or the bell that peals for Barbary Allan above the din of their new radio. But you can see it all, as you stand up there plucking like David and you tell them all that they're not as close to their roots as they should be, and that urbanisation is making them as faceless as the victims of oriental torture. Who can blame her? She's got a team in a million. And it used to be mine.

The Moonshiners vacated the stage: Hector appeared, and brandished a whisky bottle furiously at the audience. "It's Hector!" roared the Art College, the Arts Faculty and Connor's. "It's Hector!" The City took it up and screamed a salute to the Moonshiners' manager; "Come on, Hector—give us a song!"

Hector gave them "Gi'e the lass a thing that staunds" and "Helen of Kirkconnel." They rolled in the aisles during the first and sat in dolorous subjection through the last.

Johnny drank his beers far too quickly at the interval bar. His friends felt the conflict: Murdo began to sing, his reedy voice modulating the harsh hum in Johnny's head, banishing the awful sound of recent applause for others.

Johnny seized the big goblet and robbed it of its last few drops. "I can't see the second half being so good. There aren't all that many good songs left."

But Nell had more surprises for him. The second half began with the incongruity of a love song from Glasgow, but "The Bleacher Lassie o' Kelvinhaugh" was too simple and natural to fall short of magnificence. On they rode with the Texan "Brazos"; it was followed by a lusty lungful of Woody Guthrie which gave Ricky's fingers angelic licence. Johnny burrowed deeper into his seat, his eyes just wide enough to track Nell's legs as they danced around the root of the microphone. He began to applaud woodenly; a black cloud of desolation sucked his beer-comfort into its hygroscopic soul, and a strange painful wildness began to form thoughts in the vacuum of his mind. He had felt this before, after seeing Brando at his best or hearing Callas at the Festival: "Wait for me, I'm part of you. Let me do it with you! I can feel the beauty and the love and hatred. I need to express myself too!" But now he was suddenly old, sobbing contrition to the prodigal son who had made it.

Nell was singing "Red Roses." It was his favourite song, the bitch, so she sang it better than ever before. She repeated the second verse at the end of the story, using her mandolin softly against the guitar:

> "On the banks of red roses my love and I sat doon.
> He took oot his tuning-box to play his love a tune;
> In the middle o' the tune, his love got up and cried:
> 'Oh Johnny, Johnny, dinna gang and leave me'."

He hid blindly in the noise of the audience, ignorant of the fact that she was staring at him with a face pouring the tears of a year's loneliness. I'll kill you, Nell, God help me, I'll kill you; if it takes me ten thousand years I'll drag you into the deepest pit of hell. You cow, you're tearing me inside out in the only way you know how! When he raised his head he saw with surprise that she was off-stage.

But she returned, smiling wickedly to the collars and ties, and the uncalculated Revenge of the Moonshiners on Johnny Ferguson rose to its climax. There were restive shufflings at the back of the hall when the prolonged applause died on their usual farewell piece, but she stepped forward and held up her hand. "Ladies and Gentlemen," she said. "The Moonshiners would like to thank you for the wonderful reception that you've given us. We'll be going over to Dublin full of hope in the knowledge that singers who can please this audience need fear no audience at all." Self-conscious titters. "But there is a young man in the front row of the audience who gave this group its name and most of its ideas—his name is Johnny Ferguson. We're going to sing something now that he wrote himself—something that is very much a part of him. It is not a folksong in the scholar's definition, but we believe that whenever a human being writes anything from the heart that beats out the pulse of his people, he is a folk-poet. Here, then, is a poem of Glenellin." She began: "The hills are still green. . . ."

Johnny recovered his scattered wits. "The robbing bitch," he exclaimed vehemently, "I'll stop her bloody nonsense." He tried to rise, but Murdo and Jehosaphat hauled him down; people were muttering behind him.

He would not have believed it possible. They had taken the untidy rambling lines of his uncouth nineteen-year-old hand, and transformed them into a piece of genuine-sounding folk-music. Again they used guitar and mandolin together, he could not begin to understand what they were doing, but not one word of his teenage crusade against the Hydro Scheme sounded out of place. Nell and Stella sang the last verse without accompaniment; their duet lifted in straight, true harmonics to the roof of the hall:

> "There are times in the mood of a morning
> When the plunge of a pick is horrific.
> Its echo wrenched raw from the granite
> Delves deep to the root of a memory,
> Distorting in black laceration
> The flesh of a soul in its segment,
> Full-filling the end of a chapter
> With a heartbreaking hunchful of sin."

The hall exploded. "More," they screamed. "More! More!" There was no more, for the caretaker was already making angry signs at the back. Hector made a short, dignified speech, and wished the audience "Beannachd Leibh."

Murdo looked at Johnny and Jehosaphat looked at Johnny. His face was blank. "My God, that was brilliant."

"I've never heard anything quite like it," said Murdo.

Johnny smiled. There was a fulfilling warmth glowing inside him; the old Ferguson Bible of Life had been set to music, and they had loved it.

"Let's go and congratulate them," he said. "They certainly deserve it."

The little cloakroom was creaking with humanity. The Moonshiners were drinking beer in a corner; questions were being fired at Hector from all angles. Nell rose to meet them.

"Did you like it?" she asked Johnny.

Before he could reply a grubby young man holding pencil and pad grew out of the ground and stood between them. "What are your plans for the future, Miss Horton?"

Nell pointed to Hector. "Ask our manager," she said with bored contentment.

"Run away," said Johnny angrily. "We're talking."

The pale, malicious features attempted hauteur. "I was speaking to Miss Horton. *Will* you use this song, Miss Horton?"

"If this gentleman doesn't mind," she said with a mischievous grin. "He wrote the words."

The man looked spitefully at Johnny, and turned back to Nell with a disbelieving look on his pale face. "But you and Mr Slater wrote the wonderful music, didn't you? It was quite superlative, you know."

"And I wrote the words," said Johnny doggedly.

"Yes," said the reporter, scribbling away. "The words. But that lovely melody is real Moonshiners' stuff—how does Mr Slater spell his name, Miss Horton?"

"Ask him yourself," she said, for Johnny's eyes were growing flinty. "Mr Ferguson spells his with one 's'."

The reporter put his pencil in his pocket, and tried to smile like an honest man. "We haven't room for all the names, you know. I must go and talk to Mr Slater."

Johnny gripped her by the arm; the pain lashed her fingertips. "Why did you have to go arranging my poem like that? Those swine will be attributing it to you and Ricky before long. It didn't need music, you bitch. That *was* a part of me, and you've dirtied it with your sexy growling."

"Let go my arm," she said. "That was done with the best of intentions. It's one of the few things you left me; you used to repeat it so often in your cups that I didn't need to write it down. But it hasn't quite made you the man of the evening, so it's all wrong."

"Just never sing it again, Nell." He could hear Ricky going over the accompaniment for a group of pencil-wielding wolves. "I've a good mind to slap your face, you thief!"

She sighed deeply. "You're still one of us, aren't you, darling? You're eating your soul because you weren't up there tonight."

"Don't call me darling. And I never want to see or hear any of you again. In a few months I'll be doing work that's worth more than a thousand of your songs."

Stella and Ricky were coming over; he prepared to beat a hasty retreat. "Just remember, now," he said. "No more tricks, Nell. And if you dare use my poem again, I'll bloody well strangle you."

She tossed her bright black head beneath the electric light. "You won't kill me, Johnny. But you'll love me again—you and I are part of this stuff."

"How are you, Johnny?" said Ricky's warm voice behind him.

"Get lost, you bastard," he grunted, and ran to the night.

CHAPTER XIX

THE FIRST WARM KISS of April coming late in the month, and term starting—for the last time. Final term, and Final Year and the Day of Judgment. A sinister new aura accruing to pen, paper and book, and a rare new excitement deep in the belly, and a Task ahead. But first, Charities Week to start the term; a week of torch-lit processions; fireworks in the black of night, and endless dances; bus raids deep into the lovely Border country. Then finally, the big collection in the City on Saturday, with turbanned sheikhs lying in front of buses in Princes Street and drunken cavemen brutally kissing frigid City matrons in the quieter thoroughfares. The afternoon procession of lorries and floats that gives the populace its annual surfeit of risque student humour, and the final Charities Ball in the Union where cracked cherries are ten a penny.

It was not until the Saturday parade, when he met her stone drunk, and pulled her roughly on to a lorry that was simply a mobile section of Connor's, that Nora realised with a sinking heart that he had broken his promise. Their float was decked up as a public bar; Johnny seemed to forget all about her, for he promptly donned one of Lizzie's aprons and proceeded to serve beer from the large cask that sat behind the cabin. The lorry was jam-packed with a nefarious selection of people whom she had once hoped never to see again, and she was forced to sit beside Starkey Shearer, who made all manner of illegal advances on her in a minimum of space until the lorry driver, labouring under a heavy load of Connor's hospitality, took the sharp corner into the High Street far too wide and mounted the pavement. When all the screaming had died down Nora managed to wriggle away from her tormentor who turned his attentions to a large fat Art College girl in a bikini, and began to bite her thigh. The Connor's lorry continued on its way, leaving a few Scots oaths and torn nylons among the crowd.

When the waggon finally came to rest outside the Union, she jumped off quickly, feeling utterly miserable. Around the Union steps the proletariat watched in wonder as seven prostrate forms were lowered tenderly to the ground. The fat girl's flesh had been too strong for Starkey: he lay across the tailboard, heaving in agony at the road.

An ancient City grandmother pulled at her black shawl and clucked in admiration: "Look at they students" she said loudly to her angular daughter, "they're awfy guid actors—ye'd think they were really drunk."

At the evening dance Nora watched Johnny closely, probing the gestures that were more nervous and the abstract periods that were slightly longer, without receiving any comforting reply; when she tried to exploit Jehosaphat's loyalty she found him mysteriously hesitant to make clinical comment.

But her prayers were answered the following Wednesday evening. Johnny wandered down to the flat with beer on his breath and a worried frown on his face; she forbore to raise the hated name, and cooked his meal dejectedly, but when he had finished he rose and made straight for the calendar.

"Exactly six weeks to go," he said quietly. "Right, Nora, the books come out tonight and you won't see me wasting an evening until the whole damn lot's over." He came over and kissed her. "This is it, girl—I'll do it or bust."

"Oh, Johnny," Her eyes flooded and she threw herself at him. "Darling, I thought you'd forgotten your exams." She moved to kiss the tense muscle around his mouth and nostrils, but he turned quickly, picked up his large green textbook, and went to the bedroom door. "I'll study in here," he said firmly.

"I'll bring you a cup of coffee in an hour or two, love. And Johnny—" She looked at him with an appealing helplessness—"You haven't changed, have you, darling? Once all this is over we'll be making love like we used to."

"Sure," he said. "We'll be married in about six months, Nora; by this time next year you'll probably be carrying a little Ferguson inside you."

"What a wonderful thought," she said shiny-eyed.

Johnny sat down by the little bedroom window and opened a textbook. It contained over a thousand pages of print; he would be through it twice before Finals started. He was reasonably confident of Surgery, and Arnold's beautiful notes would suffice; as for "Midder. and Gynae." a few nights in the last fortnight were quite enough for anybody who had some common sense. This damned Paediatrics paper was an extra thorn in the flesh, but he was attending all the cliniques, and a little added reading would do the trick. On with the motley!

Nora's wonder and disquietude grew as May blossomed white outside on the Meadows. He appeared punctually every evening at 5.30 p.m. and was hard at work shortly after 6. She was first delighted with his complete renunciation of alcohol, but after the first fortnight she began to wonder if this fanatical addiction to his books was not a worse drug. His tenderness was steadily disintegrating before her eyes; the only humanising factor in his gruelling routine was the guitar, which he would play constantly during his relexations, and the songs became more melancholy every day. They spoke few words to each other; she accepted this at first, then came to resent it slightly and longed for the old days and the old closeness of their spirits; but there was nothing for it but to curl up in the kitchen with a book and wait out the weeks.

To sit indoors while the loving couples wandered carelessly up and down the green Meadows fringes would normally have been too much for Johnny to bear. But this time his obsession was too powerful for any deviating temptation; never had he felt the whiplash of compulsion more fiercely on his labouring back. He raced through the white leaves of his textbooks with a grim, frantic concentration that amassed facts in his brain and a great heap of cigarette ends in his ashtray: pages that had bored him before took on a sudden interest as the great plan assumed shape; hour after hour he kept at it, reading, writing down data he considered super-salient until in the early hours his brain was reeling with fatigue. The morning brought no respite for he hung on to every word that was uttered in the Children's Ward, and his lunchtime discussions were always regurgitations of "shop." Connor's was almost forgotten, and the Moonshiners and Hector were part of a fairy-tale film that he had seen as a small boy, and for which he longed hopelessly when he gave himself the luxury of a reflective moment. Nora, bless her, was always around, far sweeter than she had any right to be, on hand with coffee, fags and even a little money when necessary, never once complaining, damn her, even when he barked at her to get the hell out of the room and give him some peace to study, and was sorry he had started shouting long before he was finished. There were times just now that you seethed with hatred when you saw people tripping gaily into cinemas, or lying with arms interlocked on the grass, or simply smiling. For right now you're just not part of the human race; you know how a leper feels, or a negro in the southern states, for there's a Mark of the Beast inside you letting heaven know that you're a Final Year medic who's sitting his Finals for his sins, and you're not allowed to feel human until the whole thing's over.

And still Nora watched him; proudly, fearfully, and somehow distantly. His environment was a succession of small rooms: the Medical Reading Room, Nora's bedroom, the Study in the Union. Hours and nails were eaten by phrases and figures; by the differential diagnoses of tachycardia, the treatment of a post-partum haemorrhage, the method of reducing a Colles and a Potts, Bilroth and Polya, bile-saturated urine, and black, tarry stools. They were certainly wonderful chaps, all those pioneers of Medicine and Surgery, but for examination purposes they did far too bloody much. There's a new and wonderful vitality about the stuff now but there are hours on end when you spit on it. Then you remember Huxtable J. Peterson's Mid-Western twang that is anathema to any lover of speech, and you throw yourself back into the midden with a sob of fury, for you're damned if he's going to see you slinking away from the results list with your tail between your legs.

On with it then: "Distribution of the pain is very varied: it may radiate into the jaws and gums." . . . "Before ye get any wild, dramatic ideas, laddie, give the fundus a wee rub" . . . "a low ventral mass?—foetus, flatus, faeces, fibroid, full bladder" . . . "For God's sake, Nora—turn that bloody radio down!" . . . poor old Torquil, poor old Torquil, poor old Scotland.

As his face grew paler and thinner, and his diet became less solid and more milky, she made tentative suggestions that he should slow down a little bit. He shrugged, nodded, and proceeded to work harder than ever. Eventually, after he had done twenty-four days on the trot, she was asked to a party by a classmate. At first she refused, then with a sudden flare of rebellion she assented.

His eyes widened when he came down to the flat that evening, and saw the lemon dress, and the gleaming, groomed hair. "Well, well," he said. "Are we having a private mannequin session tonight?"

"D'you mind if I go to a party for a bit?" she said.

"What sort of a party?" His voice grated against the quiet walls.

"Oh, just a party some of the gang in the year are throwing."

Books hit the table angrily. "I've been waiting for this, Nora; you haven't got much patience, have you? There's nobody around to pay you the usual compliments, and your little ego is starving for adulation?"

She recoiled. "Oh darling," she said, "that's not fair."

"Yes, it is," he spat. 'You love me, don't you? But yours is the sort of love that goes to pieces when things are tough. I don't make you laugh any more, do I, Nora? You're growing tired of me, aren't you?"

"Simmer down," she said quietly. "I'm not growing tired of you, Johnny, but you're going through a sticky period, darling, and you're almost unrecognisable. We used to discuss everything under the sun, and it was wonderful. But now I scarcely hear your voice, except when you're swearing at me, and you hardly ever touch me, and if you do you're giving me dirty looks for days afterwards. Look, darling, I'm sure you must know your stuff by now; why don't you take me out yourself tonight, and I'll forget the—the bloody party!"

"So it's blackmail, now, is it?" he drawled. "When I wasn't studying you were nagging all the time, and now that I am, that's not right either. You're just a downright malcontent, woman, and I'm sick of the sound of your whining!"

She came close to him. "What's wrong, love?" she said "We shouldn't let things come between us like this, Johnny."

As he lit his cigarette his fingers were shaking, but his face softened to an apology. "Sorry, sweetheart, I'm far too wound up. I just can't see myself passing at the moment, and I've got the cobbly-wobblies. But tonight is Friday—we're going out, m'chicken; that is, if you can afford a couple of spaghettis."

"Of course I can," she said. "We've been out so little that my pockets are bulging. On you go and shave!"

They ate in the Scala; Maria's Bolognaise was, as ever, majestic. Johnny wiped his greasy mouth, lit two cigarettes and stared into space.

"What are you thinking, darling?" she asked. She had to repeat the question twice before he answered.

"I'm trying to remember something Colin said this morning. Somebody in the Faculty gave him a tip for the Medicine paper, but I've forgotten what it was."

"Oh, forget it for a bit, love," she said. "I'm almost tempted to take you into Connor's for a good drink; you've got to leave it all behind you sometime."

"You don't understand," he said with an irritated flick of ash. "We went over one of the old papers today, and I was lost in some of the Medicine questions."

"Stop it, Johnny," she said angrily. "Why you men all start getting excited at the last minute is beyond me. I remember, Kevin was the very same when he was at Agricultural College." She let the name slip inadvertently from her mouth; he stared into the glowing end of his weed.

"How is Kevin?" he asked.

"I saw him once or twice in April," she said. "He's all right."

"Did he get fresh with you?"

"For heaven's sake," she blurted out. "Why the sudden third degree?"

"Answer my question," he pursued. "Did he try and get his hands on you?"

"Cut it out," she said; a furnace blazed behind her eyes. "He knows that we're engaged. What's all the suspicion in aid of?"

"I'm not suspicious. But I have a good memory. You once told me that you could never trust Kevin if he was alone with you; he was always looking for a chance to grab you."

"That was a long time ago," she said.

"Yes, and he did more than grab hold of you, didn't he? What about that night at Dingle, when you nearly lost your bathing costume?"

"Johnny, what's wrong with you tonight?" she said hopelessly. "I'd never have told you any of these things if I'd realised you'd cast them up. I thought I could trust you."

"Well, I don't trust him," said Johnny. "I saw the way he looked at you at Christmas time, and you won't tell me that he's forgotten what your arse feels like."

"Johnny!" She slapped him hard across the face. The cafe was quiet: only a couple of spinster coffees beheld the blow. Nora gripped the felon hand, and cried into her spaghetti.

He turned his bitter, twisted face to the ceiling, its one red cheek burning; his Richard Widmark pose. "You don't like the truth, do you, Nora? You haven't forgotten him either; I'll bet you often think about that night in Dingle, even when you're lying beside me."

She was raining tears now. "I've never as much as kissed him in three years," she whispered, shoulders heaving. "I've never really loved anyone but you, but I can't stand any more of this, Johnny. Break it off now before you wreck me completely."

He slipped into her seat and pulled her head to his shoulder. "Forget it, love, I must have been mad. Please forget it, my white love; I adore and worship you, and I'll kiss your feet if you ask me. I'll never mention Kevin again—I swear."

She nodded, drying her eyes silently. After a minute her shoulders came off the rack and he rose to pay the bill, but Maria's sharp eyes were on Nora as she sidled past the counter and he received a sharp rap across the knuckles with a heavy pencil.

"You're a bad-a bugger," said Maria pleasantly.

"Quiet, or I'll rape you, woman," he said, and put out his tongue.

Outside the air was sweet and cool, and the east wind asleep. They wandered back to the flat at a leisurely pace, and her misery melted, for he pulled her into doorways every twenty yards to kiss her.

Two students passed them, walking quickly. Nora heard a brief breath of their conversation: "—if you make a big mistake in your Medicine Clinical it can be fatal: I remember old Collins—"

Johnny pointed at their backs. "Those are two of the blokes in the year—swots. They're still talking shop at this time on a Friday night, the blighters."

She smiled to herself. "What's all this about some Clinical being fatal?"

"You have a paper and an oral in each subject, and then a clinical exam in each by the bedside," he explained. "The whole thing takes about ten days. Some people reckon that the clinical exam in Medicine is the one that ploughs people."

"It's awful the way you boys have to go at it."

"Yes," he said, "each man secretly envying what the other knows. In garrets all over the city just now more than a hundred heads will be bowed in unrelenting effort, not giving a damn what their best friend's chances are, as long as they pass themselves; and all this to enter a profession whose ethics are second to none."

"Are you like that?"

"I'd hate Colin or Martin to fail, but if it were a case of them passing and me ploughing, I'd like it even less."

"D'you remember the wonderful nights we used to have last year?" she said irrelevantly. "When we used to go through some of my old Irish books; when you were Naoise, and I was Deirdre?"

"Yes," he said, and clutched the yielding willow of her waist. "All this damned studying blots the pleasure out of life; but don't worry, love—we'll be Deirdre and Naoise again."

She caught his arm and turned him towards the sky. The sunset was an angry rebel above the old ramparts of the Art College: a scarlet ball of courage set behind three long rashers of streaky cloud that were suffused with a mellow pink glow; the sky around and the silhouetted slate below were toned soft golden yellow.

She saw his face twitch. "Isn't it a sight for kings and heroes?" he whispered. "The last gleam of the West, a warrior even in death." He slid his arms around her, and found her willing; his lips lay peaceful in the warmth and moisture of her mouth.

She drew her head away to look at the sun; already the Art College gable had reared into the lowest segment. "This is heaven," she murmured, "and for the moment I think we *are* Deirdre and Naoise again. Johnny, I can feel all of you coming back to me." She raised her face to his smile. "I'll never forget it, darling; it's the sort of thing that would make life worth while even if we never had another night like this."

CHAPTER XX

[*The Union Snack Bar. Colin Morrison, Jimmy Anderson, Martin Clark, John Stewart Ferguson. The atmosphere tense: cigarettes smoked and stubbed out quickly. A hint of June sweat-smell at the table, and the conversation one of a hundred*].

MORRISON: "Well, that was rather a good lecture. When Sir Norman bothers he can be very amusing."

CLARK: "It was a bloody waste of time. He forgets that life isn't terribly funny for us right now. Then all this crap about following our careers with his cataractous, rheumy eye and a brimming heart—I'll bet it's a different story when he's questioning us across the table."

MORRISON: "From all accounts he really does his damndest to get you through, and that's more than can be said for some of them."

ANDERSON: "I'm sorry for you blokes. I've given up hope already—I couldn't even pass T.B. and V.D. last term. My only hope is to get some boozy old examiner who's too drunk to recognize my ignorance."

MORRISON: "It's not impossible, old boy. They say that old Johnstone was drunk as a lord last year."

CLARK: "It makes you laugh. Here we are, in the worst state of nerves we'll ever know, and some of those buggers are having a holiday out of it. Still, old Johnstone's not a bad old stick—he didn't fail many people."

FERGUSON: "That's just it—there's so much chance involved. You might not know your stuff all that well, and be lucky, or you could know it inside out and get a combination of the wrong questions and the wrong people."

MORRISON: "All the more hope for the old slackers like you, Johnny boy."

CLARK: "I've come to the conclusion that they should let everybody through, as long as I'm included. I'll go crackers if I fail. What'll you do, Johnny?"

FERGUSON: "God knows. I try to forget about it."

CLARK: "I've a feeling that myxoedema is coming up this year. They haven't had it for ages."

MORRISON: "So what? They haven't had Cushing's Syndrome for ages, or haematemesis. Stop spotting questions, old boy; you could go on all day."

FERGUSON: "I've scarcely done any neurology. I must get cracking tonight. Lord, if only I'd started a bit earlier."

CLARK: "You know, I've got one great fear. I'm terrified that at one point I'll get so flustered that I'll say one really stupid thing that'll finish me, like that girl three years ago who told the surgical external that the penis has a core of bone."

[*Laughter*].

MORRISON: "I don't think you can be failed unless you're generally below the border line."

ANDERSON: "Yes, I heard about one chap who was very dicey; they just couldn't make up their minds about him. Then they went through his record and found that he'd been ordered out of an Anatomy lecture theatre for stuffing a cadaver's tongue down a female student's neck He was passed unanimously."

MORRISON: "Oh, yes, they're human enough. Let's hope that we all make it."

CLARK: "I'm beginning to forget what a woman feels like. I wish I had something steady, like you blokes. It must help a lot."

ANDERSON: "Yes, it helps a lot. There's nothing like a bit of romping baboon. Isn't that right, Johnny?"

FERGUSON: "Yes, yes, I suppose it helps."

CLARK: "He supposes it does? If I had a girl like Nora, I'd do a lot more than suppose."

FERGUSON [*angrily*]: "Stow it, Martin!"

MORRISON: "Easy, gentlemen, let's talk about something else. Finals, for instance. I'll tell you what I'll do: I'll lay Johnny and Martin a little side-bet that they get through. How about ten shillings each?"

FERGUSON: "That's most unwise, Colin. It's tempting Providence."

ANDERSON: "Look what's climbed out of the pig's bin."

[*Huxtable J. Peterson approaches, sits down sucking Coca-Cola noisily through a straw*].

H. J. P.: "Hallo, boys—all set for the final straight? I've just been reading the latest paper on oesophageal varices. You know, those textbooks of ours are inadequate for this exam.

I'm glad I've had the sense to keep my outside reading up to scratch."

MORRISON: "We're all very impressed. What else did you want to say?"

FERGUSON: "Easy on the boy, Colin—he's lost weight. He's not a pound over 15 stone now."

H. J. P.: "Gawdammit, we're all very confident today. Have some of you been bribing the examiners?"

[*Hearty guffaw from* H. J. P.].

FERGUSON: "Yes, we've just heard that one of them is a cannibal from the University of Lagos. We're looking for the most expendable hunk of human blubber around. What about it, Huxtable?"

H. J. P. [*rising*]: "I guess you guys don't intend to be very pleasant. Well, all the best, I got no hard feelings. Most of you should get through."

FERGUSON: "Beat it, Huxtable. You're filling us with emotion."

H. J. P.: "That didn't include you, Ferguson. I'm a decent guy, but you've asked for it. You're gonna fail your Finals, and you deserve it. You think you can cram these crummy little textbooks into your head and get away with it, but you've lost too much clinical experience. You're gonna fail your Finals, and goddamn it, I'm not sorry. I'm an honest man, and I'm not sorry."

[*Johnny's green textbook assaults Huxtable amidships. He moves off bent like a clasp-knife*].

FERGUSON [*face flaming red*]: "If that pile of dirt says one more thing to me, I'll cut it apart. I'm off now, lads. All the best if I don't see you before it starts."

[*Exit*].

CLARK: "Johnny's more jumpy than any of us."

MORRISON: "He's doing more slogging than any of us—probably about 12 hours' reading in a day. He's a tough old bird. But I'm sorry for Nora—it must be hell to see as much of him as she does. Well, it's time we were all back at the torture-wheel. I've got all my abdominal Surgery to do tonight."

CLARK: "I've got my Gynae. to finish, and I could just do with a few pints."

ANDERSON: "I'm having my usual few tonight. How about coming up after nine?"

MORRISON: "Damn it, yes I will if the wife lets me. How about you, Martin?"

CLARK: "Yes, I think I can spare a few hours. What about Johnny?"

MORRISON: "Better leave him. He needs all the time he's got."

CHAPTER XXI

He was sitting by the window as usual, running his hands through the thick brown stack of his hair, and he was reading the last leaf of Arnold's Surgery notes.

There were just seven days left before his long medical case; the siege was nearly begun. A week ago you knew that for some reason you had to go through it day after day, but you still believed that Time had some mercy left and would stretch the calendar sideways to keep the dread date a thought in your mind. But the days slipped by, and the earth continued to turn. The wallflower faded, the corn speared at the sky and there was no further use kidding yourself: you still felt hellishly unready but in another seven days like the dead ones gone you would be led before your judges like a lamb to the bloody slaughter. It was real. It would happen after all.

Nora came in, carrying some sheets. "How's it going?"

"I've done about as much as I can," he said. "For the last week I'm going to do revision of the bigger chapters. You'll have to help me like you did during the winter."

"I'd love to, Johnny-o," she said. "I've felt so helpless up to now. Dear old Johnny-o, I love you."

"Talk like a woman, not a little girl, Nora!" he said, still looking down. "There was a time when your baby-talk was attractive, but now it aggravates the situation. And I could do with a cup of coffee."

In the kitchen she thought: this is getting worse all the time. At first he gave me more than his blood, then we became something less than lovers, something like friends, and I didn't want to admit it. And now he doesn't tolerate things a friend would—is he beginning to dislike me? Have pity, somebody! Get him through this spell, and when it's finished make him something like the lovely young rascal I met last year. Please, dear God, please.

She came back with his coffee.

"Have you no classes today?" he said.

"I finished yesterday," she said. "I'm finished with this University, and, I hope, with all Universities." She waited for the appropriate reply.

"You forgot the sugar," he said.

Back she went to the kitchen. "Let something happen," she whispered aloud.

She was praying on the morning of the Battle.

There was the Rectorial battle, when the anti-medical faction made an unwise raid on the bar and left a lot of their blood on the floor. There was the battle of Ollie the Bull when the big schizophrenic negro came close to murdering two policemen. There were always fights in Woods Street. But that which took place one cool summer evening seven days before Finals went down in the annals of Connor's as *The Battle,* and those who claimed to have seen it lacked for little drink in the months that followed.

An hour after Johnny Ferguson had drunk his first coffee of the day, Stan the manager was sweating his way up the cellar steps behind a heavy crate of Export. He saved his toes at the second attempt when the sound of shattering glass broke the concentration of his grip.

In his glazed front window a jagged hole had been smashed high up. The agent missile lay by miraculous chance on the counter; a whisky bottle. He raced to the deserted street. "Did you see who did it?" he screamed across the road to Maria.

"I saw him no' verra guid," she yelled back. " 'E was on yin o' them motor-bike things."

Stan crossed the street; he counted four disinterested pedestrians.

"What did he look like?"

She scratched her raven head. "I've seen 'im afore. One o' them wee-a laddies wi' the hair. I think he's a Bobo's man."

A young Highland bobby came, and took particulars.

"Ye'll find the culprit somewhere doon the road," said Stan.

The policeman shook his head. "They're barred now from half the pubs in Woods Street—they've beaten nearly all of them to pieces. The students are beginning to go back."

Stan showed him a crumpled piece of toilet paper. "What's the meaning of this, then? It was in the bottle." Scrawled in pencil were three words in crude capitals: CONNORS YOUR NEXT.

"I don't know," said the policeman. "I thought Bobo's crowd were broken. Most of them have been fined or jailed already. He can't have all that many men left."

"This is followin' a pattern," said Stan. "Some other shops who got messages like this were wrecked before the night was oot. I can see Bobo appearin' here in person today."

"I'll be around till three o'clock," said the policeman. "I'll keep an eye on things."

"It's O.K., son," said Stan. "I just want the polis to get the wee rat who broke the windae. But if things are gonnae be rough, Connor's can handle its ain troubles."

"Don't tell me," said the bobby. "But I'd better give this note to the C.I.D."

After he had left Stan had second thoughts about the situation, and realised with sudden horrified understanding that whatever the motive for Bobo's latest madness might be it contained a sinister method and intelligence. For Connor's was quieter now than it had been for weeks, and was almost naked of fighting men: Jimmy Anderson was away for the week with his blonde as a last defiant, despairing gesture—Ollie the Bull was still in jail. Most of the younger lads were in the throes of study and would not appear on a week night. Worst of all, the big spare barman had a day off. He had been caught with his trousers down and Bobo knew it. The only alternative was to call the police—perish the thought!

He opened the door at twelve, and paced around nervously for twenty minutes before a thirsty face appeared. Even the elements were keeping the customers away today; the sun could not vaporise the heavy haar, and the streets were dank and chilly.

Joe the Rat strode in just as Stan was pouring himself a large whisky. "I hear we're in for trouble tonight," he said.

Stan spilled a little spirit on the counter. "How d'you know?"

"Two of Bobo's men just told me—said they're taking over in Connor's tonight, the dirty little swine. They've certainly picked a good time for it."

"That's what worries me," said Stan. "We're a bit thin on the ground. Christ—if only we had Jimmy or Johnny around."

"Hector's back for a few days," said the Rat. "The Moonshiners are over for a wee break; I hear they're going great guns."

"To hell with the Moonshiners," said Stan. "And it's no' fair to drag a famous bloke like Hector into this—it could ruin him. If we could only get some o' the lads that are studyin'."

"Let's have a half-pint," said the Rat. He took a deep draught with an expert flexing of his elbow. "I've been round all the reading rooms," he said. "None of our boys are there; they must be working in their 'digs'. Have ye got any addresses?"

"Aye," said Stan. "But only one or two. I've got the Sinclairs; ye ken, the two big Shetlanders. And I've got Starkey's address somewhere."

A few more customers drifted in; elderly casuals. Stan served them in a hurry.

He came back to the Rat. "If you can get the Sinclair cousins they're worth two men each. Starkey's no' much, but he can be vicious at times. D'you think he'll come?"

"Of course he will," said the Rat. "He's a Connor's man."

Stan did not leave at three. He waited behind locked doors until five o'clock. He drank four doubles and smoked incessantly. A few respectable early evening customers patronised him during the first hour, but none of the recognised hard men came near.

The Rat appeared after six with the two Sinclairs and Starkey. Stan felt decidedly better at the sight of the two big northerners; they were wonderful lads, those big blue-eyed sons of Shetland; mammoth drinkers, fine singers and fearless fighters.

"Are you game?" Stan asked Starkey.

The rake nodded, brushing his fashionable suit. "I'll do what I cen, Sten. But you'd better get me tight first."

"Drinks are on the hoose for tonight," said the manager. "You're not a bad old stick, Starkey."

"I'm a louse," said Starkey. "But I cen't bear the thought of Connor's being ruined. I'm barred from every other pub in the area—if I lose this place, I'll die."

They drank whisky. A few workmen stood around the foot of the bar; good solid local men, but thirty years past their fighting prime.

After an hour Stan's face carried the threat of despair. "I think I'll have to phone the polis," he said.

"No," said Dan Sinclair. "We can handle them, Stan. Can't we, Tammy?"

Tammy Sinclair nodded. "That we will, man. We've sorted the bastards before."

"I wish we had just three more Shetlanders," said Dan. "But the Chemistry boys have all got a paper tomorrow. We can't ask them to help us."

"Look, lads," said Stan. "I reckon it's hopeless. There are four of you, there's me—a dead loss—and there's Lizzie when she comes in. Two fightin' men, two half-pissed physical wrecks, an old man an' a woman, against about a dozen of Bobo's hooligans; it's a massacre."

"No," said Dan Sinclair. "It's not as bad as that. Believe me, Bobo has been cut down to size—this is his swansong—he knows the cops have finished him and he's determined to go out boasting that he's done every bar in Woods Street."

Stan looked at the clock. "I'm gonnae phone the polis. We need some help."

The Sinclairs argued against him, determined to fight. Their argument lost its sense when Lizzie came on. They looked at her beloved attractive mother-face and remembered that a barman fifty yards away had been scarred for life with a bicycle-chain. Stan went into his office.

He came back from the phone: "I've been on to the C.I.D. We should be all right. You people can go now if you want to."

"No," said Dan Sinclair. "Whatever happens we're staying. By God, we are. We're staying. Whether the cops come or not, we'll be here."

For the first time in his life Starkey realised that the Connor's clock could tick.

Johnny reached the Scala in a flaming temper. "Twenty Players," he said rudely to Maria.

"What's wrong with you, young-aster? Are you no' working the night?"

"I have been up to now. But Nora insists that I waste an hour having coffee with her Celtic lecturer, as if I cared who he was. I'll be back in an hour, Maria; if they're in before me, tell them to wait."

"Aye, O.K. It's a good job you're a good boy now, Johnny. There's big-a trouble comin' across the road tonight."

"What sort of trouble?"

"Bobo's comin'. He's a bad-a bugger, that Bobo."

He picked up his books with a snort. "I've heard that before, Maria. I'll bet it's a false alarm. I'm going to the Reading Room."

"You have a look outside," said Franco, coming through from the kitchen.

Johnny wandered to the door. "Christ, they've broken the window! When—hey Franco! Come and have a look at this! Quick!"

Franco ran to his side and followed the line of his arm. Two hundred yards distant, outside the "Hole in the Wa'," a dark clump of bodies was moving to and fro. In the middle of it something flashed silver.

"That's King Bobo all right," said Johnny. "The big dark chap, with that funny silver bracelet thing on his sleeve. He fits it on his knuckles when he's fighting. You should see the mess it leaves."

"We told you," said Franco. "Look, they're moving this way."

The black slug moved untidily towards them. It stopped after twenty yards and most of it parted in two. Three of the Teds darted furtively into a stair; three more did the same on the other side of the road.

"Oh Lord," said Johnny. "Bobo's still using that trick he got from the films. The idiot thinks it's clever. Those six will come round the back ways, using the closes and the back greens." He pointed to the stair entry beside Connor's and the one beside the Scala to his right. "The Teds'll be hiding in there inside five minutes; Bobo'll keep himself on the road with one mate, the other six-footer. All this is supposed to fool the police, but if they're watching him, they've probably got the closes tapped. Mind you, I can't see any coppers around, can you? It's queer."

"What will Bobo do now, Johnny?"

"He and his mate'll come along quite innocently—look, here they come now. They'll go into Connor's and try to do as they bloody well please. If Stan knuckles down the other Teds'll saunter in at their leisure and take the place over. If he objects, Bobo'll start yelling or smashing glass and they'll all come running to beat hell out of everybody. It's not a very bright way of doing things, but Bobo's ruined lots of good bars this way."

"He must-a lost a lot o' his gang," said Franco. "He's only got seven men tonight."

"He's damned lucky not to have been jugged," said Johnny.

"But he has a certain gutter-sharpness and he's never been caught in the act of messing somebody up. I hope the boys give him hell tonight—they'll make a better job of him than the cops will. If they can just get him out into the lane the place won't even be damaged."

"Stan was across here ten minutes ago," said Franco. "He's only got the two Sinclairs and Starkey and Joe the Rat."

"What? Where are all the other boys?"

"I dunno, Johnny. Probably all studyin' like you. If you take my advice, kiddo, you'll take your books and go. Somebody's goin' to get hurt. Stan's dependin' on the police now."

"Then where *are* the police? There's not a sign of them. Who's the constable on Woods Street tonight?"

"Old Nick Neilson. But I saw him goin' down George Square way about half an hour ago."

"This gets worse and worse," said Johnny. "Nick won't lift a finger to help us, and I don't blame him—Ollie the Bull nearly killed him. You know what I think, Franco?" Revelation had struck him like a bolt. "The police don't intend to move in until the worst of the damage has been done. Connor's and Bobo's men have caused them more trouble than the rest of the town put together. I can see them rubbing their hands at the thought of the two lots battering hell out of each other, then they'll move in and arrest what's left!"

"Johnny, son, you could-a be right."

"Of course I'm right! But what a mess—things are so one-sided tonight that Bobo'll probably get away with it."

"On you go," said Franco. "You get your study done. There's nothing we can do. Go on, Johnny."

"Cheerio, Franco."

He walked slowly towards the Quad; he had never seen Woods Street so quiet. He turned to take a look at the dear old door on the corner, feeling sick within himself. Connor's stood still, defenceless. The stair door beside the pub opened a foot and a curly head flickered out and in again like a serpent's tongue. They were there. He walked across the road. Franco was still at the Scala door; beyond him the second door opened and shut.

And you, Ferguson, you've begged at that bar for money and drinks on the slate and you've taken all Stan's decency and Lizzie's mothering for granted, and now they're probably both in for a pasting, and you couldn't care less for it's every man for himself and your security lies in those pages in your hand. Holy cat—remember your Finals! Forget Bobo—he's not your pigeon!

He walked to the corner. His neck moved in three jerks when he stopped again. Bobo was coming himself now; a big beautiful Ted, built like a wrestler. He was coming up Woods Street with his pal, just a hundred yards from slaughter.

And you, Ferguson, thank God you're out of it all, away from those nights of whisky vertigo and fists on flesh, and Nell and shagging and Jimmy and stories and Jehosaphat and arguments and smoke and stuffiness and Murdo and Gaelic and songs and Hector—by CHRIST! Run, you bastard, RUN!

Franco turned in astonishment as Johnny pelted up to him.

"Franco, you're going to help them—and so am I!"

"Count me out, Johnny— I got-a the cafe and Maria to think about."

"Franco, you're as good a man as any round here. I've seen you sort out your own place—it was the first thing that made me respect Italians."

"Johnny, I won't—"

"Look, boy. If you don't help us now, I'll see that not one student ever uses your cafe again. I can do it, Franco. I can do it, and I will."

Franco's eyes were slits. "I won't-a forget this, Johnny. What do I do?"

"You can get into that stair next to you through your cellar door. Keep those three occupied for the next twenty minutes. You know how to do it, Franco. They won't stand up to your form of fighting."

"All right." Franco clenched his fist. "I hate-a Bobo. But you and me won't be so good-a friends, Johnny. Threats is bad things." He went inside.

Johnny glanced down the street. Bobo and partner had stopped. They were smoking, surveying him with a quiet, deadly interest. He took measured steps across the road to Connor's.

There was one elderly gentleman drinking port by the door. Saving him there were none present to bolster the tiny group round the arch.

"Ye've come to help us," cried Stan. "Here, have a whisky!"

"Make it quick, Stan." He threw his books away on a bar

stool. He was trembling with fear and excitement. "Some chaps never learn. I've been told this place would be the death of me; I used to laugh." He rapped his palm on the counter. "Listen to me. There are only eight of them counting Bobo, and with a bit of luck we can forget three. We don't need the police if we play it properly."

"D'you know what I think of the polis?" said Stan.

"Yes, I've just thought the same, but it doesn't matter now. Bobo's playing his old game. We've got to nail him and his mate before they yell for the Teds next door. Stan—open your tradesman's door to the lane, then Dan and the boys can hide in a doorway at the top of it."

Stan moved quickly to the long wall opposite the counter. A strand of thin sunlight entered the room after the iron bar clicked down. "I don't quite understand, Johnny. What are ye goin' to do?"

He swallowed his whisky. "If we can get Bobo out in the lane without the rest, we can do him quickly without wrecking the pub. I want you all out of sight, then I'm going to get him out there with me."

Dan Sinclair shook his head. "It's better if I do the challenging. Bobo's a big chap: he'll give you a doing, Johnny."

"Look," he said. "Stop arguing. If you challenge him, Dan, he'll think twice and call his mates in at once. But he's sure to think he can murder me, and the chap with him'll probably be drawn outside as well. If things go badly, I want the lot of you out of that doorway hell for leather and we'll get the pair of them. Then, if the others *do* come, we can rush them down the hill. Stan —I want you to lock the front door as soon as Bobo and his pal are outside."

There was a moment's complete silence. Lizzie leaned forward, with something like tears in her eyes. "Johnny," she said, "Johnny."

"Go on lads, please. They'll be here in a minute."

They filed out of the door, a ridiculous company ambush. Starkey clutched a soda siphon.

"Give me another, Stan," he said. The bottle gurgled.

The old gentleman stood sipping his port. Lizzie was weeping openly and shaking her head. Stan's forehead dripped with sweat. Johnny moved to the very end of the counter.

Ten minutes passed . . . fifteen . . . still they counted them. . . .

The door opened quickly to Bobo's shoulder. He stood there colossal, a heavy hunk of jungle muscle with low side-burns and a pasty face ignorant of sunshine. His small black eyes glittered with pleasure at his sparse welcome. He rubbed his stubbly chin and big fleshy nose, spat a wad of spearmint on the floor; his teeth were atrocious. Behind him stood his mate, only slightly smaller, but handsome and blonde, clad in the same tight black clothing and pointed shoes. The door clamped shut behind the fair head. The glass of port was swept to the floor. "Come oan, feyther, let's hae a nip," said Bobo with a quiet smile.

The old fellow produced a pound note that quivered like an aspen leaf and a very old voice said: "A whisky, please, miss." He looked at Stan in terror; the manager turned to Johnny who tried in vain to find his voice.

"Two nips," said Bobo. "I've got a pal here, feyther." He slapped the old man on his flat cap, pushing it over his eyes.

"Two—two nips, miss."

Lizzie served him, looking steadfastly at her hands. She went back to stand beside Stan.

Bobo wandered up the bar after her. "Nice place this," he said. "I think we'll hae a few nights here, Duke. D'you no' think?"

"Aye," said Duke from the door, barring the old man's exit. "We've often fancied Connor's."

"It's nice and quiet," said King Bobo. "Even the auld boss is no' sayin' a thing. An' this runt here's awfy quiet, tae."

Johnny smiled a weak little smile and drank his drink, fighting off the paralysis of his larynx.

But the smile of fear satisfied the Ted. He looked at Stan and slipped the heavy silver across his knuckles. He laughed, swinging his glass, and the metal clashed dully. "I'd like to play wi' you a bit later on, auld yin. But right noo, I fancy your barmaid—she's nice." He reached across the bar with animal speed and pulled Lizzie to the counter by the arm. "Come oan, hen, get up on the counter and gie's a show. Come oan, let's see the colour o' yer knickers!" His left hand clawed down for her skirt, and Stan's fist closed over a beer bottle. Duke laughed by the door; his teeth were better than Bobo's. Now!

"Bobo," said Johnny. "Leave my mother alone."

Bobo twisted round with delight in his face. "Yer mither? Away, ye wee nyaff!"

"Bobo," said Johnny, "I remember your own mother well. She was that dirty fat fishwife with the one eye that used to sell meth down in the Grassmarket, and other things as well."

Bobo straightened up and released Lizzie. His little eyes were bewildered.

"And your father too," continued Johnny, in a small, dry voice. "I mind him well—yon big collie dog down there that was a bit mad and always bitin' the kids. He was a bit better-looking than you, though, Bobo—and he didn't smell quite so bad. Come on outside, ye big slobberin' lump of shit, and I'll wipe the pox off ye with one hand."

He slapped his glass down and walked straight through the side door. The lane looked deserted, and his courage nearly failed him. He backed ten yards up the cobbles, and waited.

He was lucky. They came, just the two of them, and fairly slowly; no calls for help, and Stan should get the door locked. He threw his jacket to the ground.

Bobo halted four paces below him. "Son," he said. "You're off yer heid, but that's too bad. If I leave ony o' yer face, Duke's gonnae stand on it and we'll pit a' the wee pieces doon the barman's throat." He polished the silver lovingly with his palm and prepared to use it. Just a second too late.

Johnny took one, two steps and came at him off the slope, airborne, straight as an arrow, left elbow pointing in front, head packed in neck and gathering muscle, right hand stretching for the string tie. The knuckleduster scythed by his ear in its tardy errand of destruction, then their bodies smashed together in a collision that threw them apart like billiard balls. Johnny rolled over sobbing with the pain that was streaking down his left arm, but when he came to his feet he saw that although his head had missed its target, the little right pig's-eye was gashed and closing from the shattering impact of his elbow and that Bobo was still on his knees, gasping and clutching his winded chest where a slewing right shoulder had made a lucky strike. He sprang at the big man before he could rise, feet first.

The Ted flailed at him and the heavy weapon sliced his shins, but his heels crackled on something that yielded and as he cartwheeled to the ground a second time he knew that King Bobo would never forget him. His own breath was shortening; he scrambled desperately on to all-fours. Bobo came to his feet against the wall, sporting a nose flattened below the bridge, spouting blood from nostrils that pointed sideways at his jaw. But he lurched forward doggedly; his own law had taught him the worse-than-death of surrender.

The silver knuckles looped through the air. Johnny ducked, but they struck him on the crown and he felt his scalp tear. Dazed and bleeding he fell at Bobo's feet and caught at the narrow trousers before boot could follow. They rolled against the wall and Johnny feared he had met his master; the King was far too heavy for him and damn near indestructible. But with Bobo rolling on top Johnny surrendered to his force a little more than he expected: they overshot their revolution and performed another half so that Johnny sat uppermost; as the Ted caught him round the throat he spat and the white hands shot back in protection, then he found paunch with his knee and leaned his weight on it. Bobo uttered a terrible sound, a high-pitched panther scream, and his powerful body thrashed like a wounded crocodile's. Johnny was thrown in the air; as he landed on his back he was seized by the hair from behind and a white object plummeted down at him in the Duke's hand. He closed his eyes and screwed his face to the dust of the street; the broken cup missed and shattered into fragments that peppered his cheek; the Duke fell across him. Bobo came to his feet for the last time, but now there was a rush of pullovers and flannels and the King went down for good; fingers tore tufts from Johnny's hair and the Duke was dragged over backwards.

He sat on the road getting his breath back, while Tammy Sinclair, Joe and Starkey punched Bobo into senselessness in a fresh wave of fury: the Duke was not in the same class as his leader and screamed for mercy beneath a mutilating fusillade of blows from Dan; eventually a massive fist split his skin behind the ear and he lay semi-conscious and gibbering on his face. Tammy and his squad rose from the blood-masked Bobo. The big Shetlander held a silver object aloft. "This is your souvenir, Johnny. You earned it."

He nodded shakily, full of a strange elation. Sensation returned; his elbow was numb and swollen, and blood was trickling down the back of his neck. Then pain went with Stan's appearance at the side door: "It's the others, boys!" From the corner they could hear the rattle of the lock and the anger of feet. Round they came—smaller and perplexed. It was impossible that those two prostrate bodies could be Bobo and Duke—and where were Corky and the others from across the road?

In the stairway beside the Scala Corky lay against the wall moaning in agony, nursing the blistered skin of his thighs; a panful of hot cooking oil had just splashed through his trousers. His two friends cowered in terror under cover of the carving knives of Franco and his cook.

Johnny picked himself to his feet. "Charge them," he yelled.

They charged, and to his cost the Rat was fleetest. The first Ted met him bravely with a left boot that Puskas would not have scorned and the Rat went down heavily clutching his testicles. Starkey jumped astride his body, howling defiance through his nose: he levelled the siphon, but in his excitement failed to work the trigger. Fist drew back, and Starkey threw up the soda as a clumsy guard. Fist struck bottle and glass flew everywhere. Starkey clutched at his face, the Ted at his badly-slashed hand. They were still staring vacantly at one another, sick and afraid of the whole affair, when Stan stepped between them and slammed the long handle of his brush across the enemy's ribs. Another Boboite hit the dust.

Of the remaining two, one squat little plumber stayed his ground to grapple furiously with Tammy and succeeded in butting him in the face. The other turned and ran, pursued across the road by Dan and Johnny. Johnny hit him with a crash-tackle from behind: a car screeched to a halt five yards away. Ignoring it, the huge islander pulled the Ted to his feet and knocked him down again. Johnny grabbed Dan's arm, conscious for the first time that the fight had attracted an audience. About twenty people were standing before the wide front of the Scala, watching spellbound.

"Come on, Dan," he said, "they're finished. The police won't be long now."

Dan pulled the boy to his feet; he was no more than seventeen. "You should be in bed, sonny," he said, and rooted him towards the pavement. Johnny bowed to the driver of the car and they returned to the lane. The last Ted was still struggling madly on the ground with Tammy, despite Stan laying about his back with the broken brush handle. Johnny looked at Lizzie, who was gently dabbing Starkey's cuts in the doorway. He remembered Bobo's filthy suggestion, and a madman's fury banished the tiny vestige of clemency he had left.

He pulled the threshing arms away from Tammy's neck and found another knuckleduster. His heavy brown brogue smashed down on the armoured hand; there was a pistol crack and the loudest shriek of the Battle finished it. Stan turned hurriedly away; the Ted fainted.

Johnny looked up with red dusty eyes. "We've done it, boys. We've done it!" The words froze in his throat. No more than ten yards away at the lane entrance stood a woman, a beautiful young woman with flowing red hair and lovely green eyes that were filled with the horror of Belsen. She shook her head, coming fearfully forward. "No!" she cried brokenly. "No—I don't believe it. It's not you, Johnny. It can't be! Oh, my God—I'm going to be sick!"

"Nora! You must try and understand!"

She fled down the lane and across the road. He pounded after her. She stopped by the Scala door and hung sobbing to the arm of a tall middle-aged man with a dark trilby.

Johnny slithered to a halt. In the glass window he saw himself; face bleeding from a dozen cuts, hair plastered flat and hard with dry blood, shirt buttonless and filthy. A tramp, a bloody bar-tramp; J. S. Ferguson two years ago. He did not see three woe-begone figures limp out of the next stair. "Look, Nora, I *must* speak to you," he pleaded.

She spared him the corner of her eye, and recoiled into the other man's jacket. "Take me away. For God's sake, Mr Fisher, take me away!"

"Who are you, young man?" said Mr Fisher. "I've never seen such a savage exhibition of bullying in my life—surely this isn't your young man, Nora?"

Her look was more furtive than the last. She shivered violently. "I don't—it's—no! NO!'" Her voice rose to a piercing hysterical shriek: "Take me away, Mr Fisher—TAKE ME AWAY!"

"You lying treacherous bitch!" He reached for her arm and Fisher stepped between them. "It's the police for you, young man." His voice rose: "Would somebody please fetch me a constable?" Nobody moved. The crowd was largely student.

Johnny drew back his clenched fist, but Franco emerged from the doorway and held his wrist. "No, Johnny son, you've done enough tonight. Let her go, Johnny—it's only right."

"Sure," said a voice like his own. "It's only right."

"Here's Hector come to take care of you," said Franco.

He watched Fisher lead Nora away. What have I done? What have I done?

Hector took him by the shoulders. "Come on, Johnny. There's a police van only two minutes away. They've got Bobo and his casualties hidden away in the back green. Stan can stash you and the boys in the cellar."

He allowed Hector to lead him across the road. "Nora's gone, Hector. I think she's left me."

"Wait till tomorrow before you say that," said the folklorist. "But you've got plenty of friends right here."

The lane was as peaceful as yesterday: inside the bar people were moving against the light, for it was dusking early. As in a dream he saw a guitar-case propped by the corner, and Nell and Ricky standing beside it.

The police had been gone half an hour; they had learned nothing and cared less. The bar was closed, but the select few remained, and drinks were still on the house. An air of tired satisfaction pervaded most of the company.

Connor's had called its own consultant surgeon, and Pat Leitch was looking at Johnny's scalp which Nell was drenching with warm water. "You really need a few stitches and an X-ray, Johnny," he said.

"Go to hell, it'll be all right."

"Do as he says, Johnny." Nell's sponge was scarlet as she wrung it into the basin.

"Go to hell." His voice was stone. "Get a pad on it. It'll be O.K."

Leitch shrugged. "Heroes will be temperamental," he said, and went over to Lizzie and Starkey.

There was one deep cut close to Starkey's left eye. "You're definitely coming across to have that seen to," said Pat. "No arguments!"

"Surely," said Starkey, now very drunk. "But you mustn't

keep me in. Lizzie's got such lovely hands that I'm taking her to bed tonight."

She smiled without reproach. "After what you laddies did tonight I'd sleep wi' all o' ye."

Dan Sinclair leaned comfortably against the wall, sipping his pint. His clean, unmarked ruddy face looked scrubbed for church. "Thank old Ferguson," he said in his thick Dunrossness accent. "By God, Johnny, you're a pal."

The others murmured agreement; only Nell heard his reply, "Nora's gone, and I've lost a night's work." He said it with the tonelessness of an idiot.

Pat beckoned to the Sinclairs. "Escort me up the back. I'd better have a look at Bobo and Co."

But he returned in two minutes. "They've gone," he said. "Some poor quack's going to be busy tonight."

"That's the greatest fight I ever saw," said Stan.

"It was a tragedy," said Hector. "The working classes still have people who ruin their good name; most Teddy Boys are noblemen, true noblemen! But you lads had your work to do in the name of all decency, and by the saints, you did it well."

"There was nothing noble about these bastards," said Stan. "They deserved all they got."

Johnny looked at Hector. "I wonder what Nora will do."

"Don't worry, Johnny," said Hector. "If she's the woman she should be, she'll be back to you tomorrow."

Nell finished dressing his head. She came round the wooden bench and sat beside him. "Don't you think you're drinking too much, old son?"

He drained his seventh successive whisky. "I'm not bad: look at Joe the Rat—he's passed out."

The Rat sat dead-drunk in the corner, tears of pain still on his cheeks. His trousers were off and a wet towel covered his thighs.

"God," said Stan, "when I think of the times I've cursed the little Turk. It takes a thing like this to prove a man."

"You can come with Nell and me," said Hector to Johnny. "I'll get a taxi now."

He acquiesced without caring. They went to the door and hands were shaken all round. Lizzie gave him a long moist kiss. He turned back to Stan: "See that that poor old chap gets his money back."

"It's already done. We took it oot o' Bobo's pockets."

In the taxi the world was spinning round him like a top; he had lost all sense of orientation. Hector seized his hand. "Good night, Johnny, God bless you."

"Careful, Hector," he mumbled. "Wait till the thing stops." But Hector was gone.

The infernal noise of the engine grew louder. His head was splitting. "Where are we, Nell? I've got to get fresh air." His head slumped forward grotesquely.

Suddenly her arms were round him. "Honey, your head's pouring again. I'm not leaving you on your own—you're coming up with me to get that properly bandaged."

The taxi was shrinking, revolving faster and faster. "No. leave me, Nell. I've got to see my darling." He toppled forward to the floor.

He awoke panting, afraid, from a nightmare he could not remember. The strange room and the large bed terrified him, then he found the bedside lamp. He knew this combination of light and shadow—the blue curtains, the red contemporary wall-paper, the bust of Socrates over the fireplace with the cigar in its mouth; and the armchair with his trousers draped across.

He staggered to the mirror; his legs and elbow were stiff, but his head was clear and painless. It was swathed in a white triangle of sheet tied St John's style. His shins had both been dressed with gauze bandages, and there was iodine on his face. God damn it, she's all right!

Nell rose from the old divan in the kitchen as the light went on. She sat up shamelessly; as always she slept naked.

"How are you feeling, Johnny?"

"I just wanted a drink."

"Help yourself. There's a bottle of squash by the sink."

It was when he put the glass down that the events of the evening and the year behind it came back into focus. He was looking at the wreckage of a dream stranded and broken on the rocks of circumstance. Tears tumbled down his quivering cheeks. He stumbled to the divan and sat down, face buried in his hands. The harshness of his sobbing filled the room.

With one swift graceful movement she pulled him down beside her. "Don't, my love, don't," she crowed. "I'll not let a soul hurt you, Johnny—not ever!" Her two thin blankets were an engulfing pincer movement and he lay against her under them. But as he sobbed his heart out there was a new battle under the covers he could not win; he realised his weakened resistance all too late. She moved deftly over him, and when he ceased to fight the passion of her panting melon breasts and the thrust of her soft belly he salved his conscience with a ferocious attack on womankind. She lay under his barbarous assault almost with fear, then with pain, then with a joyous abandon beyond both, but when he had taken her to the accompanying symphony of her grunting animal bliss, he tore away from the smell of her love with a fresh burst of sobbing. Damn you, woman, and damn Nora, and every dirty female thing that ever tried to make a man walk in her way and didn't care to learn there are some things about men she could never understand!

She misconstrued his emotion. "That was beyond words, honey. Johnny, you and I can go back and master the world together."

His eyes were dead on the pillow. "I used to think it was heaven," he said.

She smiled. "And it's coming back, just like before." She went to him again, but he was already asleep.

Somewhere in his dreams he heard Nora's voice. It was singing his "Irish Lovesong" and it made him roar in his sleep. But not for her mouth to kiss: for the cock to crow three times, and get the whole ghastly thing over with. Then as he lay in the wasteland between consciousness and mercy, the voice changed in character. It was small and frightened, and it said: "Please let me in, Nell. I must see."

Nell's voice: "If you take my advice you'll go, Nora." Not unkind but a suggestion of conquest?

The door barged open.

He sat up sleepily. Nora was real enough: she stood there in her apple costume, and her face was very beautiful, and there was no horror left, only the ultimate of death and defeat; and in her eyes tears, and he was sick to Christ of tears.

"Hello darling," she said quietly.

He buried his head in the blankets.

Nell's voice: "How did you know, Nora? Why are you here?"

Quiet, thick, unmistakeably Nora's. "I have a telephone. Allan Prentice saw you getting into the taxi, and followed you. It's all very simple."

He looked up. "It's not what you think, Nora," he said, wondering at the lack of interest in his voice.

"Isn't it? Isn't it, Johnny? Look at me—isn't it?"

He hid his head deeper. This can't happen to me. I'm dreaming—please let me waken up! And still he could not move.

Nora's voice. "Good-bye, Johnny."

It was the clatter of the outside door and the roar of a motor that broke the spell. Freed, he leapt to his feet. "Wait!" he yelled.

Nell came close to him in the passage. "She's gone, darling. She had a taxi. Now let's get on with what we call living."

The back of his hand carried her five yards; she slumped sitting against the bathroom door. He pulled her to her feet and slapped her back and forward across both cheeks till he could not bear the pain in his hands. She fell moaning at his feet.

"You whore," he said quietly, madly. "To think that I've lost her because of you. She was the sweetest person you ever saw."

"And you no longer love her." Blood trickled from her mouth. "Am I wrong, honey? Do you love her, Johnny? *Do* you?"

He looked wildly around for solace. "I—Lord God! I don't know!"

CHAPTER XXII

He found Nora after an hour's search that began in panic, and mattered less and less with the sun's steady climbing. She was sitting on the grass in the early morning sunshine, in the middle of the Meadows. She had been crying fit to break her heart; now her face was dry, dirty, rather pretty. He sat down beside her.

"I've found you at last, Nora."

"Does it matter?"

"It's finished, isn't it?"

"After this morning that's an unnecessary question."

"After last night, too."

She plucked at the dewy stems. "I came back looking for you last night, after I got over my hysterics. You've had your revenge now. There's nothing more to say."

Deep in the quick of him there was no grief, only the confirmation of a void. "What went wrong, Nora? It was so perfect, but now it's gone to pieces. First a few cracks, then a dreadful great gulf between us. I used to think that I had less moral strength than most, but last night you were terrible. I just don't understand it."

"There was a dream," she said, "and we both loved it. But you and I are not of dreams, we're flesh and blood. We couldn't force each other into the scheme we created. I'm sorry for my part, but my name isn't Deirdre, it's Nora O'Brien."

"D'you want to try again?"

"If I do, I'll forget it, and you'll never hear me admit it. No doubt we could be happy in a way, but we'd still love the dream and we'd hate each other for being outside it. You go back to Nell."

"I'll never see the bitch again. I hate her. Are you going back to Kevin?"

"I'm going home tomorrow; I must get myself sorted out. I don't know about Kevin—he's a darling, but I hurt him badly."

"It's been wonderful, Nora."

"Yes. And terrible."

"It's been coming a long time, this I mean. I can see it all now. We were scared to admit it."

"Were we? I don't know, Johnny, I just don't know."

"D'you still love me?"

"I can't say—it's not a fair question. Do *you* love *me*?"

"If I can love anybody, I do. But I don't know either. There are so many things in the way."

"Where are you going now, Johnny?"

"I'll take my things to Colin's flat. I've lost a lot of working time." A silly thing to say, and she began to cry again.

He stood up. "It's hopeless?"

"I think so."

"I'm sorry, Nora."

"So am I." A few more steady racking sobs.

He kissed her for the last time. Her lips were morsels of frozen slimy flesh; pathetic denizens of a fishmonger's slab.

"Goodbye, Nora."

"Goodbye, darling."

He ran for the shelter of the trees. There was no heartbreak, bitterness, no relief. Nothing.

Twice she thought of calling him, but she had no sound to give the air. A third time her voice broke through the phlegm; she bent her face and bit green meadow to stop herself.

CHAPTER XXIII

THEY'VE TAKEN A LOT away from me: The Moonshiners, Glenellin, and the Scotland I wanted. Now they've taken Nora. But they haven't taken my pride, they haven't, and as long as I've got that and these bloody horrible books I've got a chance. I've got four stinking days left, and I'll pack them with the labour that built the pyramids. I'm going to be a doctor, d'you hear? Nothing on earth is going to stop me; my name is Johnny Ferguson, and I'll die before I'll retreat.

Colin and Jean received him into their flat with a sympathetic, judicious lack of enquiry. He closeted himself in his own bedroom and rarely saw them. He threw himself yet again at the pages he hated and ate their knowledge with venom. He began when the light strayed across his clothed body and finished when he could no longer see print, usually about three or four in the morning. When thoughts of auburn hair and green eyes and love in the bracken made his face wet he bought whisky and studied with its comfort; on the third day he stole Colin's brandy from the kitchen cupboard. He drove the words behind him with relentless energy; as he shaved on the morning of the fourth day he had to stop and steady his hand.

On the eve of the exams Colin came into the stale sweaty room. "I came in to wish you luck. I'm sure you'll do it."

Johnny cackled irritably. "Thanks old boy, so will you. Now away you go—I'm still at it."

"Don't you think you've done enough? You look terrible, old son."

"You mind your own business. I've had enough advice to last me a lifetime."

"You've had bad luck," said Colin. "You should forget everything and have a good night's sleep."

"I *have* forgotten everything," he shouted.

Colin moved away with a puzzled frown on his face.

"I'm sorry, Colin," he said. "Here, test me on my Therapeutics; the bloody stuff's got me all nervy."

Colin picked up his own notebook. "You really need some pit. You're driving yourself to a breakdown."

"That'll be the day. Come on! Let's have a few questions."

"Right. What's the treatment of subacute nephritis?"

"Let me see now. You need a high protein diet as free of salt as possible. What's that salt-free protein called? Honestly, Colin, I knew it!"

"It's 'Casilan'," said Colin soothingly. "Now what about steroids?"

"Oh yes, you use hydrocortisone. Colin—I've forgotten the dose!"

He banged his fists on the bedside table and a bottle of ink sprawled its contents over the carpet. "Try something else. The stuff'll come back to me. Quick, man!"

Colin tried several maladies; it was the same story every time. Facts that had been firm in his mind for days had fled. He cursed and tore his hair.

Colin put the book down firmly. "You're going to bed—I know the signs when a brain's overloaded. Get your head down right away! And good luck, Johnny." He left the room.

But Johnny did not go to bed. He read subacute nephritis quickly then shut the book. This time he remembered it. He lit a cigarette with trembling fingers and turned to idiopathic steatorrhoea. The mercurial word-picture shot out of his mind as soon as the book was closed. Terrified, he went to rheumatoid arthritis. Things got worse and worse—he could remember nothing. I've had it! I'm breaking up—no I won't—Colin was right, Johnny, a good sleep, Johnny, a good sleep, boy, bed, bed, BED!

He threw off his shoes and slacks and leapt in. Not even sleep would abide with him. Dismembered words and phrases floated through the morass of his brain: I love you, Nora—no, I don't. I can't remember how you treat it—open the bloody book. The old man'll be down to see me capped, I'll do him really proud—you're gonna fail your Finals, GET AWAY, HUXTABLE! You're gonna fail your Finals, YOU'RE GONNA FAIL YOUR FINALS—NO!!

He jumped out of bed and dressed. He had one last liquid line of defence. And if that didn't work he could always break a leg or something. Of course, he needn't sit this time at all!

He ran up to Woods Street past the Royal City. Breathlessly he lit a cigarette by the East gate and found another one already burning in his hand. He threw them both away and went to the Scala for more.

Maria's pupils dilated in horror at the sight of his hairy yellow face and sunken cheeks.

"Twenty cigarettes, quick," he rapped out.

She gave him them, speechless. "You pay me now, Johnny? I can wait."

"Nora's left me," he said. "But I'll be a doctor soon. So long, Maria."

Jimmy Anderson raised a welcoming glass in Connor's. "The man of the moment," he shouted. "Come and have a drink, Johnny!"

"Stay away," he screamed.

The boys rebounded from his rasping voice, muttering to one another.

"Here, Lizzie," he shouted. "Whisky! No, not a measure —fill the bloody glass up!"

He threw the blazing tumbler into his stomach; at first he thought he was coming apart. He stepped back and wiped the tears from his face. They were coming to him again. "Stay away!" he shouted.

"Johnny," said Lizzie, crying again for some reason—*why will women cry*?—"you're ill, laddie. Ye should have had that X-ray last week. Come into the office and sit wi' me."

"No," he said. "I must go now, for a walk. Lend me a pound, Lizzie."

Without a word she opened her purse. "Please stay for a wee while," she said.

"No," he said, taking the note. "I must go."

He fell to his knees opening the door, bolted upright, and ran like a stag towards the next bar. Lizzie's pound bought him two pints in the "Bishop's Ingle" and a dram in the "Hole in the Wa'." He staggered on to the Royal George and drank a Guinness in three seconds. He left hurriedly when he threw the glass to the floor. "Bobo'll get you," he snarled at the irate barman. "He'll be back."

He was as pissed as a newt, but it wasn't fair; he was beaten. He was still shaking and frightened and he still couldn't remember the treatment for subacute nephritis. Get away Huxtable! Get away! Come on, big friendly bar, save me, save me! I need you, mother, God help me. What's the dosage of hydrocortisone?

Jehosaphat found him sitting against the wall beside the Royal George.

"What are you doin' here?" said Johnny.

"They're worried about you in Connor's. I've to keep an eye on you."

"Do you know the treatment for subacute nephritis?"

"No."

"Neither do I. Get me up, Jehosaphat, I'll show you how to break a leg."

"Of course, Johnny. You show me."

Johnny turned into the High Street. The first pub on the left-hand side was the Cairter's Horse. It was crowded.

"I can't buy you a drink, Jehosaphat," he said. "My need is greater than thine."

"You're gassed, Johnny. Come on home."

A little tart watched him sink the big whisky. "Gie's the price o' an Export, son," she said.

"Nora's gone," said Johnny. "And I don't need you. But the Lord is with me. He'll help me through Finals or he'll break my leg, madam, or perhaps he will restore to me the years that the locust hath eaten."

"Fuck off," said the tart. "Ye're nuts."

"Come on," he said to Jehosaphat. "I haven't much time."

He sprinted down the High Street. Jehosaphat tried to follow, but the late pavement crowds were the harvest wheat of Auden's ballad. Johnny was halfway down the High Street when Jehosaphat found him leaning breathlessly on a lamp post.

"This is for the last time," said Johnny, grabbing Jehosaphat's arm. "How do you treat subacute nephritis?"

"I don't know. Come on home."

"That settles it; I'll show you." Johnny could not see clearly now, but the High Street was the friendliest thing he had seen in years. That friendly square tower and the white clock and the old stone, they could save you from your Finals. And those big—. By God! He shot off the pavement. Jehosaphat pawed for his shoulder and lost it, uncertain of his purpose.

The driver of the number 45 bus had had a heavy day. He

was twenty minutes from a mug of tea and beans on toast as he raced down the hill slightly faster than usual. He braked in a sweat, but women screamed and the thud went clean through him after he had the brief, impossible vision of a twisted, stubbly, little devil's grin that seemed to lean thankfully into his radiator.

He climbed from his cab pleading like a child for the mercy of the Name he had cheerfully blasphemed for years. With two flat feet on the ground he stopped. In the middle of the throng of pop-eyed spectators a scruffy youth was weeping on his knees beside a scatter of shillings and pennies; before his wheels lay the broken neck of Johnny Ferguson.

Jehosaphat threw himself across the still form, for people were closing in on it. "Get away, you vultures!" he hollered. "Oh, Johnny, what a bloody silly thing to do!"

They stood in Connor's three days later.

"When's the funeral?" said Stan.

"Tomorrow," said the Rat from above his rum. "Jimmy and I are catchin' the Crieff train tonight."

"Lizzie'll come with you," said the manager. "I cannae manage; it'll be heavy here the night."

"It's funny," said Pat Leitch. "He should have been finishing his Medicine paper right now. I saw it this morning; it's one of the easiest in years."

"I wish I'd bothered to sit it," said Jimmy Anderson drunkenly. "I might have managed ten per cent."

"He could fight," said Stan. "He was far bigger than he looked."

"I'm sorry I missed that fight," said Jimmy. "I wanted to get my mitts on Bobo. But in a way it's just as well—I have no intention of remembering Johnny by anything better."

"Aye," said Stan. "It'll be a cosy wee memory for the future."

Starkey was drinking with his gloves on. "It's been a great year so far," he said. "I've never hed so many good stories to tell."

"This beer's flat today, Stan," said Pat. "Things will have to improve."

The manager smiled. "The day you pack up this beer I'll shut the shop."

"I wonder why he did it," said a little First Year medic.

"Who?" asked Jimmy.

"Johnny. The Ferguson."

"That's a silly question, son. Maybe Finals knocked him a bit queer. Or maybe he did it for one of his mad sentimental Celtic reasons—who knows? Johnny could do things really well if he tried, and he made a lovely job of it. Real quick. I hope I have his luck one day—and I hope I'm as pissed as he was."

"He could sing," said Stan. "I used tae get near greetin' when he played 'Arlin's Fine Braes'."

"Let's have another round," said Murdo. "Here's to the song we had with him."

Jehosaphat and Nell sat in the corner. "They don't care," he said. "I can't stand it. I'll strangle them."

"If you had been a bit more careful," she said, "I wouldn't be so keen on strangling you." But as the clown's head hit the table and a sheaf of dirty hair swam in his beer, she pulled him upright. "Here, stop blubbing, you're making me lonely. I've bawled myself dry." Her haggard features softened in a smile. "Come on outside, you can cry on my shoulder."

In the cool of early evening they walked to the corner and came to a standstill by the main gate of the medical Quad.

"I've had enough of Connor's," he said. "They scarcely seem sorry."

"Shut up with your honey of sorrow," she said. "You've not been in Connor's long enough. You're not really one of them yet."

"What d'you mean?"

"They're right. They understood him even better than we did. Everybody has his own anodyne in this rotten world; Johnny's was Connor's, and his guitar. I was useful for a bit: so was Nora, and so were lots of people, but not in the same way."

"Why, Nell? He had so much to do."

She shook her scarecrow mop. "Drivel. They're right back in there—they know. I don't know what it was, but there was a terrible blackness somewhere that we could never feel. But they know. They've got it too, maybe for different reasons, but it's there. He hadn't much more to do, anyway. No doubt he could have become a doctor—and he could have settled down and lived in clean hospitals and flashy houses and worn nice suits. And inside he would have cried himself to something worse. He's better where he is."

"—the years that the locust hath eaten," whispered Jehosaphat.

"What's that got to do with it?"

"It was one of the last things he ever said. It's a biblical text, but I can't remember all of it."

"What a ruddy coincidence," she said bitterly. "It's one of the few I know: 'The floors shall be filled with wheat, and the presses shall overflow with wine and oil, and I will restore to you the years that the locust hath eaten'."

"I wonder what he meant, Nell?"

"You're not as clever as you think. Away from Connor's and his songs he was in a state of famine. The idiots were all locusts, trying to make him what they bloody well thought he should be —they ate his spirit—his mother and his respectable tutors—and that woman, her most of all. And they'll still be at it. His mother will say that he forsook the way of the Lord, and the Dean'll be shaking his head and saying how tough the course is, and Nora'll have hysterics and hope he did it because of her, and the Scottish Free Party will find some ethnic reason. They'll all have their little nibble at Johnny for weeks to come. But you heard Jimmy Anderson: he won't have any locusts in Connor's, bless him."

"Are you going back to the Moonshiners?"

"I don't know. I'll tell you a secret, Jehosaphat. I still hate him, especially because he's dead. I fought so hard! I felt his hands on me again, and I'm sure that in time I could have had him back for good. Then he had to go and do this."

"Nell," said Jehosaphat. "You're twisted."

"This morning," she said, "I was ill and I'm never ill. And I'm a day late, and I'm never late. And I've got a funny feeling, and my funny feelings are almost never wrong. Do you still think I'm twisted?"

He put an arm round her. "What are you going to do?"

"I don't know. But he won't have the last laugh on me. I'll probably go and see somebody. Then, wherever he is, he won't laugh so bloody much."

"If you do that," said a suddenly cool, grave Jehosaphat, "I'll kill you."

She laughed. "I've heard that before. And yet you're probably right. I was more crackers about him than anybody." She touched his arm almost playfully. "If I don't do anything, you'd better be around—I'll need your help."

He smiled. "Of course."

"I'm going now," she said. "I want to think it over and I haven't had a good cry all day. I must walk myself into the mood."

"Cheerio, Nell." She walked away from him; her seams were very crooked.

Two young student lovers, both good-lookers, passed him. "You poor buggers," he said loudly, peering through his wet eyes with an air of resurrection. They giggled back at him, pointing with their healthy young heads.

It was Friday, pleasant, but an irresistible unseen force was pushing the east wind into the streets from the sea, ruffling his hair and freshening the faces of the cheerful, grubby-faced little Scotsmen who brushed past him, clutching their week's redemption in a transparent paper packet.